Bohumil Hrabal was born in 1914 in Brno-Židenice, Czechoslovakia. Receiving a degree in law, he worked as a stagehand, postman, clerk and baler of wastepaper. He is internationally known and loved for such books as *Closely Observed Trains* and *I Served the King of England*. The former was made into a hugely successful movie of the same name by Jiri Menzel.

Bohumil Hrabal died in 1997.

D0229998

By the same author

I SERVED THE KING OF ENGLAND
CLOSELY OBSERVED TRAINS
THE DEATH OF MR BALTISBERGER
TOO LOUD A SOLITUDE

Cutting It Short

and

The Little Town Where Time Stood Still

Bohumil Hrabal

Translated from the Czech by
James Naughton

Introduction by
Josef Škvorecký

An *Abacus* Book

First published in Great Britain by Abacus 1993
This edition published by Abacus 1994
Reprinted 1995, 1997, 1999

Cutting It Short
Copyright © Bohumil Hrabal 1976
Translation copyright © James Naughton 1993

The Little Town Where Time Stood Still
Copyright © Bohumil Hrabal 1973
Translation copyright © James Naughton 1993
Introduction copyright © Josef Škvorecký 1993

The moral right of the author has been asserted.

All rights reserved.
No part of this publication may be reproduced,
stored in a retrieval system, or transmitted, in any
form or by any means, without the prior
permission in writing of the publisher, nor be
otherwise circulated in any form of binding or
cover other than that in which it is published
and without a similar condition including this
condition being imposed on the subsequent purchaser.

A CIP catalogue record for this book
is available from the British Library.

ISBN 0 349 10540 5

Printed in England by Clays Ltd, St Ives plc

Abacus
A Division of
Little, Brown and Company (UK)
Brettenham House
Lancaster Place
London WC2E 7EN

Translator's Note

Cutting It Short follows the text of the first edition of Postřižiny as published by Československý spisovatel, Prague, 1976. Its sequel, The Little Town Where Time Stood Still, follows the text of the author's original 1973 typescript Městečko, kde se zastavil čas, as used for the editions by Odeon, Prague, 1991, Sixty-Eight Publishers, Toronto, 1989, and Comenius, Innsbruck, 1978.

Contents

Introduction

One of the first authors – certainly the oldest and the most popular – of the political thaw that reached Czechoslovakia at the end of the 1950s and lasted until the Soviet ambush in 1968, was Bohumil Hrabal (b.1914). Yet to appreciate fully what a revelation his first books were to the Czech reader, the Westerner would have to have some knowledge of the socialist-realist portrayal of the working class, of its deadly foe, the bourgeoisie, and its wavering ally, the intellectual. In the terminology of the "method", which only the Devil understood (as Sholokhov once remarked), these social categories translated into the Positive, Negative, and Wavering Hero. Classical socialist-realism knew no other human type. The formula was permeated by a social determinism more deterministic than anything written by American naturalists in the nineteenth century. The positive character in these fairy tales was *always* a worker, the negative *always* either a capitalist or his middle-class lackey; the wavering hero was *always* either an old, feeble-minded worker, unable to comprehend the beneficial nature of revolutionary change, or a bourgeois intellectual who, to paraphrase Marx, found it difficult to cross in ideology the limits he was unfit to cross in life.

Into this thoroughly fictitious world of wishful thinking came – as a ray of light – Hrabal's stories, peopled by unmistakable proletarians who were not necessarily always likeable, by unmistakable middle-class characters, not necessarily unlikeable, and by "atypical" intellectuals who discussed E.A. Poe or Jackson Pollock in a tavern over a mug of beer. Gone was the determinism, gone was the lifelessness of the cardboard world of the once mandatory "method". Hrabal's colourful folks were triumphantly alive, they displayed the politically incorrect classlessness of raconteurism, they lived in a universe lighted by fireworks of imagination. The "low" material of rough life recorded in beerhalls merged with the "high" concepts of great art; this union was blessed by surrealism and the silent two-reelers of early American cinema; everything was sifted through a creative intellect blessed by the profound democracy of extraordinary talent. The poetic products of this talent were anathema to everything the socialist-realist establishment stood for, although nowhere did the author trouble himself with the ponderous issues of ideology, and very rarely was there a direct criticism of the particular sores of socialist life. But the entire oeuvre, by its miraculous existence, was a critique of the canonized vision, enforced, in the bad old Stalinist days, sometimes to the point of incarceration.

In the early fifties, the man who did all this was realist enough not to attempt submitting his fictions for publication. He read them aloud to a group of friends who constituted one of the very few active literary undergrounds of the Stalinist era. I was a member of this circle, so was the great jazz composer, the late Jan Rychlík; so was Zdeněk Urbánek, later one of the most courageous dissidents of the seventies and eighties; so was Věra Linhartová, the gentle experimentalist of fiction, who later left the country for Paris; and last but not least, the then unpublished poet Jan Zábrana. The *spiritus agens* of the sessions was Jiří Kolář, a great and influential force in modern Czech literature, who did in verse something similar to what Hrabal did in prose. It was Kolář who first helped Hrabal to see his name in print. He found a loophole in the censorship of the day: the fact that officially sanctioned organizations were allowed to print newsletters for their membership. Since such materials were not sold to the general public, the censor applied much lighter control. In 1956, Kolář convinced the Bibliophiles Club to print a supplement to one of their issues, entitled *People Talking (Hovory lidí)* and containing two of Hrabal's stories. In this limited way Hrabal reached his first readers outside the underground circles.

Then the post-Stalin thaw began to be felt in Prague publishing houses, and the first collection of Hrabal's stories, *Lark on a String (Skřivánek na niti)* was to be brought out by the Writers' Union Publishing House. But before it could be released in 1959, my own novel *The Cowards* exploded in the ideological trenches and was used by the Stalinist faction of the Party as a warning example of what happens if the grip of orthodox censorship is loosened. Hrabal's collection was one of the many casualties of the ensuing purge.

But that was the last, cramp-like attempt by the Stalinists to regain full control over literature. The liberal forces quickly recovered, Hrabal's book eventually came out in 1963 with a new title, *Pearl on the Bottom (Perlička na dně)*, and launched its author on a meteoric career that elevated him to peaks of popularity no other Czech writer had enjoyed before him. It also brought him almost universal critical acclaim.

Soon, too, came the first international success when his short novel *Closely Observed Trains (Ostře sledované vlaky)*, was filmed (directed by Jiří Menzel), and received an Oscar in 1967. The novel's theme – the merging of sexual suffering with anti-Nazi sabotage – was another challenge to accepted norms: this time to the officially ratified portrayal of Czech wartime resistance as something sexless, saintly and thoroughly removed from the mundane affairs of common people. It was Hrabal's first step towards more expressly political themes, and gradually issues related to the repressive and often destructive party measures began to seep through the palavering texture of surreal raconteurism. The trend culminated in another film, and in another novel. The film, shot again by Jiří Menzel and based on Hrabal's most "controversial" book to date, *An Advertisement for the House I Don't Want to Live In Anymore (Inzerát na dům, ve kterém už nechci bydlet*, 1965), but, symptomatically, given the slightly altered title of the book banned in 1959 *Larks on a String (Skřivánci na niti)*, is the story of a group of female political prisoners, of "bourgeois elements" sent to work in a huge junkyard, and of the *mésalliance* of a young worker with one of the jailbirds. It was banned before release and locked, with many similar films, in the vaults of the Barrandov Studios whence it finally, twenty-two years later, emerged unscathed to receive recognition at the San Francisco film festival in 1990.

The novel was *The Little Town Where Time Stood Still* (*Městečko, kde se zastavil čas*). Written in 1973, it went through two emigré editions (in 1978 by Comenius, Innsbruck and in 1989 by the Sixty-Eight Publishers, Toronto), but it was never, in its entirety, brought out in Prague until after the Velvet Revolution of 1989.

It is, perhaps, Hrabal's most powerful text: essentially a dirge for the "old times" before the advent of cruel European dictatorships – times that, whatever they were, possessed at least a human face.

Why was it never published at home until after the collapse of communism? I suspect that Western readers will hardly find anything so politically unacceptable in the text as to give the authorities a reason to smother a book which brims with life (and it is not the life of the leisure class). But the Stalinist mind does not possess the superstructure of the unconscious, but of pathological suspicion. And, in the meantime, Soviet tanks arrived in Prague.

The best writers either left, or went underground where they founded several samizdat publishing ventures; or simply remained silent; or even began writing inconspicuous crime stories. When Hrabal turned sixty in 1974, a group of his friends published, in the samizdat form, a *Festschrift*, and Hrabal was generally seen as a dissident writer, alongside Václav Havel, Milan Kundera (who at that time still lived in Czechoslovakia), Ivan Klíma, Ludvík Vaculík and others. But Hrabal, who under the guise of a "tough guy" is a very sensitive and vulnerable man, was selected and focused on by the establishment hacks. These included both the secret policemen who, playing the traditional role of the "bad" cop, regularly took the sick author in for interrogation, and the Marxist literary critics, who tried to convince him that it was his duty to do something so that the thousands upon thousands of his devoted readers could again read his books. One such critic, Mr Jiří Hájek, playing the traditional role of the "good" cop, eventually persuaded Hrabal to give him an interview which was printed in the Party's cultural weekly *Tribuna*. It's a lukewarm text, conceived in generalities, talking, for instance, about socialism which Hrabal "never had anything against", without specifying what kind of socialism he had in mind. His devoted readers naturally understood him; what he certainly did not have in mind was the post-invasion abomination which Party ideologues labelled "truly existing socialism". Seriously ill and under constant pressures of this kind, Hrabal finally published his interview in exchange for permission to return to print.

And return he did – but something happened. When he submitted *The Little Town Where Time Stood Still* there was considerable embarrassment in the Writers' Union Publishing House, judging at least by the time lapse between submission – some time in 1973 – and the publication of *Lovely Wistfulness* (*Krasosmutnění*, 1979) and *Harlequin's Millions* (*Harlekýnovy milióny*, 1981) which contain fragments of the as yet unpublished *Little Town Where Time Stood Still*. Under new pressures, this time from editors (acting as preventive censors), Hrabal rewrote the text considerably, removing most of the powerful conclusion, changing the narrative voice to that of his mother, and chopping the text into pieces which he then mixed with other material, and published in the two above mentioned books.

The removal of essential parts of the requiem for the *temps perdu* naturally changed the tone and also, to a great extent, the meaning of the text which was still further disfigured by other "editorial" changes. A good example is one of the central episodes, the sacking of Francin after the arrival of the "new times" (i.e. after the communist takeover). In the "unedited" text; now fully restored in this English language edition, Francin, after being rather rudely thrown out of his job, begs to be allowed to keep at least two old office lamps with green shades as souvenirs of his long years in the brewery. However, "when Dad left the office, this was what the workers' director had been waiting for, he took both lamps with their green shades and he threw them out of the window on to a heap of lumber and scrap, and the green shades and cylinders smashed to pieces and Dad clutched his head and there was a crumpling sound inside, as if his brain had been smashed. 'The new era's beginning here too,' said the workers' director, and he went into his office." In *Harlequin's Millions* the same episode is rendered in the following way: when Francin asks for permission to keep the two lamps, the working-class director (renamed "chairman of the brewery"), a kindly, almost apologetic, certainly not rude character, first also refuses, but then turns to the other members of the committee with the words: "Well, what do you think, comrades? Shall we be magnanimous? Take the lamps as souvenirs of old times which were good to you." The difference between the two versions certainly needs no explanation. Hrabal, in order to have the book published at all, simply used the Writers' Union mandatory method, and from a surrealist became a realist with an adjective attached. In fact, in one of his several books banned and seized by the censors after the Soviet invasion entitled *The Buds (Poupata)* he predicted, with bitter self-irony, his own fate: "a cab driver drove me this year from the Barrandov studios, and suddenly he asked me, laughing, 'You're Mr. Hrabal?' I said, 'Well, I am.' And he said, 'Heh-heh, so they've outsmarted you, haven't they? You wanted to be a *poète maudit*, and they've turned you into a socialist-realist. That's what I call an achievement.'" A cabbie displaying knowledge of nineteenth-century French literature was nothing very extraordinary in those times in Prague. Many "bourgeois elements" found refuge from the uranium mines behind the wheel. And, for that matter, it's not so very extraordinary in New York today, albeit it's not political oppression that makes such fine contemporary Czech writers as Iva Pekárková drive a taxi in the Big Apple.

Besides *The Buds*, at least two other works by Hrabal fell victim to the post-invasion book-burning: *Homework (Domácí úkoly,* 1970), a collection of highly original essays, and *Three Wistful Grotesques (Tři teskné grotesky)* which contained his early pieces written in 1944-53. The first fruit of his compromise with the establishment, to come out in 1976, was *Cutting It Short (Postřižiny).* There are, however, no traces of any *artistic* compromise in this crystalline text of subtly erotic beauty, a refined and moving love song for his pretty and witty mother. Hrabal simply did not include things that do not belong in a love song, and approved the omission of two other texts contained in the samizdat edition of 1973. These two stories, however, *The Bridesmaid (Družička)*, and *The Handbook for a Palaverer's Apprentice (Rukověť pábite ského učně)* are self-contained tales, and the charming novella *Cutting It Short* in no way suffers by being published separately. In the present edition it is printed together with *The Little Town Where Time Stood Still*, which is logical and most appropriate – the same lovingly depicted characters appear in both, and the dirge for old times assumes a new, polyphonous and more universal quality.

After the publication of *Cutting It Short*, the book market in occupied Prague was flooded with various new and old texts by Hrabal, but these were not the result of further compromises but of censorial selection. Hrabal has always been very prolific, and so, from the deluge of writings, the "normalized" editors, with an unerring hand, excluded the best. *Too Loud A Solitude* (*Příliš hlučná samota*, 1976), his poetic condemnation of the banning of books, was never published (except by emigré houses), and neither was his incomparable three-volume autobiography *The Weddings in the House* (*Svadby v domě*), *Vita Nuova* and *Vacant Lots (Proluky)*. They cleverly use the narrative voice of the writer's loving but puzzled wife who cannot comprehend what is it about her beer-swilling, pork-guzzling man that makes people think he is a genius. And, at the very end of the "new era", shortly before the collapse of communism, Hrabal returned to the ranks of samizdat authors. Another masterpiece, *I Served the King of England (Obsluhoval jsem anglického krále*, 1975) was rejected as inappropriate, and eventually published in 1983 by a courageous group of people, members of the semi-legal Jazz Section of the Czech Musicians' Union who tried to use the same loophole Jiří Kolář had discovered a quarter of a century earlier. They brought the book out in their "members only" series *jazzpetit*, endorsed by Hrabal's dedication "To the Jazz Section", and it proved to be the last drop in the establishment's cup of patience. For years they had been trying to suppress the Jazz Section, and so, finally, in 1987, the Section's leaders were put on trial and sent to jail for "unauthorized publishing activities". Shortly afterwards, communism went bust.

Hrabal, now approaching the eightieth year of his life, is still the favourite of Czech readers. He is certainly one of those contemporary Czech writers without whom the knowledge of the literature of that distant land would be lamentably incomplete.

Josef Škvorecký
1993

Cutting It Short

La Bovary, c'est moi
GUSTAVE FLAUBERT

ONE

I like those few minutes before seven o'clock at night, when, as a young wife, with rags and a crumpled copy of the newspaper *National Politics*, I clean the glass cylinders of the lamps, with a match I rub off the blackened ends of the burnt wicks, I put the brass caps back, and at seven o'clock precisely that wonderful moment comes when the brewery machinery ceases to function, and the dynamo pumping the electric current around to all the places where the light bulbs shine, the dynamo starts to turn more slowly, and as the electricity weakens, so does the light from the bulbs, slowly the white light grows pink and the pink light grey, filtered through crape and organdie, till the tungsten filaments project red rachitic fingers at the ceiling, a red violin key. Then I light the wick, put on the cylinder, draw out the little yellow tongue of flame, put on the milky shade decorated with porcelain roses. I like those few minutes before seven o'clock in the evening, I like looking upward for those few minutes when the light drains from the bulb like blood from the cut throat of a cock, I like looking at that fading signature of the electric current, and I dread the day the mains will be brought to the brewery and all the brewery lamps, all the airy lamps in the stables, the lamps with round mirrors, all those portly lamps with round wicks one day will cease to be lit, no one will prize their light, for all this ceremonial will be replaced by the light-switch resembling the water tap which replaced the wonderful pumps. I like my burning lamps, in whose light I carry plates and cutlery to the table, open newspapers or books, I like the lamp-lit illumined hands resting just so on the tablecloth, human severed hands, in whose manuscript of wrinkles one may read the character of the one to whom these hands belong, I like the portable paraffin lamps with which I go out of an evening to meet visitors, to shine them in their faces and show them the way, I like the lamps in whose light I crochet curtains and dream deeply, lamps which if extinguished with an abrupt breath emit an acrid smell whose reproach inundates the darkened room. Would that I might find the strength, when the electricity comes to the brewery, to light the lamps at least once a week for one evening and listen to the melodic hissing of the yellow light, which casts deep shadows and compels one into careful locomotion and dreaming.

Francin lit in the office the two portly lamps with their round wicks, two lamps continuously bubbling on like two housekeepers, lamps standing on the edges of a great table, lamps emitting warmth like a stove, lamps sipping paraffin with huge appetite. The green shades of these portly lamps cut off almost with a ruler's edge the areas of light and shadow, so that when I looked in the office window Francin was always split in two, into one Francin soaked in vitriol and another Francin swallowed up in gloom. These tubby brass contraptions, in which the wick was adjusted up or down by a horizontal screw, these brass skeps had a huge draught, so much oxygen did these lamps of Francin's need that they vacuumed up the air around them, so that when Francin placed his cigarette in the vicinity of the lamps the brass hive mouth sucked in ribbons of blue smoke, and the cigarette smoke, as it reached the magic circle of those portly lamps, was mercilessly sucked in and up the draught of the glass cylinder, consumed by the flame, which shone greenishly about the cap like the light given off by a rotted stump of wood, a light like a will-o'-the-wisp, like St Elmo's fire, like the Holy Spirit, which came down in the form of a purple flame hovering over the fat yellow light of the round wick. And Francin entered by the light of these lamps in the outspread brewery books the output of beer, receipts and outgoings, he compiled the weekly and monthly reports, and at the end of every year established the balance for the whole calendar year, and the pages of these books glistened like starched shirt-fronts. When Francin turned the page, these two portly lamps fussed over every motion, threatening to blow out, they squawked, those lamps, as if they were two great birds disturbed out of their sleep, those two lamps positively twitched crossly with their long necks, casting on the ceiling those constantly palpitating shadow-plays of antediluvian beasts, on the ceiling in those half shadows I always saw flapping elephant ears, palpitating rib-cages of skeletons, two great moths impaled on the stake of light ascending from the glass cylinder right up to the ceiling, where over each lamp there shone a round dazzling mirror, a sharply illumined silver coin, which constantly, scarcely perceptibly, but nevertheless shifted about, and expressed the mood of each lamp. Francin, when he turned the page, wrote again the headings with the names and surnames of the public-house landlords. He took a number three lettering pen, and as in the old missals and solemn charters, Francin gave each initial letter in the headings ornaments full of decorative curlicues and billowing lines of force, for, when I sat in the office and gazed out of the gloom at his hands, which anointed those office lamps with bleaching-powder, I always had the impression that Francin made those ornamental initials along the lines of my hair, that it gave him the inspiration, he always gave a look at my hair, out of which the light sparkled, I saw in the mirror that wherever I was in the evening, there in my coiffure and the quality of my hair there was always one lamp more. With the lettering pen Francin wrote the basic initial letters, then he took fine pens and as the mood took him dipped them alternately in green and blue and red inks and round the initials began to trace my billowing hair, and like the rose bush growing over and about the arbour, so with the thick netting and branching of the lines of force in my hair Francin ornamented the initial letters of the names and surnames of the public house landlords.

And when he returned tired from the office, he stood in the doorway in the shadow, the white shirt cuffs showed how he was exhausted by the whole day, these shirt cuffs almost touched his knees, the whole day had placed so many worries and tribulations on Francin's back that he was always ten centimetres shorter, maybe even more. And I knew that the greatest worry was me, that ever since the time he had first seen me, ever since then he had been carrying me in an invisible, and yet all too palpable rucksack on his back, which was growing ever heavier by the day. And then every evening we stood under the burning rise-and-fall lamp, the green shade was so big that there was room for both of us under it, it was a chandelier like an umbrella, under which we stood in the downpour of hissing light from the paraffin lamp, I hugged Francin with one hand and with the other I stroked the back of his head, his eyes were closed and he breathed deeply, when he had settled down he hugged me at the waist, and so it looked as if we were about to begin some kind of ballroom dance, but in fact it was something more, it was a cleansing bath, in which Francin whispered in my ear everything that had happened to him that day, and I stroked him, and every movement of my hand smoothed away the wrinkles, then he stroked my loose flowing hair, each time I drew the porcelain chandelier down lower, around the circumference of the chandelier there were thickly hung coloured glass tubes connected by beads, those trinkets tinkled round our ears like spangles and ornaments round the loins of a Turkish dancing girl, sometimes I had the impression that the great adjustable lamp was a glass hat jammed right down over both our ears, a hat hung about with a downpour of trimmed icicles . . . And I expelled the last wrinkle from Francin's face somewhere into his hair or behind his ears, and he opened his eyes, straightened himself up, his cuffs were again at the level of his hips, he looked at me distrustfully, and when I smiled and nodded, he plucked up courage and looked right at me and I at him, and I saw what a great power I had over him, how my eyes entrapped him like the eyes of a striped python when they stare at a frightened finch.

This evening a horse neighed from the darkened yard, then there came another whinny, and then there resounded a thundering of hooves, rattling of chains and jingle of buckles, Francin jerked up and listened, I took a lamp and went out into the passage and opened the door, outside the drayman was calling out in the dark, "Hey, Ede, Kare, hey whoa!", but no, the two Belgian geldings were pelting away from the stable with a lamp on their breastplate, just as they had returned weary, unharnessed from the dray, in their collars and with the traces hung on the embroidery of those collars and in all their harness after a whole day delivering the beer, just when everyone thought, these gelded stallions can be thinking of nothing else but hay and a pail of draff and a can of oats, so, all of a sudden, four times a year these two geldings recollected their coltish days, their genius of youth, full of as yet undeveloped but nevertheless present glands, and they rose up, they made a little revolt, they gave themselves signals in the gloom of dusks, returning to the stables, and they shied and bolted, but it wasn't shying, they never forgot that still and ever up to the last moment even an animal can take the path of freedom . . . and now they flew past the tied houses, on the concrete pavement, under their hooves sparks were kindled like flints, and the lamp on the chest of the offside gelding furiously bucketed about and bobbed and lit up the flitting buckles and broken reins, I leaned forward, and in the tender light of the paraffin lamp that Belgian pair flew past, stout, gigantic geldings, Ede and Kare, who together weighed twenty-five metric quintals, all of which they now put in motion, and that motion constantly threatened to turn into a fall, and the fall of one horse entailed the fall of the other, for they were harnessed together with ties and leather buckles and straps, yet constantly in that gallop they seemed to have a mutual understanding, they bolted simultaneously and alternated in leadership by no more than a couple of centimetres . . . and behind them ran the unfortunate drayman with the whip, the drayman dreading that one of the horses might break its legs, the brewery management would dock it from his pay for years to come . . . and the loss of both horses would mean paying it off till the end of his life . . . "Hey, Ede and Kare! Hey whoa!", but the team was already dashing into the draught of wind by the maltings, now their hooves softened in the muddy roadway past the chimney and malting floor, the geldings slowed down also, and again by the stables, on the cobble-stones, they speeded up, and on the concrete pavement, illuminated by sharp-edged shafts of light from passages lit by paraffin lamps, on that pavement, drawing hissing sparks from every buckle dragging on the ground, every chain, every hoof, those two Belgians gathered speed, it was no longer a running pace, but a retarded fall, puffs of breath rolled from their nostrils, their eyes were crazed and filled with horror, at the turning by the office both of them skidded on that concrete paving, like a grotesque comedy, but both rode along on their rear hooves, with sparks flying, the drayman stiffened with horror. And Francin rushed to the door, but I stood leaning on the doorpost, praying that nothing would happen to those horses, I knew very well that their incident was also my story too, and Ede and Kare once more in synchrony trotted alongside one another into the draught from the maltings, their hooves grew quiet in the soft mud on the road past the malting floor, and again they gave themselves a signal, and for the third time they flew off, the drayman leapt and the lamp, as one of the horses tugged the bridle, flew in an arc and smashed against the laundry, and the crash of it gave the Belgians new strength, first they neighed one after the other, then both together, and they pelted off along the concrete pavement ... I looked at Francin, as if it were me who had changed into a pair of Belgian horses, that was my obstinate character, once a month to go crazy, I too suffered a quarterly longing for freedom, I, who was certainly not neutered, but hale and healthy, sometimes a bit too hale and healthy ... and Francin looked at me, and saw that the bolting Belgian team, those fair blowing manes and powerful air-drawn tails streaming behind their brown bodies, they were me, not me, but my character, my bolting golden coiffure flying through the darkened night, that freely blowing unbound hair of mine ... and he pushed me aside, and now Francin stood with upraised arms in the tunnel of light flooding from the passage, with uplifted arms he stepped towards the horses and called out, "Eh-doodoo-doodoo! Whoa!", and the gelded Belgian stallions braked, from beneath their hooves the sparks showered, Francin jumped aside and took the offside horse by the bridle, snatched it and dug it into the foaming maw of the animal, and the motion of the horses ceased, the buckles and reins and straps of the harnessing fell on the ground, the drayman ran up and took the nearside one by the bridle . . . "Sir, sir . . ." stammered the drayman. "Wipe them down with straw, and take them through the yard . . . forty thousand crowns that pair cost, do you follow me, Martin?" said Francin, and when he came in the front door like a lancer, and he served with the lancers in the time of Austria, if I hadn't jumped aside he would have knocked me down, he would have stepped right over me . . . and out of the dark came the sound of the whip and the painful whinny of the Belgian horses, swearing and blows with the wrong end of the whip, then the leaping of horses in the dark and cracking of the long whip, wrapping itself round the Belgians' legs and slashing into the skin.

TWO

But my portrait is also four pigs, brewery pigs, fed on draff and potatoes, and in the summer, when the beet ripened, I went for the beet leaves and chopped up those leaves and poured yeasty liquid and old beer over them, and the pigs slept twenty hours and put on as much as one kilogram a day, those piggies of mine used to hear me going off to milk the goats, and straightaway they bellowed with joy, because they didn't know that I was going to sell two of them for ham and have two of them slaughtered at home for sausages. As I was milking the goats my porkers would cry out in delight, because they knew that all the milk I got would be poured out right away for them. Mr Cicvárek only glanced at the pigs and said immediately how much those pigs weighed, and always he was right, then he took those two piggies in his arms and threw them into a kind of basketwork gig, a butcher's buggy, drew a net over them and said, "Those little beggars fight you back just like the old woman the first time I kissed her as a lass."

Bidding them farewell I said to my piggies, "Tatty

bye, little old piggie-wiggies, you're going to make ever such lovely hams!"

The piggies had no particular desire for such glory, I knew, but all of us have the one death coming to us, and nature is merciful, when there's nothing for it, then everything alive that has to die in a moment, everything is gripped by horror, as if the fuses go, for both man and beast, and then you feel nothing and nothing hurts, that timorousness lowers the wicks in the lamps, till life just dimly flickers and is unaware of anything in its dread. I didn't have much luck with butchers, the first one I had put so much ginger in the sausages that he turned them into confectionery, whereas the second drank so much from first thing in the day that when he lifted the mallet to stun a pig he smashed his own leg, there I was standing with the knife ready, I practically slit that butcher's throat in my fury, then I had to cart him off to the hospital, what's more, and get hold of a replacement. Whereas the third butcher brought his own invention, instead of scalding he had taken to scorching the bristles off with a blow-lamp. I should've junked that butcher in the WC instead of the soup, because for one thing the bristles stayed in the skin, and more important, the pig stank of petrol, so that we had to pour the soup down the drain, because not even the pig that was left would eat it.

Mr Myclík, he was a butcher now, a butcher to my taste. He asked for some marble sponge cake and a white coffee, and had himself a rum, but only once the sausages were in the cauldron, a butcher who brought all his tools wrapped up in napkins, brought with him three aprons, one for slaughtering and scalding and gutting, the other he donned when putting out the offal on the chopping board, and the third apron when everything was almost finished. It was Mr Myclík too who taught me to get one extra spare cauldron and keep that cauldron only for boiling sausages and blood puddings and brawn and offal and heating fat, because whatever cooks in the pan leaves something of itself behind, and a pig-slaughtering, lady, it's the same as a priest serving mass, because, after all, both are a matter of flesh and blood.

And while we baked the bun dough for the sausages and blood puddings, and while we brought the tub, and into the night I boiled the barley and prepared on plates a sufficient quantity of salt and pepper and ginger and marjoram and thyme, the pig had got nothing to eat at midday and began to sense the smell of the butcher's apron, the rest of the livestock too were subdued and quiet, trembling already in advance like aspen leaves, all the other trees are calm and still, the storm is somewhere off in the Carpathians or the Alps, but the aspen leaves tremble and vibrate, like my pig, who is to be slaughtered on the morrow.

I was always the one to go and bring the pig out of the sty. I didn't like them to bind up the piggie's mouth with a rope, why this pain, when I brought the pig treacherously out for the butcher I scratched it on the dewlap, then on the brow, then on its back, and Mr Myclík came from behind with his axe, raised it and knocked down the pig with a mighty blow. For safety's sake he aimed two or three more wet knocks at the pig's splintered skull, I handed Mr Myclík the knife and he knelt down and stuck the blade in its throat, searching a moment for the artery with the point of the blade, and then a gush of blood poured out and I placed the pan beneath, and then another big cauldron. Mr Myclík always, obligingly, while I was changing the containers, stopped up the gushing blood with his hand, then let it go again. Now I had to mix the blood with a wooden whisk to stop it from clotting, then with the other hand too, with both hands simultaneously, I beat at the wonderful smoking blood, Mr Myclík with his helper Mr Martin, the drayman, rolled the pig into the tub and poured boiling water on to it from jugs, and I had to roll up my sleeves and with splayed fingers feel through the cooling blood, take the clotted lumps of blood and throw the stuff to the hens, with both arms up to my elbows in the cooling blood – my arms failed, I waggled them about as if I was on my last legs with the pig, now the last clots of coagulated blood, and the blood settled down, grew cool, I pulled my arms out of the pans and cauldron, while the scalded, shaven pig rose slowly on a crook to the beam of the open shed.

The pig's head lay severed with the dewlap on the board, just then I brought across two shoulders. And now I ran through the yard, my hair tucked under a scarf, so as not to miss a moment, because by now Mr Myclík had rolled out the guts and told his helper to go and turn and wash them, while he himself rummaged in the pig's innards, from memory, like blind Hanuš in the clock, slicing into something else every time, and the spleen and liver and stomach came loose, finally also the lungs and heart. I held the jug ready and all those wonderful lights tumbled out, that symphony of wet colours and shapes, nothing gave me such ecstasy as those pale red pig's lights, wonderfully swollen like crêpe rubber, nothing is so passionate in colouring as the dark brown colour of liver, adorned with the emerald of gall, like clouds before the storm, just like tender cloud fleeces, there running alongside the guts is the knobbly leaf fat, yellow as a guttered candle, as beeswax. And the windpipe too is composed of blue and pale red cartilaginous rings like the suction hose of a coloured vacuum-cleaner. And when we tumbled out that wonderful stuff on to the board, Mr Myclík took a knife, whetted it against a steel, and then sliced off, here a piece of still warm lean meat, here some pieces of liver, here a whole kidney and half a spleen, and I held up a large pan with browned onion and put those pieces of pig straight in the oven, after carefully salting and peppering it all, so that the goulash from the slaughtering would be ready by midday.

Taking a sieve, I strained out the boiled pig's offal, the shoulder, the halved head, turned it on to the board, one piece of meat after another, Mr Myclík removed the bones, and when the meat had cooled a little, I took in my fingers a piece of dewlap and a piece of cheek, instead of bread I chewed some pig's ear, Francin came into the kitchen, he never ate any, he couldn't stomach a thing, so he stood by the stove and had some dry bread and drank some coffee with it, and looked at me and was embarrassed on my behalf, and I ate with relish and drank beer straight from the litre bottle. Mr Myclík smiled, and just for politeness' sake took a bit of meat, but changed his mind and sipped his white coffee and tasted his marble cake, then he took his mincing knife, rolled up his sleeves, and with powerful motions of the knife the lumps of meat began to lose their shape and function, and with the half-moon slicings of the rocker blades the meat gradually became sausage-meat. And Mr Myclík proffered his palm, and I poured scalded spices into it, Mr Myclík was the one butcher whose spices I had to drench first in boiling water, because, he said, and I understood him quite palpably, it makes for a greater dispersion and delicacy of aroma. And then he added the soaked bread-roll crumb and again mixed it all thoroughly and ran through it with his powerful hands and fingers and mixed it through and through, then he tugged the sausage-meat off both his hands, dug into it, tried it for taste, gazed at the ceiling, and at that moment was as handsome as a poet, he stared at the ceiling in delight, repeating over to himself: pepper, salt, ginger, thyme, bread-roll, garlic, and as he pattered over that quick-fire butcher's tiny prayer, he dug into the sausage-meat and offered me some. I took it on my finger and put it in my mouth and tasted it, staring likewise at the ceiling, and with eyes brimful with piggy delight I unfurled and relished on my tongue the peacock fantail of all those aromas, and then I nodded my assent, that as the mother of the household I approved of this gamut of flavours, and nothing now stood in the way of getting down to making the sausages themselves. And so Mr Myclík took the trimmed skins, spaled with a splint at one end, with two fingers of the right hand he parted the aperture and with the other hand just stuffed, and out of his fist there grew a wonderful sausage, which I took and fastened with a spale, and so we worked, and all the while as the sausage-meat declined, so in their jointed vessels of skins the heap of sausages rose.

"Mr Martin, where have you got to again?" Mr Myclík called out every other while, and every time this Mr Martin, the drayman, maybe all the days of his life, whenever he had a moment, he had loitered, in the shed, in the stable, behind the cart, in the passageways, he drew out a little round mirror and looked at himself, he was so enamoured of himself, he was always overpowered by whatever it was he saw in that little round mirror, for hours on end he could linger in the stable, forgetting to go home, all because he was plucking bristles from his nose with the tweezers, plucking hairs from his eyebrows, he even dyed not only his hair, but even coloured his eye-lashes and powdered his face. I'd tell myself, next time Francin would have to get me another helper from the brewery. "Mr Martin, for Christ's sake where have you got to again? Slice up this gut fat, we're going to make barley and breadcrumb puddings, where have you been?"

Mr Myclík loaded the barley puddings, by now he'd drunk his second pouring of rum, then, quite out of the blue, he just dug into the blood-soaked sausage-meat and smeared a bloody smudge on my face with his finger. And quietly he started to laugh, his eye glinting like a ring, I dipped into the bloody pan myself, and when I tried to smear the butcher one on the face he ducked aside and I planted my palm on the white wall, but before I'd wiped it off Mr Myclík had given me another smudge, then he carried on skewering the pudding. I dipped into the blood again and made a dash at him, Mr Myclík ducked me several times like a Savoy medley, then I smeared his face with blood, and went on skewering the barley puddings, and laughed when I saw the butcher laughing with his great hearty laughter, it wasn't just any old laughter, it was a laughter from somewhere way back out of pagan times, when people believed in the force of blood and spittle. I couldn't resist scooping up some barley blood and smearing it again in Mr Myclík's face, and he ducked me again, I missed him, and with a great big chuckle he planted me another smudge, and carried on skewering the puddings. Mr Martin brought a crate of beer over from the bottling room, and as he bent down carefully I smeared him in the face with a full palm of bloody sausage-meat, and Mr Martin the drayman drew his little round mirror out of his pocket, looked at himself, and probably he was even more enamoured of himself than usual, he gave a hearty laugh and scooped up three fingerfuls of red sausage-meat. I dashed into the living room, Mr Martin ran after me, I shouted out, not even realising that behind the wall the brewery management board was in session, you could distinctly hear the scraping of chairs and calling of voices, but Mr Martin besmirched me with blood and laughed, the blood brought us closer together somehow, I laughed and sat myself down on the sofa, holding my hands out in front of me like a puppet, so as not to mess up the covers, Mr Martin likewise held his messy hand up in the same gesture, while the rest of his whole body gradually dissolved with laughter, shook, and his throat burst into a choking, jubilant, coughing chuckle. And Mr Myclík dashed up and scooped with a full palm at Mr Martin's face, the barley grains glistened in it like pearls, and Mr Martin stopped laughing, he went solemn, it seemed as if he wanted to hit someone, but he only drew out his little round pocket mirror, looked at himself in it, and seemingly found himself even better looking than he had ever seen himself before, and he guffawed with laughter, opening wide the sluice gates of his throat and bellowing with laughter, and Mr Myclík, an interval of a third lower, chuckled away with a small-scale laughter which matched the little teeth under his black moustache, and so we roared together with laughter and didn't know why, one look was enough and off we went, bursting into stitches of mirth which hurt in the side. And now the door opened and in rushed Francin in his frock coat, pressing his cabbage-leaf-shaped tie against his chest, and when he saw the blood-smeared faces and the terrible laughter, he clasped his hands, but I couldn't restrain myself, I took three fingers of bloody sausage-meat and smeared Francin in the face, to make him laugh in spite of himself, but he took such fright that he ran, just as he was, into the boardroom, two members of the board of management collapsed on the spot, because they thought a crime had been committed in the brewery. Doctor Gruntorád himself, the chairman, ran by the back entrance into the kitchen, looked about him, and when he saw that broad laughter on the blood-smeared faces he sighed a sigh of relief, sat himself down, and I, with my hands messy with sausage-meat, made a red stripe on the doctor's face, and for just a moment we all went quiet, gazing through tearful eyes at our chairman Doctor Gruntorád, who rose to his feet and clenched his fists and thrust out his bulldog jaw ... but all of a sudden he bayed with laughter, it was that force of blood, that sacral something which, in order to be averted, was discharged from time immemorial by this smearing with pig's blood, the doctor dug into the sausage-meat and rushed at me, I ran laughing into the living room, the doctor missed me and landed his hand on the ready made-up bed, he went into the kitchen and scooped up a fistful and returned, I ran round the table, the white cloth was full of my palm prints, every other moment Dr Gruntorád dotted the tablecloth with blood, he headed me off and I ran squealing into the passage connecting our flat with the boardroom, the lights were on in the room and I ran into the meeting, golden chandeliers and beneath them a long table covered with green baize, upon which files and reports lay outspread. And Gruntorád, chairman of the board, rushed in after me, all the members of the management board thought their chairman was after my blood, that he'd tried to kill me already. Francin sat on a chair and mopped his brow with a bloodstained hand, and the chairman chased me several times round the table, I shrieked and the sweat poured from both of us, when suddenly my foot slipped and I fell, and Doctor Gruntorád, chairman of the municipal brewery, and limited-liability company, splodged a full hand in my face and sat down, his cuffs drooped and he started to laugh, he laughed just like me, we laughed together, but that laughter only enhanced the consternation of the members of the management board, because they all thought we had gone quite dotty.

"Gentlemen, if I may be so bold, I invite you all to our slaughtering party," I said.

And Doctor Gruntorád declared:

"Manager, have ten crates of bottled lager brought over from the plant. No no, make it twelve!"

"Come along, this way, gentlemen, if you please, but you'll have to eat the pork goulash with a spoon from a soup bowl, right up to the brim! And in a little bit we'll have sausages too with horseradish, and barley and breadcrumb puddings. Gentlemen, come this way please," with a motion of my blood-spattered hand I invited my guests in by the rear entrance.

It was late at night when the members of the management board dispersed to go home in their buggies. I accompanied each with a lamp in my hand, the vehicles drove up in front of the entrance, glowing carriage lamps fitted on mudguards illuminated the dimly gleaming hindquarters of horses, all the members of the management board squeezed Francin's hand and clapped him on the shoulder. That night I slept alone in the bedroom, cold air streamed in through the open window, on planks between chairs the sausages and puddings glittered on their rye straw, right by the bed on long boards lay cooling the dismembered parts of the pig, the boned and apportioned hams, the chops and roasting joints, the shoulders and knees and legs, all laid out according to Mr Myclík's orderly system. As I got into bed I could hear Francin in the kitchen getting up and pouring himself some lukewarm coffee, taking some dry bread to chew with it, it had been a tremendous blow-out, all the members of the management board ate abundantly, only Francin stood there in the kitchen drinking lukewarm coffee and chewing dry bread with it. I lay in the feather quilt, and before I fell asleep, I stretched out a hand and touched a shoulder, then I fingered a joint and went dozing off with my fingers on a virginal tenderloin, and dreamed of eating a whole pig. When towards morning I woke, I had such a thirst, I went barefoot to fetch a bottle of beer, pulled off the stopper and drank greedily, then I lit the lamp, and holding it in my fingers, I went from one bit of pork to the next, unable to restrain myself from lighting the primus and slicing off two lovely lean schnitzels from the leg. I beat them out thin, salted and peppered them and cooked them in butter in eight minutes flat, all that time, which seemed to me an eternity, my mouth was watering, that was what I needed, to eat practically the whole of the two legs, in simple unbreaded schnitzels sprinkled with lemon juice. I added some water to the schnitzels, covered the pan with a lid, out of which angry steam huffed and puffed, and now I laid those schnitzels on a plate and ate them greedily, as always I got my nightdress spattered, just as I always spatter my blouse with juice or gravy, because when I eat, I don't just eat, I guzzle . . . and when I had finished and wiped the plate with bread, I saw through the open door how, there in the twilight gloom, Francin's eyes were staring, just those eyes reproaching me again for eating as ill becomes a decent woman, and it was as well I had eaten my fill already, for that look of his always spoilt my appetite, I bent over the lamp, but then I remembered the reek of the wick would affect the flavour of the meat, I carried the lamp into the passage and blew it out with a powerful puff of breath. And so I climbed into bed, and feeling the shoulder of pork, dropped off to sleep, looking forward in the morning when I woke to making two more plain schnitzels.

THREE

Bod'a Červinka always took great pains with my hair. He said, "That hair of yours is a hark back to the golden days of yore, never have I had such hair under my comb before." When Bod'a combed out my hair, it was as if he had lit two burning torches in the shop, there in the mirrors and bowls and glass bottles the fire of my hair blazed up, and I had to admit that Bod'a was right. Never did I see my hair look so beautiful elsewhere as it did in Bod'a's shop, when he washed it in camomile infusion, which I boiled myself and brought along in a milk can. While my hair was still wet it never had the promise of what began to happen to it when it dried out; the moment it started to dry it was as if in those streaming tresses thousands of golden bees were born, thousands of little tiny fireflies, the crackling of thousands of little tiny amber crystals. And when Bod'a first drew the comb through this mane of tresses, there came a crackling and a hissing from them, and they swelled and grew and seethed, till Bod'a had to kneel down, as if he were grooming the tails of a couple of stallions with a currycomb. And his shop was

24

illuminated with it, cyclists jumped off their bikes and pressed their faces to the window to confirm and explain what had so startled their eyes. And Bod'a himself dwelt in the cloudy expanse of my hair, he always locked and closed the shop so as not to be disturbed, every now and again he sniffed at the scent of it, and when he had finished combing he breathed out blissfully, and only then did he bind the hair, just as the mood, which I trusted, took him, sometimes with a purple, at other times a green, or else a red or a blue ribbon, as if I was part of a Catholic rite, as if my hair was part of some feast of the church. Then he unlocked the shop, brought me my bicycle, hung the can on the frame, and helped me ceremoniously up on to the saddle. By then there was a crowd of people in front of the shop, everyone stared at that hair smelling sweetly of camomile. When I leant on the pedals Mr Bod'a ran alongside for a bit and held up my hair to prevent it from catching in the chain or the spokes. And when I had got up enough speed Mr Bod'a tossed up a corner of my tresses in the air, as you would throw up in the air a star or a kite up into the sky, and breathless he returned to the shop. And I rode off, and as my hair blew behind me, I could hear its crackling, like someone rubbing salt or silk, like when rain trickles off down a tin roof, like Wiener schnitzel frying, so that torch of tresses blew behind me, as when boys at dusk with burning pitch broomsticks run about on the Mayday night of Philip and James or burn witches, so the smoke of my hair blew behind me. And people stopped, and I wasn't surprised that they couldn't tear themselves away from that blowing hair as it came and accosted them like an advertisement. And I felt good myself when I saw how I was seen, the empty can of camomile jangled on the handlebars and the comb of streaming air swept my hair back. I rode through the square, all glances converging on my flowing tresses like spokes on the wheels of this bicycle on which my moving Ego trod the pedals. Francin met me twice flowing along like this, and each time this blowing hair of mine took his breath away, he didn't even acknowledge my presence, he was quite incapable of calling out to me, he just stood there numbed by my unexpected apparition, pressing himself to the wall and obliged to pause a moment to get his breath back. I had the feeling he would have keeled over if I had spoken to him, it was his loving adoration which pressed him to the wall, like the picture by Aleš of the orphan child in all the school readers. And I trod on the pedals, knocking my knees alternately against the can, cyclists riding the other way halted, some turned their bikes and sped after me, overtook me, only to turn their bicycles round and ride again to meet me, and they greeted my little blouse and milk can and my blowing hair and me in my entirety, and affably and understandingly I granted them this show and only regretted I did not have the ability to ride to meet myself like this one day, so that I could also take pleasure in what I took pride in and could not be ashamed of. I rode once more through the square, and then up the main thoroughfare, there stood the Orion motorcycle in front of the Grand, in front of it Francin holding a spark plug in his fingers, there he stood with that motorbike of his, and certainly he saw me, but he pretended not to, his Orion was always playing up with its ignition and whatnot, so that Francin carried always in the sidecar with him not only all his spanners and wrenches and screwdrivers, but also a little treadle lathe. And next to Francin stood two members of the management board of our limited-liability brewery. Before slapping my shoe on the pavement I reached behind me and drew my hair forward, and laid it in my lap.

"Hello, Francin," I said.

And Francin blew into the spark plug, but when he heard me the spark plug dropped from his fingers, his face had two smudges on it from the repairing.

"Good day to you," the two management board members greeted me.

"Good morning, lovely weather, isn't it?" I said, and Francin blushed to the roots of his hair.

"Where have you dropped that spark plug, Francin?" I said.

And I bent down, Francin knelt and searched for the spark plug under the sidecar, I laid a little hankie on the pavement, knelt down and my hair fell beside me, Mr de Giorgi, master chimneysweep, took up my hair tenderly and threw it across his elbow, like a sacristan taking a priest's robe, Francin kneeled and fixed his eyes under the blue shadow of the motorcycle sidecar, and I saw that my presence had so disconcerted him that he was searching only in order to regain his composure. When we had our wedding it was the same thing again, as he was putting the ring on me his fingers trembled so much that the wedding ring dropped out and rolled away somewhere, and so first Francin, then the witnesses, then the wedding guests, first bending over, then on all fours, and finally the priest himself, all of them were crawling on all fours about the church, until the server found that wedding ring under the pulpit, a little round ring that had rolled off quite the opposite way to where the whole wedding had been searching, down on its hands and knees. And I laughed that day, I just stood there and I laughed . . .

"There's something over there by the gutter," a child said, passing by and bowling his hoop on down the main street.

And there by the gutter the spark plug lay, Francin picked it up in his fingers, and when he tried to screw it into the engine his hands shook so much that the spark plug chattered in the threads. And the doors of the Grand opened and out came Mr Bernádek, master blacksmith, who drank a keg of Pilsner at a sitting, and he carried out a glass of beer.

"Come on, young missus, don't be shy, have one on me!"

"Cheers, Mr Bernádek!"

I sank my nose in the foam, raised my arm as if to take the oath, and slowly and with relish I drank down that sweetly bitter liquid, and when I had emptied the glass, I wiped my lips with my forefinger and said, "But our own brewery beer is just as good."

Mr Bernádek gave me a bow:

"But the Pilsner beer, young missus, is nearer to the colour of your hair, allow me . . ." mumbled the master blacksmith, "allow me to go back in and continue drinking in your honour some more of that golden hair of yours."

He bowed and left, a presence that weighed a

hundred and twenty kilos, and whose trousers made huge flaps at the back, flaps like those of an elephant.

"Francin," I said, "are you coming back for your dinner?"

He tightened the spark plug at the top of the engine, feigning concentration. I bowed to the two honourable members of the management board, trod on the pedals, tossed behind me those streaming tresses of Pilsner, and gaining speed rode off down the narrow lane on to the bridge, and the land beyond the balustrade unfurled in front of me like an umbrella. You could smell the scent of the river, and there in the distance rose the beige-walled brewery with its maltings, our limited-liability company municipal brewery.

FOUR

On the lid of the muscle builder box was the message: You too shall possess the same fine physique, powerful muscles and stunning strength!

And every morning Francin would exercise his muscles, which were just as magnificent as the gladiator's on the box lid anyway, but Francin saw himself as just a puny little skinned rabbit. I put the pot of potatoes on the stove, took the box with the photo of the great muscle-man on the lid, and read out loud:

"You too shall have the strength of a tiger that with one blow of its paw kills prey much larger than itself."

At that moment Francin glanced out to the pavement, and the muscle builder withered in his fingers, and Francin straightaway collapsed on the ottoman in a heap and said, "Pepin."

"Now at last I'm going to see that brother of yours, at long last I'm going to hear something from my little old brother-in-law!"

And I leant against the window frame, and there on the pavement stood a man, with a small oval hat on his head, wearing check breeches tucked into green Tyrolean stockings, with an upturned nose and on his back an army rucksack.

"Uncle Jožin," I called out to him from the doorstep, "come on in."

"Which one are you?" asked Uncle Pepin.

"Your sister-in-law, you're right welcome!"

"Christ, I'm a lucky lad, to have such a fine winsome sister-in-law, but what've you done with Francin?" Uncle enquired, rolling on into the kitchen and living-room.

"Here he is, but what's up with the man? Lying down are you? Good God, man, I've come to pay you a visit, I won't be staying more than a fortnight," Uncle ran on and his voice boomed and sliced the air like an army banner, like a military command, and Francin felt an electric shock hit him with each word, and he leapt up and wrapped himself in a blanket.

"All of them sends their love, except Bóchalena, she's a goner, some joker put gunpowder in her woodpile, when the old thing popped a log on the stove, it went off, lammed her right in the mug, and that was that, she just snuffed it."

"Bóchalena?" I clasped my hands: "Your sister?"

"Sister? No. Local woman, old girl that crammed herself all day with apples and buns, for thirty years she'd always be saying, 'Oh, you young folks, I'll be gone soon, I dinna want to do nothing, just sleep . . .' me neither, I'm no exactly one hundred percent," said Uncle, untying the cords of his haversack and tumbling all his cobbler's tools out on the floor, and Francin, hearing the clatter, covered his face with his hands and groaned, as if Uncle had tumbled all that shoemaker's equipment out into his brains.

"Uncle Jožin," I said, shoving the baking tin in front of his face, "have yourself a bun."

And Uncle Pepin ate two buns, and declared, "I'm really no a hundred percent."

"Surely no," I fell on my knees and clasped my hands over those lasts and hammers and leather-cutting knives and other cobbler's bits and pieces.

"You just watch it!" Uncle Pepin cried with alarm. "Dinna go and mess it up with that hair of yours, but listen Francin lad, Zbořil the priest's broke his leg at the hip sae bad he'll just be a cripple for life. Uncle Zavičák, he was up doing the roof of the church tower when the cradle slipped and him with it and down he went, but he grabs a hold of the hand of the clock, and there he is, holding on to this hand on the tower clock, but the hand shifts, it slips from a quarter past eleven right down to half past, and so, as Uncle goes hurtling, his hands lose their grip on the clock hand and he just plummets, but there's lime trees growing down there, so Uncle plonks into the top of one of they, and Zbořil the vicar, as he just stands there watching, he's wringing his hands to see Zavičák drop from branch to branch, and then he falls on his back on the ground, and Zbořil comes rushing over to congratulate him, but he overlooks this step, see, he falls and breaks his leg, so old Zavičák has to load up Zbořil the minister, and off they cart him to the hospital in Prostějov."

I picked up a wooden last for a lady's shoe and stroked it.

"These are really lovely things, aren't they, Francin?"

I said, but Francin groaned, as if I was showing him a rat or a frog.

"Aye they're right beauties," said Uncle and pulled out his pince-nez, placed it on his nose, and there were no lenses in the pince-nez, and Francin, when he saw that lensless pince-nez on his brother's nose, he whimpered, he almost wept and turned to the wall, then he tossed about and the springs of the sofa moaned just like Francin.

"And what's our Uncle over in the Great Lakes doing?" I asked.

Uncle gave a dismissive wave of the hand, and took Francin by the shoulder and turned him round to face him, and related to him in a great voice full of glee:

"Well now, Uncle Metud over in the Great Lakes he's begun to get a wee bit strange, and one day he read a notice in the paper: Suffer from boredom? Get yourself a racoon. And Uncle Metud, what with having no kids and that, he replied to the ad, and in a week's time the beast arrived, in a packing case. Well that was a thing now! Just like a child, it made friends with anybody going, but there was one special thing about it, you see, the German for racoon is *Waschbär*, and whatever that racoon saw, it simply had to wash it, and so it washed Uncle Metud's alarm clock and three watches, till nobody could put them together again. Then one day it washed all the spices. And again, when Uncle Metud took his bicycle to pieces, the racoon went and washed the parts for him in the nearest creek, and the neighbours were coming along saying: Uncle Metud, would you be needing this piece of junk at all? We just found it over in the creek! And after they'd brought him several bits like that, Metud went to have a look himself, and that racoon had gone off with practically the whole bang shoot. My those buns are good though. And that racoon he would only do his business in the wardrobe, so the whole building stank of his pee, in the end they had to lock everything up from him, they even had to start whispering when they spoke together. My those buns are good, pity I'm no one hundred percent. But the racoon kept watching to see where they put the key, it went and unlocked whatever they were keeping from him. But the worst of it was, the animal kept a look-out in the evenings, and soon as Uncle Metud gave Auntie a wee kiss, the racoon went for him and wanted to have some too, so Uncle Metud had to go down to the woods wi' Auntie Rozára courting like before they were married, and still they had to keep turning round in case the racoon was right there behind them. And so there was no time for boredom, till once they went off for two days and the racoon was sae bored that this one Whitsun holiday he dismantled the whole big tiled stove in the living room, made such a muck of the furnishings and the feather quilt and the linen in the commode, that Uncle Metud sat down and wrote him an ad to *The Moravian Eagle*: Suffer from boredom? Get yourself a racoon! And ever since then he's been cured of his melancholia."

Uncle Pepin went on, and as he talked he ate one bun after another, and now he felt into the baking tin, he fingered the whole baking tin, and finding it empty he waved a hand and said:

"I'm no quite one hundred percent."

"Like Bóchalena," I said.

"What nonsense are you blethering?" Uncle Pepin broke into a shout: "Bóchalena was just a poor old thing that crammed herself with apples, except she also had visions . . ."

"Was it the apples?" I interrupted.

"Bollocks! Visions, these old lassies get visions, she got it from the church," Uncle Pepin said choking, "a great big horse flying in the night over our wee town, and the mane and tail of that horse blazing with fire, well and as Bóchalena said at the time, 'It'll be war,' and it was war too, but Francin lad, last year the whole town was in a right tizz! The old women were falling down on their knees, I saw it too, over the square and over the church, this baby Jesus figure flying through the air! But then it all came out, that tootsy wee chappie Lolan had been out watching his lambs, and the airyplanes exercising overhead, lugging after them some kind of punchbag and potting at it with their popguns, they clean forgot about the rope, you see, and as it dangled along the ground, so it got tangled up all round Lolan's leg, and him a braw wee child too, with his dainty fair hair, and as the airyplane flew upwards, the rope went up and Lolan with it, and right over our wee town Lolan went, flying through the air, but the old women they thought it was baby Jesus, specially when the rope got hooked up on a lime tree by the church, and this baby Jesus fell down like Uncle Zavičák, tumbling from branch to branch, and then wee Lolan falls to earth and says 'Where are all my poor wee lambs?' and the old women knelt down for him to bless them."

So Uncle continued, and his voice was resounding and triumphant and blared right through the room.

Francin got dressed, pulled on his coat, his frock-coat, tied with his fingers his tie shaped like a cabbage leaf, I adjusted his gutta-percha collar with folded-down corners, raised my eyes and gazed into his, and gave him a little peck on the tip of his finger.

"A fortnight?" he whispered. "You'll see, he'll stay a fortnight right enough, and maybe just the rest of his life!"

When I saw how unhappy he was, I planted a proper kiss on his lips, and he was embarrassed, he looked at me reproachfully, a decent woman doesn't behave like this in public, even though the only public present was actually Uncle Pepin, and Francin extracted himself from my embrace and went off through the back entrance to the office. Through the wall I heard the glazed swing doors burst open, ah, Francin and his "decent behaved woman", ever since I married him, he's been raising the matter, raising the spectre of this decent woman, sketching out the pattern of his model woman, which I never was and never could be, I that so much loved eating cherries, but when I ate them my way, greedily and ravenously, he reddened to the roots of his hair, and I couldn't fathom the cause of his annoyance, until I saw for myself, that a cherry held in my lips was indeed a reason for his discomfiture, because a decent woman simply doesn't eat cherries quite so greedily as that. When in the autumn I scrubbed the heads of corn on the cob, again he looked at my scrubbing palm and the tiny glints of fire in my eyes, and there again, a decent woman just doesn't scrub corn on the cob quite like that, and if she does, well not with such great laughter and flaming eyes as mine, if some male stranger were to see this, he might see in my hands scrubbing that corn on the cob some sort of a sign favourable to his hankerings.

Uncle Pepin laid out his precious cobbler's treasure on a little stool, then he took off my shoe, and elaborating to me on all its parts, he replaced his lensless pince-nez and said to me grandly:

"And since you're a lady of such outstanding intellectuality, I'm going to mend you all your broken shoes, because I've made footwear for the official supplier by appointment to the court, that was patronised not only by the imperial court, but all throughout the world, that delivered shoes . . ."

"By bicycle," said I.

"Bollocks!" roared Uncle Pepin. "Do you think your court supplier is just the same as your common or garden rat-catcher, or peltmonger? He delivers by ship and by rail, if the Emperor ever met his sort riding on a bicycle . . ."

"Did the Emperor ride a bicycle too?" I clasped my hands.

"What are you twittering on about, you twittering magpie?" Uncle shouted. "I'm telling you, if the Emperor met the likes of your court-appointed supplier riding on a bicycle he'd have taken his . . ."

"Bicycle off him," I said.

"Bollocks! Taken his court appointment off him and the eagle out of his crest!" Uncle Pepin choked and spluttered, but then, taking a look at the stool, he gave a blissful grin, took out a pot, opened it, sniffed and gave it to me to sniff too and waved his hand:

"Feast your eyes on this, sister-in-law, it's cobbler's

glue alias shoemaker's gum," said Uncle Pepin, placing the open pot on a chair.

Through the wall you could hear the rattling of chairs in the boardroom, subdued conversation, the shuffling of heels, then the chairs went silent and Francin opened the meeting in a quiet voice with a report on the state of the brewery over the past month.

"Uncle Jožin," I ventured, "so this man really supplied shoes to the court and the estates?"

"Bollocks!" roared Uncle Pepin. "What are you twittering on about like a silly bairn? What's a court supplier got to do with farming and cattle-estates? A court supplier's a pretty touchy character, now old Kafka, he was that touchy, always on edge, once when his wee daughter kept bashing her head on every sharp edge of furniture, old Kafka, that court supplier by appointment, he took a whole basketful of shoulder pads out from the workshop and he stuck a pad on every single corner of the furniture, but then what with him being so mighty on edge, he went and flung the door open that sharp, he knocked his wee lassie right out with the door, so Látal now, he advised him just to put another pad on his daughter's forrid."

"Látal, would that be Francin's cousin, Uncle Jožin?" I said.

"Balls!" Uncle Pepin cried. "Látal the school-teacher! Last year he fell out of a first floor classroom right in the middle of demonstrating uniform time and motion . . . like it's when a train just keeps chugging along and along and along and along and along . . . and Látal struck out with both arms flailing and like a train he pounded along over to the open window, and then he fell right out the window, and the whole class rushed gleefully to the window, surely teacher must've broken both his legs in the tulip bed, but Látal wasna there, he'd cut round the yard and nipped up the stair, and again, there his train was, chugging along and along and along . . . and in he came to the classroom, behind the backs of the schoolkids that was still leaning out of the window."

In the boardroom through the wall you could hear the voice of the chairman, Doctor Gruntorád:

"Manager, who's making that infernal roar out there?"

"Sorry, Sir, my brother's here on a visit," said Francin.

"Well, Manager, just you go and tell your brother from us to pipe down! This is our brewery!"

"Now that Látal fellow's wife was Mercina, your cousin, wasn't she, Uncle Jožin?" I said doucely.

"Not a bit of it! Mercina's the one married Uncle Vaňura, chef on the Balkan express, ye know, lived in Bohemia, hereabouts, somewhere in Mnichovo Hradiště, and when that Balkan express went through Mnichovo Hradiště once a week regular, Mercina used to let the dog out every time at half ten, it went down to the station, Uncle Vaňura leant out of the Balkan express and dropped it a muckle parcel of bones, and the dog took it off home, but one day this year, when Vaňura let go the bones, the parcel went and clobbered the stationmaster one, and old Vaňura had to pay for fouling up his uniform!" Uncle Pepin hollered on.

And again he picked up my shoe and put on that lensless pince-nez and roared out radiantly, "But never you heed this nonsense, I'll explain it you once all over again, then I'll hand it to you to have a try! So this here is Pariser Schnitt, and this is the vamp or *Gelenk*, alias ankle upper. This here is the sole, alias bottom leather, and this is your heel or *Absatz*. Mind you, sister-in-law, anyone that wants to be a shoemaker or a cobbler has to have a certificate of apprenticeship, and that's like getting your school leaving certificate or a college doctorate. Now that court-supplier Weinlich . . ."

"Ulrich?" I said, cupping my ear with my hand.

"Weinlich!" roared Uncle. "Wein as in wine, there's this idiot scuffs up his shoes and brings them to this court-supplier chappie Weinlich and the supplier says: 'Good God man, these shoes are wrecked, what am I supposed to do with them?' And the idiot says, 'Sell 'em to the Jews.' Now Weinlich was Jewish himself, and he starts roaring, 'So Jews are swine, are they?' "

"Peps," I said softly.

"Balls!" thundered Uncle, rearing threateningly over me. "I've had nothing but glowing testimonials, and what would a fancy gent like that be associating with me for! What d'ye mean Peps? Sister-in-law, you're as daft as in a school test afore noon!"

And Uncle gave himself such a clout on the brow with his fist that his pince-nez flew under the cabinet, but one glance at my shoe simmered him down, he seated himself and pointing with his fingertip continued with his vociferous schooling:

"And this as we've said already's the *Absatz* or heel, and on that heel or *Absatz* there's the heel-piece, heel-tap, and edge-piece otherwise known amongst the footwear profession as the rand!"

I picked up a long iron spoon, whose end was as rough as an ox's tongue, and I said, "Uncle Jožin, this is the *Abnehmer*, isn't it?"

"What?" Uncle roared woundedly. "The *Abnehmer* is this thing here, *Abnehmer* alias remover, but the thing you're got in your hand is a rasp or a file or a scraper!"

And the door flew open, and in the doorway stood Francin, pressing his tie down with his palm, he spread out his arms and bent his knees, he bowed to Uncle Jožin and then to me, bowed to the waist and said:

"You two uhlans, what are you yelling away like that for? Jožko, why all the howling?" and he put his hand in the open pot of gum.

"It's no me," mumbled Uncle Pepin.

"Who is it then? Is it . . . me for instance?" Francin pointed to himself with both hands.

"It's somebody in here, inside of me," said Uncle Pepin knitting and twisting his fingers with embarrassment.

"Cool down, the brewery management board is meeting, the chairman himself sent me to give you the message," Francin raised his hand and retreated into the passage . . .

Then you could hear Francin's quiet voice again, carrying on with his report, in which he explained how the debits for the month which had just expired would be evened out by the proceeds of the month to come. I brought over a pot of pork dripping and spread slice after slice of bread for Uncle Pepin, each time as he was about to speak I handed him another slice, but through in the boardroom Francin's voice came to a halt, you heard the shuffling of heels, then exclamations, the legs of the Thonet chairs rattled, as if all the members of the management board had risen to their feet, I thought it must be the end of the meeting, but the voice of the chairman of the brewery management board, Doctor Gruntorád, boomed out: "Meeting adjourned for ten minutes!"

The door connecting the office with the passage flew open as if with a kick, and into the room rushed Francin, pressing his hand to his tie and shouting:

"Who put that glue on the chair there for me? Crivens! I've got one sheet of paper stuck down so hard I couldn't even turn the page! Mr de Giorgi tried to help and he got so messed up he couldn't even get his hands off the green baize! And the chairman's got it on his pince-nez, it's stuck fast to his nose! And my fingers, what's more, have stuck to my tie, look at me!" Francin pulled away his hand and the elastic bands holding his tie went taut.

"I'll bring you a bit of warm water," I said.

But Francin jerked his hand forward abruptly and the elastic bands stretched and burst, and the hand with the tie shot forward while the elastic bands jabbed Francin in the neck, and he moaned softly like a little boy: "Oooh!"

Uncle Pepin took the lid off the pot, presented it to Francin and announced proudly:

"This stuff is manufactured by that Mecca of the footwear world, the Vienna firm of Salamander and Co.!"

And Uncle held up his lensless pince-nez to his nose.

FIVE

Every month Francin went to Prague on his motorcycle, but every time something broke down, so he had to mend it. All the same he would return radiant, handsome, and I always had to hear down to the last detail all the things he had had to do to make his unroadworthy Orion into a motorcycle again, one that always made it to its destination. Made it means that the motorcycle got back to the brewery, even though sometimes he had to push it the last stretch. But he never cursed and swore, he would push the whole contraption ten, fifteen, or maybe only five kilometres, and when he pushed the Orion in from Zvěřínek, a village three kilometres away, Francin enthused about how much better it was getting. Today Francin returned from Prague pulled by a yoke of bullocks. When he had paid the farmer he rushed into the kitchen, and as always I gave him a hug, we stepped again under the rise-and-fall lamp, and anybody peeping in the window would have had to wonder. For when Francin returned from Prague, each time there was this particular ritual, Francin shut his eyes and I reached into his breast pocket, but Francin shook his head, and then I unbuttoned his coat and reached into his waistcoat pocket, and Francin still shook his head, and then I reached into his trouser pocket and Francin nodded his head, and all the while he kept his eyes blissfully closed, and always I drew out of some place of concealment in his clothing a little tiny parcel, and out of that parcel, which I slowly unwrapped, feigning astonished surprise and delight, I unpacked a little ring, sometimes a brooch, once a wristwatch even. But this ritual was not the first, before, when Francin returned from Prague, where he went once a month to visit Brewers House, when he came in, he always waited till it was getting dark, told me to shut my eyes, and I used to shut my eyes the minute he came into the kitchen, Francin led me off to the living room, sat me in front of the mirror and made me promise I wouldn't look, and when I promised, he put a wonderful hat on my head, and Francin said, "Now," and I looked into the mirror and took that hat in my fingers and adjusted it to my own taste, then turned round and Francin enquired of me, "Who was it bought you this, Maryška?" and I said, "Francin," and kissed him on the hand and he stroked me. And other times he brought me something which he put round my neck and which chilled me, and I opened my eyes, and there in the mirror was glittering a necklace, a piece of Jablonec jewelry, and Francin would ask me, "Who was it bought you this?" And I kissed him on the hand and said, "You, Francin." And then he asked, "And who is this Francin?" And I said: "My little hubby." And so every month I got some present or other, Francin had all my body measurements, he knew them off by heart, he always used to ask me casually, in advance, what might I possibly like to have? And I never said it out straight, I always chatted on about something and Francin got the message. And then, the first time he brought me a ring, he stepped under the rise-and-fall lamp and taught me for the first time to search through his pockets, greater and lesser, and I always guessed where the present probably was, but always I went for that place last, to make Francin happy.

Today, when he returned drawn by the yoke of bullocks, he asked me to shut my eyes. And he carried something through into the living room. And then he put the light out in the living room and took me by the hand and led me through with closed eyes, he sat me down on the little armchair in front of the mirror, then he went and drew the curtains. I heard the lid snap open and thought he'd bought me a hat-box, but then I heard him stick the plug in the collar of the socket, I thought he'd bought me some sort of mixer, patent cooker or solar lamp, and then I heard a sizzling, slowly ascending rumble. Francin laid his hand gently on my shoulder and said "Now." And I opened my eyes, and what I saw was marvellous to behold. Francin stood there like a magician, in his fingers he held a tube, in which there shone a pale blue light, a kind of thick purple violet light, which shone on Francin's hands and face and clothes, a purple violet dampened fire in a glass tube, which Francin put close to my hand, and my arm went magnetic, I could feel purple sawdust sizzling out of that light, immaterial sparklets, which entered me and imbued me with fragrance, so that I had the scent of a summer thunderstorm, the air in the room had the scent too, like air after lightning strikes, and Francin slowly lifted the wonderful thing and put it close to his own face, I saw again that handsome profile of his, Francin stood solemnly here like Gunnar Tolnes, and then ran that tube over the open case, and there on the red plush, lining the lid as well, were set in a fan shape all kinds of brush heads, pipes and bells, all of it was made of glass and enclosed like bottles, dozens of instruments of glass, and Francin pulled off the tube and took out of the case and fixed into the bakelite holder one wonderful object after another, and each time that glass vessel glowed and filled with purple violet light, which fizzled and passed through into the human body just as required. Francin changed and experimented with all these electrodes with their neon gas content, saying quietly, "Maryška, now Uncle Pepin can bawl his head off, now they can make trouble at the brewery, now people can insult me as they please, but here . . . here are these sparks of healing which turn into health, high frequencies which give you a new joie de vivre, fresh courage in life . . . Maryška, this is for you too, for your nerves, for your health, this one here is a cathode which treats your ears, this cathode here massages the heart, imagine, a heart-enhancing sizzling phosphorescence! And this one is for hysteria and epilepsy, this violet ozone removes your desire to do in public things a decent person can only think of or do at home, and other electrodes are for styes and liver-spots, torn muscles, and migraine, the fifteenth one is for hyperaemia of the brain and hallucinations," said Francin talking quietly, and in front of me spread those neon-filled forms, each one different, these electrodes were more like great pistils or stamens or orchid blooms than curative instruments. I listened to all this and for the first time ever I was speechless with surprise, even though those electrodes for hallucinations and high frequencies for hysteria and epilepsy concealed a direct reference to me, I had no reason to resist, so benumbed I was by that purple violet beauty. Francin put on an electrode in the form of an earpiece, he put it close to my forehead, I looked at myself in the mirror, and there was a stunning sight! I looked like a beautiful water maiden, like those young ladies in Art Nouveau pictures, purple violet, with ringlets singed by the evening star! Vacuum flasks with a purple violet storm of polar radiation! And again Francin leaned over the case and into the bakelite holder he stuck a neon comb, this neon comb glowed like an advertising sign over some ladies' accessories shop in Vienna or Paris, and Francin came close to me, planted that sizzling comb in my hair, I looked at myself in the mirror and I knew that there was nothing more I could wish for but to comb through my tresses with that comb. And Francin slowly, as if he knew it, ran that shining comb through my tempestuous hair, reaching down to the ground, and again he reared up and again he ran through them with the high frequency fed comb. I began to quiver all over, I had to hug myself, Francin breathed out quietly, every time he couldn't stop himself from plunging his whole face into those tresses of mine, which felt so good in that purple violet cold storm that when the comb returned the hair ends rose with it, and again that purple violet comb forging down through my hair, that bluish dinghy plunging through the rapids, that cascade of my hair, that purple violet marrowed hollow glass comb! "Maryška," Francin whispered and sat down behind me and again slowly drew the comb through my electric charged hair, "Mary, this we're going to do every day now, I brought this to assuage life's hubbub with its blue shading, quieten your nerves, while for me the electrodes will rather be coloured red, to quicken the blood circulation and invigorate the living organism . . ." said Francin talking softly. And from the boxroom behind the kitchen hammer blows rang out, and an annoyed and ever crosser and crosser voice rose up, Uncle Pepin, who had come for a fortnight, and had been with us now for a whole month, and Francin, when I stroked him under the lamp and smoothed away his trepidation with the curve of my hand, he told me he was horrified by the idea of Pepin staying with us twenty years, and maybe the rest of his life. And Uncle Pepin mended us our boots and shoes, in the boxroom where he also slept, but they weren't just shoes for him, they were something alive, which Uncle Pepin wrestled with, boxed to the floor, he cursed and swore for days on end, and I heard swear-words I'd never heard before, and also every half an hour Uncle took the shoe he was mending, and when he'd cursed and sworn at it, he'd slam it down, chuck it away, and then he'd sit on his stool and sulk. When he'd settled down, he would turn round slowly, take a look at the shoe, ask its forgiveness and lift it up again, stroke it, then go on pegging it and threading it tight, and having somehow clumsy fingers, he always yelped out, so that I came running, thinking he'd stuck the knife in his chest, but it was only the thread which wouldn't pull through the sole, and the whole shoe threatened to rebel, indeed did, like a wound-up spring jumping out of a gramophone, so that shoe shot away like soap out of your palm, and it leapt right up on to the cupboard or the ceiling, as if there was a little motor in it, and when it flew out of Uncle's hand, Uncle flung himself after the shoe, like a goalkeeper making a flying save of the ball . . .

And now Uncle yelled out, "Damn! Blast!"

Francin put away the neon comb, on top of the instruments in the case he laid the sheet of plush, took a look in the direction of Uncle's cry and said:

"Those fulgurating currents have given me added strength already." And he put the case away in the cupboard, then I pulled on the button and the window blind flew up and the china button clicked lightly against my teeth. Across the orchard I could see the beige maltings, a maltster was walking with a squat lamp in his fingers up the steps to the first floor, then he disappeared, and the lamp appeared again one storey higher, again it disappeared, and reappeared, and all the time with each stair the lamp rose as if it was walking through the dusky brewery by itself, a lamp stepping all on its own up the staircase, then the lamp disappeared, but again reappeared and walked from window to little window over the covered bridge connecting the maltings with the brewhouse. But who was that stepping along at random like that, who was carrying that lamp about, just so that it might seem to rise up through the maltings and brewery all by itself? And I stood by the window and lurked like a hunter in

wait for the buck about to come out on to the clearing
. . . and my expectation made me quiver. Now the lamp
appeared right up on the cooling-floor, where nobody
ever goes at this hour, where there is a vat the size of an
ice-hockey rink, a tank in which a whole brew of beer is
put to cool, the young stuff . . . and now the lamp is
walking there, a lamp that acts as if it knew I was
watching it, a lamp carried just for me, the ten great big
four-metre cooling-floor windows are fitted with
louvres, open just a crack, like shutters in Italy and
Spain, and that lamp walks steadily on, interrupted by
those hundreds of louvres, the thin slivered motion of
the kindled lamp, which now halts. I saw the window
frame with its louvres open and someone with the lamp
came out on to the roof of the ice chamber, where there
is a mountain of ice piled four storeys high, twelve
hundred cartloads of frozen river, of icy ceiling, which
cart after cartload is heaped up in the chamber by a
bucket-hoist, an ice chamber which is covered on top
against the heat by half a metre of sand and river
pebbles, on which from spring till autumn houseleeks
grow, hundreds and thousands of houseleeks amidst
cushions of green moss . . . and there stands now the
squat lamp, which one of the brewery workers has
brought up there, a maltster . . . I opened the window
and heard from above a pleasing male voice, as if the
kindled lamp were singing: ". . . the love that was, it is
gone, 'twas for but a short while, golden lassie, not for
long, now she is no more . . . her life is o'er . . . to the
deep linn by Nymburk town she's gone . . ." And from
the boxroom came Francin's shouting: "For God's sake,
give over, please, Jožko!" And slowly I went out of the

room, I didn't even look today as the electric current slowly ebbed, like that love which drowned in the deep linn. Francin had lit the lamps, I went out into the passage and there sat Francin on a chair, both hands pressed to his chest and urging Uncle to leave it all be, and since he's here, couldn't he read or go to church or the pictures, just so long as there's some peace and quiet in the house . . . Francin wanted to get up, but somehow he couldn't, he tried once more, but he was intimately joined to the chair, I put my hand over my mouth, such was my alarm, because I knew that Francin had sat in the pot of cobbler's glue. Pepin was mortified, he would have liked so much to mend all of his brother's shoes, he talked about it such a lot because, of whatever he had ever felt affection for in this world, he felt affection for his brother the most, Francin tried to force his way up off the chair, but he couldn't prise himself free and he bent forward and keeled over, he lay there on the floor and the chair with him. I knelt down and tried to prise Francin free, but the cobbler's glue alias gum had stuck Francin down so firmly that he looked like an overturned statue of a seated Christ. Uncle Pepin pulled Francin's shoulders, I tried lying down behind Francin and pulling the chair in the opposite direction, but it seemed more likely that my husband and Pepin's brother would be torn in half than that we would liberate him from this situation. I rose up and something else rose with my hair, I took my hair in my fingers, drew it on to my lap and saw that my hair had got stuck in the other pot of cobbler's glue or gum, I took the scissors and snipped off the pot of glue along with the end of hair, there the little container now lay like the Golden Bull of Sicily dipped in the strings of my hair. When Francin saw what had happened to my hair, he pranced up like a horse and a lovely sound of tearing fabric ripped through the boxroom. Francin rolled over free and stood there handsome once more, his eyes filled with healthy predatory sizzling wrath, he took the lasts and pots and boxes of pegs, and Uncle Pepin, I thought the look would be enough to break his heart, but Pepin handed his brother with alacrity everything combustible, and Francin with an ever greater and growing sense of relief chucked it all in the stove. The cobbler's glue burned up so violently it lifted the stove plates, and the flame was sucked up through the flues into the chimney, a practically two-metre-long flame it was, long as my hair.

SIX

Uncle Pepin liked sitting best out beyond the malting floors, sheltered on one side by the orchard, on the other by the chimney stack, beside which oak staves of all sizes were stacked, staves out of which barrels were made in the cooperage, kegs, quarter hectolitres, halves and hectolitres and two hectolitres alias doubles, according to need, and then great big fifty-hectolitre and hundred-hectolitre casks, in which whole brewings of beer were stored in the fermenting rooms and cellars, casks in which the beer matured into either ordinary beer or lager. Here Uncle Pepin, when he couldn't do his cobbling, found a stick and walked up and down by the malting floors practising parade ground marches, bayonet duels. So as he wouldn't shout so much, Francin asked me to keep an eye on him.

"Am I glad to see you, sister-in-law," said Pepin, "your Francin's a bit of a nerves twister, a right bundle of nerves, now in Mr Batista's book he ought to give his privates a good soaking in lukewarm water or take more fresh air and exercise. But as you're here the now, we'll have a wee training session alias *Schulbildung*, seeing as I had nothing but top marks, certified commendations, no like one dunderhead, a lad from Haná, stepped out on parade and says to Colonel von Wucherer, 'Mister, here's yer bullets and buns, I'm gaun home, I'm quittin' the service . . .' and the Colonel yells at the officer in charge, 'Have you got the cholera or what?' "

"Peps," I said.

"Balls!" bellowed Uncle Pepin. "I was ever an example to all, and anyway d'ye think von Wucherer knew who I was at all? D'ye expect him to remember thousands of men like that? Once he was gaun off after the leddies, and two sodgers, dunderheads, hailed the carriage for to get a lift, then they see von Wucherer lolling back in the carriage there, and the sodgers saluted, and von Wucherer he says kindly like, 'Where are you off to then, soldier lads?' And they says, 'We're gaun on leave.' And von Wucherer says, 'Anybody gaun on leave has to have his *Urlaubsschein*, his pass, where is it?' And the sodgers felt themselves over and von Wucherer says to one of them, 'What's your name, then?' and the sodger said, 'Šimsa!' And von Wucherer asked the other sodger, 'And what's yours?' And the other laddie said, 'Řimsa!' And the sodger that said his name was Šimsa started belting off into the field, and so von Wucherer commanded, 'Řimsa, bring me back that Šimsa, pronto!' Only Řimsa belted off along with Šimsa, and Colonel von Wucherer turned the carriage about and drove the stallions back to the barracks and right away he asked, 'Which platoon are Šimsa and Řimsa with?' And there was no Řimsa or Šimsa in the records, so Colonel von Wucherer, that said his memory was like a photographic camera, had the whole barracks called out on parade and he went from sodger to sodger, took him by the chin and stared him close in the eye, as if he would give him a kiss any moment, for about two days, but he never recognised the one who said he was Řimsa, nor the one that called himself Šimsa, so how d'ye expect a colonel like that to remember old Peps?"

"Pssst," said I, "there's a meeting of the management board this afternoon."

"Right enough," said Uncle softly, "but now I'm going to learn ye how many parts there are to a rifle," and Uncle took the stick he was practising with, took it just as carefully and expertly as if it were a real army gun, pointed out on it and one by one listed off all the parts, finishing with, "and so this is the *Kolbenschuh* or butt-end shoe, and this is the so-called *Mündung*, muzzle or mouth . . ."

"Of the Elbe," I said.

"Balls! What are you twittering on about like a young magpie? Elbow's elbow, but this is the *Mündung*, muzzle or mouth, if you'd said the like of that to old sergeant Brčula, he'd have socked you one and you'd have flopped over flat as a rabbit!"

From beyond the orchard you could hear the irate slamming of windows in the office and Francin ran out of the counting-house in a white shirt. I could see him dashing through the long grass, dodging the branches of the trees, it was a lovely sight to see the man running along, jumping over obstructions with leg outstretched to keep his footing in the grass, the other above the grass in an almost horizontal posture, his legs repeating alternately all of that wonderful top-of-the-grass-hopping motion. When he reached us I saw that in his fingers he was clutching a number three lettering pen.

"You pair of uhlans, what are you getting up to again?"

"We're playing at being soldiers," I said.

"Play whatever you like, but be quiet about it, the girl in accounts has just spilt a whole bottle of ink!" Francin shouted softly.

"Where are we supposed to play then?" says I.

"Wherever you like, climb up the chimney if you want, just as long as we can't hear you ... she's spattered a whole journal with ink!" cried Francin. The sleeves of his white shirt were tucked up at the elbows with elastic bands, he turned about, no longer running now, he waded through the tall grass, I looked after him, and he turned back, I kissed my hand and blew that kiss like a downy feather after him.

"The chimney?" said Pepin with surprise.

"The chimney," I said.

And Francin disappeared behind the branches, his white shirt now went into the office.

"So then: Direktion!" exclaimed Uncle Pepin, mounting the first cramp-iron, and then, thinking better of it, he jumped down and said, "After you."

And that which I had dreamed of since my very first day at the brewery, finding the strength to climb up the brewery chimney stack, there it was protruding and rising up before me. I leaned my head back and took hold of the first cramp-iron, the perspective ran back upwards in ever diminishing and diminishing rungs, that sixty-metre chimney from that foreshortened angle resembled an aimed heavy gun, I was allured by the

fluttering green leotard which someone had tied to the
lightning conductor, and that green leotard, while there
was a breeze below, that green leotard fluttered and
right through the open window I could hear that green
leotard making the din of rattling tin, and I caught hold
of the first rung, freed a hand and untied the green bow
that bound my hair together, and quickly I went up
hand over hand, my legs like coupled axles took on the
same rhythm. Halfway up the chimney I felt the first
buffet of streaming air, my hair was buoyed up, almost
ran ahead of me, suddenly all of me was centred in my
loose trailing hair, which spread out and enveloped me
like music, several times my hair landed on a rung, I
had to watch out and slow down the work of my legs,
because I was stepping on my own hair, ah, now if
Bod'a had been here, he would have held up my hair for
me, he would have been changed to an angel, and in his
flight he would have kept watch to see that my hair
didn't get caught in the spokes and chain, this chimney
climbing of mine was a bit like my bicycle riding. I
waited a moment, the wind seemed to have taken it into
its head to get a taste of my hair, it lifted and ruffled it so
that I had the feeling I was hanging by my hair on a
knot tied several rungs above me, then the wind
suddenly lulled, my hair untied itself and slowly, like
the loosened golden hands on the church tower clock,
my hair was falling, as if out of my head a golden
peacock spread open wide and then slowly closed its
tail. And I used this lull and quickly went up hand over
hand, coordinating the motion of my legs with the work
of my arms, until I laid my whole hand on the chimney
rim, for a moment I recovered my breath like a

swimming competitor at the end of a race in the pool, and then I pulled myself up with both arms as if out of the water, cast a leg over the rim, caught hold of the lightning conductor and slowly, as if out of syrup, drew up my other leg. I gathered my hair behind me, sat myself down and tossed my hair over my lap. And suddenly a wind rose and my hair slipped out of my hand, and my golden tresses fluttered out just like last year before the first spring day, my hair flamed out like tendrils of weed in a shallow swift stream, I held on to the lightning conductor with one hand and felt as if I was the goddess of the hunt Diana with a lance, my cheeks burned with rapture and I felt that if I did nothing else in this little town but climb up to the top of this chimney, that might not be much, but I could live on the strength of that for numbers of years, maybe even a whole lifetime. And I leaned forward and from the depth I saw how tiny Uncle Pepin was, just a little wee angel with a head and arms, I wondered how up till now I had had the impression that Uncle Pepin's hair was thick and curly, but now I saw his bald head rising towards me with its sparse circlet of hair, now that head laid itself on the very rim, out from under it pulled another palm and caught hold of the edge, he looked at me and his face likewise beamed with happiness. He pulled himself up on to the chimney, and as if unconsciously propped one arm at his waist and shaded with the other his eyes.

"Good God, sister-in-law," he said with amazement, "this would make a brilliant *Beobachtungsstelle* or observation post."

"Alias viewing tower," I appended.

"Bollocks! A viewing tower's for civilians, but an observation post alias *Beobachtungsstelle*'s for the military, for the military in time of war to follow the movements of the enemy! Sister-in-law, and you such an intellectual beauty too, if Captain Tonser heard you say that, he'd sock you with his sabre, yelling out, 'I'll have your frigging nuts for mincemeat!' "

"Peps," said I, splashing my legs in the wellspring of air.

"For Christ's sake, what would he be having my nuts for mincemeat for? He liked me, I used to carry his sabre!" choked Uncle Pepin, leaning over me, and his face was ominous and threatening like a stone gargoyle on the church roof.

"Och never mind!" I gave a wave of the hand. "Isn't it beautiful up here, Uncle Jožin?"

And I looked over the low-lying landscape, edged with hills and woodlands, I looked at the town and saw how you can only get into our little town by crossing water, how it's really an island town, above the town the river which flowed around the town divided in two and past the walls two watercourses flowed, which joined up again beyond the town in one river, I saw how actually each road leading through the town and out has two bridges, two crossings, while across the river there is a white stone-built bridge, on which people were standing, leaning on the side-wall and looking over to the brewery chimney, looking at me and Uncle Pepin, at my hair flapping in the breeze, and in the sunlight that hair of mine glittered and shone like a papal banner, while down below the air was calm and still. Across the river there towered the big church, and at the height of my face was the golden clock-face on the tower, and round the church in concentric circles stretched the streets and lanes and houses and buildings. Festooned from every window like feather quilts, petunias and carnations and red pelargonias projected themselves, the whole of this small town was edged with a lacework of walls and from above it resembled a cut chalcedony. And on to that white bridge the fire tender hurtled with its hose, the firemen's helmets glittered and the bugler held his golden trumpet and bugled "Fire!" and all the firemen wore white hessian uniforms, the red tender thundered across the bridge like an orchestrion, the firemen held on to the rungs standing upright on that clattering fire-engine altar that now dipped behind the buildings and gardens.

"Is it true, Uncle Jožin, you used to graze goats right up at the front line?" I said.

"Whoever told you that?" bellowed Uncle Pepin and sat down on the rim, then lay down on his back, folding his arms behind his head.

"Melichar, the tobacconist," I said.

"What would a tobacconist and invalid to boot be doing in the war?" roared Uncle.

"Melichar was a captain apparently in the war, yesterday Captain Melichar said, 'God forbid it should come to war and I should have that Pepin chap drilling under me,'" said I, holding on to the lightning conductor and looking down at the brewery. And again I wondered to see how the brewery was right outside the town, how it was surrounded all round by a wall, with the little town on the other side, but how along the walls there are tall trees of maple and ash, which also form a square shape, and how this brewery resembled a monastery or a kind of fortress, or prison, how every wall was topped not only with barbed wire, but each and every wall and pillar had set in concrete on its topmost bricks jagged fragments of green bottles, which glittered from above like amethysts and amaranths.

"How would he have seen me anyway . . . even if I did graze those goats?" said Uncle, and went on lying there gazing up at the sky, one leg hooked over his bent knee and swinging the free ankle.

"With a telescope," said I.

"But would the Emperor lend a telescope to any old tobacconist?" said Uncle.

"As a captain Melichar was issued with two telescopes," I said, and saw how on the bridge there were now as many people as swallows about to migrate and someone was peering at me from the bridge through a telescope. I gave a smile into that telescope and out of the depths a wind arose and my hair started to splay out like a fan of ostrich plumes, I saw how around my eyes streams of hair were closing in upwards, round the whole of my sitting figure there was a kind of halo like the one on the plague column for the Virgin Mary, Our Lady of the Seven Sorrows, on the column in the town square . . .

"And if it came to war, what would happen if Melichar was to have me under him, eh?" enquired Pepin and it seemed to me he was grappling with ever growing torpor.

"He said, if war came again, he'd just crook his little finger on drill like so . . . and call out, *'Pepin zu mir!'* And you'd come rushing over with your tongue hanging out and paying your respects and go down before him on one knee," said I, and when I took a look, Uncle Pepin was asleep, he'd fallen sound asleep, he was lying on the rim of the chimney, which had a slight sway in it, I only noticed it now from that recumbent statue of Uncle Pepin, how we were both perceptibly swaying, as if we were sitting on some kind of pendulum hung in the sky. And the firemen sped from the cross, the horses looked from above as if they had bolted, their back legs were strung out in the harness and their fore legs were shooting straight out in front of their heads, like snails sticking out their horns, the whole of that fire-fighting contraption glittered like a child's plaything and threatened any minute to fall apart and the pieces of the vehicles would go scattering just like that military vehicle in Truhlářská Street when the grenades it was carrying exploded. And there at the chief's post stood the chief of the firemen, Mr de Giorgi, member of the management board of the brewery on whose chimney I was seated, a chimney sweep who was also the fire-chief, for instead of just a flat to live in he had a fire-fighting museum, everything that had ever burned down Mr de Giorgi had photographed, he even got hold of photographs from before the blaze, and so on all the walls of his flat he had photographs, always in pairs, a cow before the fire and after it, a dog before the fire and after, an adult male before the fire and after, a barn before the fire and after it, all things, all animals, all persons burnt or affected by fire, all these Mr de Giorgi would photograph, and now to be sure he was only riding off to the brewery because, if it collapsed, he would have a photograph of the brewery manager's wife before the collapse and one after the collapse . . . and now this fire-fighting orchestrion entered the bend in the road at the brewery gate, the wheels grated and the fire-engine disappeared behind the office, and I was just thinking the firemen must have overturned along with the horses, when they rode out again nobly and trumpeting and then the fire-engine drove right up under the chimney . . . I thought they'd probably start to use their hose in a minute, they'd shower the water right up as high as the top of the chimney, Mr de Giorgi would request me to step out on to the very summit of that gushing geyser, and then slowly they'd start to turn down the tap and I would descend from above on the declining peak of the water spout, but the firemen dashed out of the engine, knelt down, saluted each other with axes and suddenly spread out a big sheet, six firemen stretched out that sheet, they leaned back and gazed upwards, but the sway of the chimney stack was evidently such that the firemen with the sheet had to shift this way and that according to the probable likelihoods of my fall.

And the members of the management board came riding along in their traps, before they came at a trot, but today those traps came rattling along the roads, from the villages and the town, the horses peltering along at a canter and a gallop. And all those traps not as before, when they stopped outside the office, this time all of them gathered in the brewery yard, where the coopers and the bottlers and the maltsters and everybody stood and all of them gazing upwards with their heads thrown back, as if expecting from on high

Jesus' return or the descending of the Holy Spirit upon them. And now the chairman of the brewery, Doctor Gruntorád in person, rode in from the cross, feudal scion and admirer of the old Austria, as always he sat there on the box holding the reins in his deerskin riding gloves, his inimitable hat elegantly poised over his eyes, smoking his cigarette and biting into its amber holder, and driving the black stallion on into the brewery, while his coachman with a rueful smile lolled back on the plush seat like a lord . . .

And down below Mr de Giorgi issued vain instructions to the firemen to climb the chimney, finally Mr de Giorgi determined to climb the chimney himself. And his white uniform ascended, pausing often, but continuing again to climb up the rungs, until his helmet finally emerged at my feet.

"Uncle Jožin," I shook Uncle who was lying at my feet and Uncle sat up, rubbed his eyes, and leapt up in shock clutching the lightning conductor. Mr de Giorgi hopped up on to the rim, regained his breath, removed his helmet and mopped the sweat with his hand-kerchief.

"In the name of the law," he said, "missus, please climb down. And your brother-in-law too."

"Mr de Giorgi, don't you feel giddy?" says I.

"I say, in the name of the law, climb down," repeated Mr de Giorgi.

"And I say, Mr de Giorgi first?" says I.

"No," said Mr de Giorgi gazing into the bowels of the chimney, "for training reasons I shall descend by the inside of the stack," he appended.

I held on to the lightning conductor, put my foot on

the rung, turned about and my hair blazed up, again that draught from the depth inflated my tresses, they fanned out for the last time, as if they knew it, one last time that golden mane of mine flamed above the brewery chimney, again I blessed with my hair like a huge golden monstrance all those who looked upon me at that moment, and Mr de Giorgi himself was affected by what he saw.

"We are witnesses to an extraordinary incident, missus, what a pity ladies can't serve as firemen," he said and picked up his trumpet, a tiny little trumpet which resembled a ticket conductor's clippers, he blew on it, but that blowing was so melancholic, like a trussed kid bleating in the slaughterhouse trap, then he kissed my hand and I descended, quickly I hurried down, so as to keep ahead of my hair, which I threatened to tread on, getting embroiled and sending myself plummeting to the depths. And suddenly I saw around me the tops of trees, then I seemed to descend into the branches and from out of the branches I finally laid my foot on terra firma.

"That was just beautiful," said Doctor Gruntorád with delight, "but you deserve twenty-five of the best . . ."

"On the bare bottom," I said.

"What were you doing there for goodness' sake?" enquired the Doctor.

"Well, as you said, it was just beautiful, and as it was beautiful, so it was dangerous, and as it was dangerous, so it was just absolutely truly made for me . . ." I said, and Francin stood there pallid, his head on his chest, in his frock coat, white cuffs and gutta-percha collar and his tie in the shape of a cabbage leaf.

And the mechanics opened the great doors of the chimney, soot came tumbling out, and that black glittering cavern was as large as a summerhouse. Uncle Pepin leapt off the last rung and said:

"So the Austrian Soldat wins another glorious victory, eh?"

But all were staring into the black chamber at the base of the chimney.

"What regiment were you? Who were you under?" Doctor Gruntorád enquired.

"Freiherr von Wucherer," Uncle Pepin gave a salute.

"*Ruht*," barked the Doctor, and added, "Manager, what is your brother able to do?"

"He qualified as a shoemaker and worked three years in a brewery," answered Francin.

"Well then, Manager, take your brother and put him up in the maltings quarters. The best cure for loudmouths is work," said Doctor Gruntorád.

And in the black cavern a white trouser leg emerged, almost right up at the ceiling of this bower overgrown with soot, the leg groped for the rung, but evidently there wasn't one, so the leg gyrated away there as if Mr de Giorgi was pedalling a bicycle. And the deputy chief of the firemen issued a command and the firemen ran with their rescue sheet into the chimney, spread the sheet out, and the deputy chief called up into the sooty grime, "Chief, let go! We're here! We've brought the rescue sheet!"

And Mr de Giorgi let go of the rungs, first of all soot and coal-dust poured out of the chimney, poured out in front of the chimney, tender soft curly little molehills of soot, then coughing resounded and the firemen ran out totally blackened, bearing something in their rescue sheet, as if they had landed some huge pike fish or wels, and they laid the sheet on the ground and out of the soot and dust popped up the totally black figure of Mr de Giorgi, laughing, with white creases of laughter wrinkling all the way across his black visage. Mr de Giorgi drew out his trumpet, blew on it, and declared, "And so we may deem the rescue work accomplished."

And he came forward out of the heap of soot and stretched out both arms and extracted congratulations and walked about the place all self-assured and joyfully stiff and wooden and I saw that Mr de Giorgi would live off the memory of that descent by the inside of the chimney not just a couple of years, but all the remainder of his days.

SEVEN

At the corner of the maltings there was always such a draught, such a wind, that I had to walk practically leaning forward, or turn round and lie back into the gust as into a rocking chair. That gusting sucked up my hair like a hungry smoker sucking on a cigarette. But no sooner had I pushed through this stumbling-block of air, by the door to the maltings there was such a breathless calm, that I fell straight over on my knees or back. And yet I always looked forward with pleasure to this air combat, in which I had to fight for possession of my towels. Once the wind snatched away a bouclé bath wrap, all I could do was grab at it with my hand, and the draught, having its sense of humour, flicked it away from me, I reached out again when the bath towel was very nearly about to touch my hair, but the gust hopped away nimbly a bit further with that great towel wrap, and when it floated down again, I leapt after it, but the gust carried it away up with drawn-out laughter, like a kite that bouclé towel bobbed up in the autumn sky, a white zig-zag-dancing wrap moving to the rhythm of the wind, and it vanished in the darkness over the maltings. And yet it was beautiful, to let yourself be handled on the lips of the breeze, to let yourself fill with the aroma of that windy bath like a peppermint sweet. Then when I felt the doorhandle, the draught from the other side of the door leaned bodily against the door so that I too had to press bodily on that door, but the draught, which had its sense of humour, suddenly stopped and I fell into the dark passage on to my knee. Once I staggered and crashed into a maltster, who fell, but in his fall still kept holding the burning lamp so neatly that it didn't break. Then, with palm outstretched as though to ward off a storm, I felt the handle to the engine room, the smell of oil and hemp engulfed me warmly like a bath, I closed the door, felt for the key and locked it. Then I lit a candle. The huge distribution wheel sketched out a silvery arc in the spindrift half-darkness, the taut distribution cables gleamed and glittered with oil. The dynamos and motors were like fat African beasts, the oil cans like birds pecking insects off those hippos. Slowly I undressed, turning on the taps of hot water, which ran from a huge boiler into a hundred-hectolitre barrel cut in half. I took off my clothes and listened to the draught whistling through the floors of the maltings right up to the drying-room and rattling the shutters there. And I got into that great big wooden bath, the water is always so hot that I have to turn on the cold water taps, I sit there squatting and the hotness of the water hurts me till my teeth chatter, until the cold water mixes in with the boiling hot, then slowly I settle down and lie back, stretching myself right out. I lie there in that barrel cut in half like the needle in a compass box, I gaze up above myself to the beams where the white boiler vanishes, and I dream, I start to dream, I slowly dissolve in the hot water, like soap powder I float in the hot water, all my limbs relax, I untie all the cloths and sheets into which my past life is wrapped and bound, I open all the baskets and cases and cupboards in which there are images which happened long ago, but which are ever willing to visit me again, beautiful, but colourless images which only in the bath acquire their finishing touches and precise colourings. These are my moving pictures, projected on the screen of my closed eyes, the film whose script and direction were shot by my own life, the film in which I play the lead role, I, who have come now to this spot, this wooden bath, in which I lie . . . I am a little lassie with straw plaits, I play chuckie stones in the middle of the road, I sit cross-legged and scatter the four stones again, ready to take one and throw it up and gather up the three remaining ones in time to catch the first as it falls. Approaching thunder, I fall on my back the moment after scattering the four pebbles, the sky darkens and above me loom terrible maws and buckles and reins, hooves flash over me with their glittering shoes, I close my eyes, dried mud spatters over me, the thundering moves away onward, I get to my feet and see the clattering vehicle drawn by bolting horses, I see the blue sky and out of it leaning over me the head of my worried dad. I am a little lassie, playing on the field track with chuckie stones, my dad always took me off behind the building for safety's sake, so nothing would happen to me. I see two soldiers running from the woods, I see them running along the meadow path where I am playing, these soldiers are running like two bolting horses, I lie down on my back so as not to be run over, I see the soldiers leaping up, I see above me the soles of the boots full of studs, then the shadow of the soldiers thundered across me and the thump of the army boots dinned and departed down the meadow track. I sat up and saw the soldiers running to the stream – they stop, instead of a footbridge there is a beam hung on chains, the soldiers splay their arms like the two guardian angels over my bed their wings, and then they run over to the other side and run on, in the curve of the track I see their rising shining studs for the last time, now they vanish in the forest bend. The soldiers vanished long ago, but I am still thinking of them. I see myself now, I toddle down to the stream, I put my little shoe on the log, I see the water swirling in the stream, I splay my arms and run along the log, but right in the middle the log slips from under me and I fall into the water – I pedalled away in the depths like mum on her sewing machine, but I couldn't get a footing on the bottom, at first I drank water, but then I had probably drunk enough water to make me drown, all I saw was how my hair fell free and fluttered along the bottom of the stream and mingled with the green tendrils of weed and water flowers without blooms, I wanted so awfully much to sleep, I couldn't close my eyes, and everything was full of light and I seemed to be seeing the sky above me through thick spectacles . . . and then I awaken, I see how beautiful it is to be drowned, as if I were at home, lying in heaven in a little bed just like the one we had at home – I saw my hands resting on the feather quilt with forget-me-nots printed over it just like the one that Mummy has, and opposite me hangs a picture of a guardian angel, just like the one we have, and then Mummy came in and said, "Just come on in, children, come along in . . ." and into the kitchen came the little girls from the neighbourhood, and now I knew I was drowned, because the girls, who called me Mary and I called them Hedvig and Evie and Boženka, those girls put holy pictures next to my hands on the quilt, all over my bed there were so many little pictures of guardian angels, and Hedvig said to me, "Mummy told me you were drowned . . ." and she put down another holy picture, and I said, "Why are you giving me that picture then?" And Hedvig said, "You put them in little dead girls' coffins . . ." and I was crying, because that meant I was really quite quite dead, but then my mummy came in, bringing candies, and when she saw so many little holy pictures Mummy said, "But girls, Mary's not dead, Doctor Michálek poured all the water out of her and breathed new life into her with his breath . . ." and the little girls were disappointed and sorry that there wasn't going to be a funeral, that I hadn't died, because they already saw themselves in their white dresses made of curtains and burning in their fingers a big candle decorated with myrtle, and the brass band would play such melancholy music and the girls would go in the procession and they would have their hair all in little curls and they would be crying because I had drowned . . . but now it's off, this procession, and the crying, all because of those two women who went out to soak their laundry and pulled me out and took me home . . . Dad was so infuriated that time, ah, my dad could be angry like nobody else, Mum bought four wardrobes a year, old cupboards from the secondhand dealer, and whenever Dad got really cross, Mum took him off quick to the summer-house and put an axe in his hand and first Dad would break up the back walls, and then he would smash and curse at the rest of the wardrobe, ripping out the door with such zest and then demolishing the whole cupboard from the side like a matchbox, and after half an hour, when he'd chopped up the wardrobe into splinters, Mum always had such a lot of firewood for kindling and heating . . . and I heard Dad shouting and carrying on about how I'd drowned myself, how I still couldn't behave like a decent little girl should, because the other girls don't do such things, I got such a fright that I slipped out of the quilt, put my clothes on and ran out into the yard, and there stood a goods lorry, I clambered up on the back, there by the rear window stood a barrel, I sneaked into that barrel, and it was warm in there, I fell asleep, and when I awoke, I could hear the goods lorry going along, and when I got up I could see through the window that it was getting dark, that close by the rear window was a man's cap, when I looked from the side I could see it was Mr Brabec, and I stuck my hand through and scratched Mr Brabec behind the ear and said, "Mr Brabec, I'm in here . . ." and Mr Brabec let go the steering wheel and yelled out, and the lorry stopped so sharply that the barrel rolled over in which I was crouched up to the shoulders, and I tumbled out on to the floor and off the floor on to the ground, and I picked myself up from the road and dusted off my wee skirt, and Mr Brabec ran this way and yelled and stamped, and I said, "Mr Brabec, really, it's me it is." But Mr Brabec moaned and keeled over,

and when the officers came, they put a blanket over Mr
Brabec, but that wasn't enough, one of the officers had
to strip almost naked and lie on top of Mr Brabec to
keep him warm, later at the police station one of the
officers told me I could have been the death of the man,
and I remembered Dad and how he would have to
smash up another wardrobe, and the officer laid me a
fur-coat on the floor and then he took a rope and tied
me by the leg to the table leg, and there I lay and wept,
above me rocked the soles of boots full of studs, one leg
crossed over the other, and I was tied there by the leg to
the table leg, and then I fell asleep and Dad appeared
over me, kneeling and resting on both arms like legs,
they untied me from the table, and when they pulled
me out by the arm the officers were so accusing that Dad
took the rope and tied that rope round my neck and I
burst into tears and called out, "Daddy, I don't want
you to hang me. I don't want to die on the branch so
long . . ." you see, once the cat ate Dad's liver and Dad
hung the cat on a branch for doing that, and the cat he
didn't die till the next day . . . and Dad led me off on the
end of the rope to the train, and when we arrived home,
Dad led me like a calf on the end of the rope, explaining
to everyone how I wasn't a decent little girl and how he
had to lead me on the end of a rope like a bad dog . . .
and at home Dad, as soon as Mum saw Dad,
straightaway she handed him the axe, I expected Dad to
chop off my head just like he did to the turkey cocks
and hens, but Dad hurled himself straight at the
wardrobe and with one blow smashed through the back
wall and with one more swipe of the body, sideways, he
smashed through the rest of the cupboard, so that it all

fell flat on the ground, like trampling a carton ... All
soap-suddy, I lie there covered in foam, lathering
myself and not even noticing, thinking and remembering the images lying deep in the depths of time,
images constantly returning, clarifying, augmenting
one another. I am a six-year-old girl with loose flowing
hair, on the crown of my head it is just caught with little
blue ribbon bows, Dad hasn't broken a single wardrobe
on my behalf for a whole year, it's Sunday noon and I
am walking through the little square, in the open
windows curtains flutter, you hear the chinking of
cutlery and plates, the draught draws out the savour of
food, yesterday Dad bought me a sailor suit and
umbrella, I stand in front of the water fountain, then I
lean over and look at my mirrored hair, coins gleam on
the bottom, we think if you throw some money into the
water fountain you may have a wish come true, for
safety's sake I threw two twenty-heller bits into the
fountain and wished that I should never drown again,
never run away from home, and always be a decent
little girl, especially when Daddy bought me such lovely
clothes and an umbrella. I hopped up on the edge of the
fountain to see better how nice I looked in that sailor's
jacket, I looked about, no one was coming, no one was
looking out of the window to complain to Daddy, I
hopped up on the fountain, and when I leaned over,
I saw the lovely pleated skirt and little white sockies and
shiny polished shoes, I shook out my hair, and when
I looked again at myself reflected in the water, I
overbalanced and fell into the fountain, and the water
swallowed me up like a great fish when it swallows a
tiny little one, again I tried to find the bottom with my

shiny little shoe, but the bottom of the fountain was deeper than I was tall, and again I surfaced for air, but I was too frightened to call for help, because Daddy would be too cross, and I was on my way to join the angels, again I was enveloped in a bright sweet world, as if I were a bee fallen into honey. I saw how my head fell slowly to the bottom, beside my eye I saw that twenty-heller coin which I had thrown into the fountain with the wish that I should never drown again, my skirt welled up so grandly and my hair washed across my face and again so slowly the hair grandly returned, and then I wanted to sleep and only moved my legs about very slowly, much more slowly than Mummy pedalling on her sewing machine, and for the last time I saw the little bubbles rising from my mouth, as if I was a bottle of soda or mineral water . . . but again I didn't drown, one lady saw me, Mrs Krsenská, who had been ten years in a wheelchair and had stomach ulcers, she had been looking out of her window just at the moment I fell in, and one gentleman came running over, Mr Pokorný the photographer, who jumped in after me still with his knife and fork and napkin tucked under his chin, and pulled me out. I woke up on the steps of the fountain, I had the impression it was raining, I took my little umbrella and spread it open, but actually the midday sun was shining and the bell finishing striking the midday hour, Mr Pokorný was leaning over me, water dropped from his napkin and a couple of frizzles of cabbage with it, Mr Pokorný was threatening me with the knife and fork in turn, saying if his dinner had got cold he was going to see to me again, because nice little girls if they want to drown themselves, do it at a proper time and not on the dot of twelve, when the first of the goose is on the table, and I looked and there in all the windows stood the townspeople in their shirts and waistcoats and all holding a fork in one hand and a knife in the other and all of them were looking down at me with annoyed expressions on their faces and indicating that what they'd really like to do was stick me on their forks and cut me up with their knives, and so I stood up and so much water gushed out of me that I thought the clouds had burst, I bowed, not that I wanted to make fun of them, but meaning that I recognised the point and knew I shouldn't have done it just when the first of the geese were on the roasting pans on a Sunday at noon . . . Now I lie in the brewery bath, in that hundred-hectolitre barrel cut in half, someone walks from the malting floor up to the lodgings where Uncle Pepin now lives too, and out of that hall resounds his frightful roar, "Doh re mi fa so la ti doh . . ." and then again the descending scale, "Doh ti la so fa mi re doh," just as the water runs out with the dregs of soap deposit. Someone climbs from the malting floor up to the lodgings, probably it's the young maltster, sweat-soaked and with a ring under one eye, as if he'd fallen on top of a telescope, a ring neatly stamped like a round postmark, it's bound to be him, now he climbs slowly with his shirt tossed over his shoulder and in one hand he's carrying the squat lamp like an emperor his imperial orb, and in the other hand the turning shovel like an imperial sceptre, so he climbs upwards, pauses on the landing and sings that sweet song . . . "the love that was, it is gone, 'twas for but a short while, golden lassie, not for long, now she is no more . . . her life is o'er . . . to the deep linn by Nymburk town she's gone . . ." Quickly I got dressed, tied my hair up in a towel, blew out the candle with a mighty puff and went out into the dark, with my palm stretched out before me, till a dim light trickled out at the bend in the passage from the depths of the malting floor, with yellow lines it edged the angles of the damp steps. From the malting floor resounded the melodic tender tapping of the turning shovels on the wet floor, the rhythmic hiss of the shovelled barley . . . and again that song like a rising sea-tide . . . "the love that was, it is gone . . ." for a moment I stood in the half-darkness, then I descended a couple of steps, the warmth of the germinated barley slapped me on the cheeks, two tubby lamps lit up the beds of barley, paraffin lamps on wooden tripods in the middle of fields of barley, the young maltster stripped to the waist was skipping along with short little paces, gathering shovelfuls of barley from one side and tossing that malt on to the other side and leaving a furrow behind him, as if that labouring wooden shovel were the keel of a boat that cleaves the waves in front but leaves behind smoothness closing in, that handsome maltster lad with every step turned over a shovelful of golden barley and with every shovel his back gleamed more and more with sweat . . . "the love that was, it is gone . . ." the male voice went on filling the low vault of the malting floor, a vault resting on four avenues of black iron pillars . . . now the young lad stood erect like King Barleycorn, the ring beneath his eye sparkled like a spectacle rim, his trunk was altogether swathed in the shining quicksilver of sweat . . . and I went on hearing that song, someone else was singing that elegy now, someone working several fields of barley away, where that second tubby paraffin lamp stood on its wooden tripod ... the young maltster wiped his face with the full of his palm and discarded a whole handful of sweat ... I walked on further, my legs were wobbling under me, there a little wee man was turning the barley, he looked more like a pensioned-off jockey, in overalls and beret, he'd just finished one heap, now he took the shovel, scooped up the barley at the edge, and then again those swift little maltster's paces, the man was almost running, he ruffled the scooped-up barley and the shovel left an exactly cut border in its wake. When this little wee maltster finished off this job and bent and placed in the corner his crossed shovels as his trademark, he straightened up and sang beautifully ... " 'twas for but a short while, golden girlie, not for long, now she is no more ... her life is o'er ..." This was Mr Jirout, the little maltster, who when he met me greeted me always guiltily and with a constant smile, Francin used to tell of him that in his younger days Mr Jirout had been an artiste, shot out of a cannon at fairs, to the rolling of drums they tied him up live in a little blue satin suit, put him into the wooden gun-carriage, then the impresario applied the bluely smouldering fuse, and when the deafening bang came, flame spouted from the mouth of the cannon and then Mr Jirout in person, arms tensed, who upon reaching the apex of his trajectory, spread his arms out wide and fell into the waiting trampoline, scattering smiles and coloured paper roses and blown kisses. When he landed, he jumped up, bounced on the trampoline and bowed and received his ovation, at every fair and every country wake. Once they packed little Mr Jirout into his cannon, and when they shot him out and Mr Jirout reached the apex of his trajectory, he spread his arms out wide and as he fell head foremost slowly downwards he saw he had already gone far beyond the trampoline, the impact in the gun-carriage was stronger than it had ever been before, but all the same Mr Jirout went on smiling and scattering his smiles and coloured paper roses and blown kisses, only to smash himself up beyond the fencing in a pile of timber. After they'd spent a year putting Mr Jirout back on his feet, he found he'd lost the desire to go on scattering his blown kisses and roses, he withdrew from the life of an artiste like a banknote no longer in circulation, and for the last eight years, after getting fully back in the pink, he's been working in the brewery as a maltster . . . "the love that was, it is gone, 'twas for but a short while . . ."

EIGHT

Uncle Pepin had been working in the brewery for three weeks now; the coopers took him on, and from then on there was merriment in the brewery. When I had a chance, I took some buckets for draff and went across the brewery yard, the foreman looked at me searchingly to see if he should bring a two-litre pot of beer, I nodded, and while I collected the draff from the wagon, the coopers were having their morning break, Uncle Pepin was lying on his back and on his chest an empty cask of keg, the cooper men were laughing fit to burst, choking on crumbs of spread slices of bread, and Uncle Pepin sang, "Doh re mi fa so la ti doh!"

The assistant cooper knelt over Uncle, saying, "Now, Mr Josef, let's have that scale backwards, just like Caruso and Mařáček used to practise it!"

And Uncle Pepin cleared his throat and screeched horrifically, "Doh ti la so fa mi re doh . . ."

And when the workmen had had their fill of this din, the assistant cooper said, "And now, Mr Josef, give us a high C."

And the cooper men stood up, leaned over Uncle

Pepin, who screeched out that high C, and the cooper men roared with laughter, lay on their backs with their spread slices of bread, and hopped up again and choked over their crumbs and rested against the cooperage and chuckled and chuckled, to avoid asphyxiating with mirth.

And in the middle of the yard the old maltster Mr Řepa roasted the malt for the dark ale, he sat on a chair and turned the black drum on its shaft, and under that drum the charcoal burned bluely and pinkly and redly, and the old maltster, with his scattering of grey hairs, majestically and regularly revolved the soot-caked globe like some god from an ancient myth of earthly spheres.

And the assistant cooper leaned over Uncle and said, "And now once again, one last breath exercise, sing us another high C, and this time sing it in the head . . . but watch you don't do a job in your pants, or give yourself brown trousers!"

And Uncle Pepin breathed in, screwed up his nose, and the cooper men leaned over him and Uncle sang inside of himself that high C, the kind of long drawn-out note made by a creaking gate, he sang that high C with all his might and main, he kept that inward singing note going a whole minute, and then he was so exhausted, he spread his arms and breathed out and the cask on his chest heaved, just like in the music academies when the pupils lie on their backs on the carpet and the teacher piles books on their chests.

And I stepped along with my pails of draff past the open door to the boiler house, there in the half-dark glowed the lower hemisphere of the boiler, the ash-box shining with the saffron shade of the burning coal on the grate, down through the glowing ash-box tumbled red and purple violet burning coals and green-blue cinders, and right next to it in the darkness glowed the open boiler with its beige tinge, and there the workman crouched like a child in the mother's womb tapping the scale out of the boiler in that cramped position, two light bulbs lit up sharply that workman crouched there in an arc, as he worked in the dust and sang with it, encircled by cables of the electric circuit like an umbilical cord. Each time I glimpsed out of the sunlight that sharply lit oval and that workman tapping away bit by bit with a hammer, I thought that anyone going past would be startled by this image framed in the lunette, but no one even paused for thought, no one was sorry, nor was he sorry for himself either, that man who spent a fortnight on end like a woodpecker tapping saltpetre in his crouched position, on the contrary, he sang with it.

And the coopers had finished their break, the foreman cooper stood like a shepherd among sheep, around him hundred of barrels, he leaned over one of them, examined it with a searching eye, then he straightened and pulled up a burning candle on a twisted wire from the wame of the barrel, and again he leant over another barrel and dangled the candle into its interior scanning it with a watchful eye to see whether the barrel was fit to be filled with beer or whether it had to be caulked, that is to say pitched. Uncle Pepin stood by the enormous stove and stoked it with anthracite and coke, heated up the pitch, the stove thundered darkly away and out of its short bent chimney there erupted a red fire hemmed with blue borders, flames ornamented with a sizzling green corona, like the flame on a blow-lamp used to thaw out frozen joints or burn off old paint.

The carters loaded the wet barrels of beer into the carts, and carried out casks of ice. The foreman handed me a measure of orange-coloured beer, a measure full of drops of condensed steam. And I knew the foreman didn't like me, and that he would have given me not one, but five measures of beer, and more, as long as I would drink them, drink them down, and the workmen would see what an inclination to drunkenness the manager's wife possessed. But I was young, and hence above all that, whatever I did, I did, only asking prior permission of myself, and always I nodded my own assent, and that inward nodding of mine, that sign from my mentor, who was somewhere in my heart inside, that consent went straight to my blood, and my hand stretched out and I sipped with gusto, with such gusto, that the carters stopped stacking the barrels and stared at me. So I stood by the ramp, alongside the horses, Ede and Kare seemed to have an understanding with me, their manes and great tails had that same colour of golden beer. And old Řepa in the middle of the brewery yard now pulled out the crank-shaft, examined expertly the contents of roasted malt and nodded to himself, pulled a handle and swung that black globe on the mechanism away from the red-hot coals, loosened the lock carefully with a small hammer, turned the handle, and the hot roasted malt tumbled out on to the black griddle and the aroma of malt shot off on all sides. It must have reached the square by now, and the passers-by will be turning their heads towards the brewery, where in the middle the old maltster mumbles contentedly and rakes through the roasted malt with a black wooden poker.

And Uncle Pepin stood by the pitching stove and smiled at me, he wore a leather apron, the furnace behind him thundered and threatened red-hot to explode into the air like some kind of fantastic rocket from a Jules Verne novel. That flame which sizzled out after Uncle Pepin was so terrifically beautiful, that I took a look about me, but no one was marvelling at the display. And the master cooper came and began passing the barrels down the skid to Uncle Pepin's feet, and Uncle Pepin took every barrel, heaved it on to his knee and stuck it on the pin of the nozzle, pressed the foot lever, and boiling pitch squirted into the barrel, and Uncle Pepin lifted the barrel and let it go in a free fall, and the barrel slowly birled over with blue smoke trailing from its filling hole, enlacing the barrel with a blueish ribbon, like a rabbi winding the holy phylactery ribbons round his arm, and when the barrel stopped at the bottom, the assistant cooper took it, or sent it on its way with a kick, and the barrel came to rest on the slowly turning shafts of the rotary mechanism, one barrel alongside another, now all the barrels were turning and blueish smoke twisting round them like those circlets which bob round the heads of sanctified figures.

I watched, and as always when I watch work with fire, I got thirsty, my tongue stuck to my palate and instead of saliva I had nothing in my mouth but the like of cigarette papers. I raised the measure and received a shock, the pot practically shot up in the air, I had thought it still heavy with beer, but it was altogether light, because I had already drunk it all. The foreman squatted down and took the measure from me and laughed and went into the conditioning cellar, I knew he would draw me my beer with one pull, put a good top on it, maybe fill half the can with lager and finish it with dark garnet, a mixture that sends your body purring all over with approval. The Belgian geldings swished their fair tails like barley and whinnied, the drayman came out of the conditioning cellar bearing two cans, and gave one to each gelding, they took those cans in their teeth, pulled on the bridle and drank, as they drank they raised their necks high to let the very last drops of beer drain down their throats, and when they had finished, they tossed aside their cans and uttered a joyful neighing sound and pawed with their hooves and from their shoes pittered hardly visible sparks, the drayman laughed and nodded to me, I nodded back and the horses nodded too, the foreman squatted down and handed me the measure from the ramp, I sniffed at the foam and nodded, and Uncle Pepin began to sing, "Oh ye lindens, o-o-oh ye li-i-inden trees!"

And the assistant cooper called out, "Mr Josef, you know what a glorious day that will be when you sing Přemysl in the National Theatre?"

And Uncle Pepin nodded, stacking the barrels on to the sprayer of boiling pitch, tears dropped on to his apron, and the assistant cooper continued, "And I warrant you this, when the first night comes, the folks from the brewery alone will make a whole busload to

Prague, but you must keep training, now instead of the quarter we'll give you an empty half size on your chest."

"A hectolitre, or a double if you like, long as it gets me up to the standard of Caruso and Maráček," Pepin shouted back.

"Half-and-half," I told myself into the can and then I sipped in and gradually, holding back the desire to pour down the whole measure at once, ever so slowly and sweetly I swallowed down that light lager mixed with dark garnet, that half-and-half, mutra the maltsters called it, I drank ever so slowly and tenderly, just like when on a summer's early evening out there beyond the brewery, on the margins of the fields of rye, someone sits sweetly blowing a mournful song on the trombone, just for himself, with closed eyes and the tremor and quiver of the gleaming instrument in his brassy hands, just for its own sake till nightfall with his head leaning gently backward, playing for himself his melancholic song.

The assistant cooper waved his hand over his head, "And, Mr Josef, do you know who'll be in the box? Your brother and your sister-in-law, then Mr Jandák the mayor, that goes to the bars to check if the young ladies' calves are nice and firm as per regulation, what a pity your parents didn't live to see that day of glory, your mum and dad! What a joy it would've been!"

And Uncle Pepin wept, wiping the tears into his apron and nodding, and the assistant cooper went on mercilessly, "Then after the performance the young ladies, Mr Josef, they would be throwing you bouquets of flowers and the newspaper men would be asking, where did you acquire all that talent, sir? And how would you answer them, Mr Josef, eh?"

"I'd say it was the gift of God," cried Uncle Pepin pressing both hands to his face and weeping, and the barrels on the rotary mechanism turned and through its filling hole each barrel went on trailing out its tender saliva, which as each barrel rotated shaped around it a bobbing blueish circlet, a violet wheel, a neon necklace.

The assistant cooper went on triumphantly, "But then you would have to tell the newspaper men, that your voice technique was learnt from a certain Austrian Captain von Meldík, that sang in the Vienna Opera House in his youth, that . . ."

And the assistant cooper didn't finish, Uncle roared and shook both his hands in the air, "Balls! The Emperor wouldn't employ a tobacconist in the Opera, and if he did, only in the lavatories, and not even that. Just ye wait, Meldík, next time I pass the shop, I'll give ye a wee box in your window."

The assistant cooper turned a barrel, held it, and the smoke rose up the cooper's chest and twined round his face, and the cooper called, "Only Meldík said, the minute he spots you, he'll have the pepper ready, and as you bend over, he'll puff the pepper in your eyes, and then Meldík said . . ."

"Aye, what did he say, what?" roared Uncle Pepin.

"Mr Meldík said then he'd just run up and be able to do whatever he wants with you. Says he'll just give you a kick up the backside all the way back to the brewery," the assistant cooper said daringly.

"What? And me an Austrian sodger, that was offered a rank and didna take it, me that carried the Captain's sabre? We'll soon see about that! Soon as I gets to the shop, over the bridge she goes, the whole jingbang into the Elbe!" shouted Uncle taking a barrel and heaving it up with his knee, and as he put it on the pin, the sprayer missed the opening and Uncle Pepin pressed on the foot lever and I put aside my measure of beer, laid it on the ramp and wiped my mouth, and at first I thought that the mixed lager with dark garnet must be making me see things, the assistant and the master cooper and the passing mechanic and old Řepa who was turning his shaft with a new lot of malt, all of them started to jig about and as they danced and capered they plucked at their cheeks and slapped their legs, they were like Moravian Slovaks dancing fancy figures, but old Řepa had to stay with his handle, so he went on turning the shaft, plucking at his face and alternately brandishing his hand and with the other turning the black globe, the drum in which the malt was roasting, till eventually, he tugged at the handle and shifted the drum away from the heat of the thirsty charcoal and like the coopers he jigged and capered, slapping his calves, as though being bitten by thousands of mosquitos.

The assistant cooper shouted, "Mr Josef, turn off that pitch!"

And Uncle Pepin stamped his foot, but kept missing the spot, till finally he hit the lever, and only now did I see how, squirting from the spray nozzle in every direction, the tiny droplets of redhot pitch suddenly wilted, and all those delicate little thin amber tendrils, over which flew those little spatterings tiny as millet, or golden rice, or obtrusive insects, all these wands all at once sank into the dust of the brewery yard, and the coopers peeled off drying gobbets of pitch from their cheeks and the backs of their hands and necks and stared crossly at Uncle Pepin, as he stood there beside that huge stove that was still spluttering, hawking and belching thick short fire out of its bent chimney. Uncle Pepin knitted his scorched fingers and stared at the ground.

The master cooper said, "Right, lads, it's back to work, so that Mr Josef here can get off soon to visit his young ladies."

NINE

The new fashion began at the Hotel Na Knížecí.
Soldiers brought in some apparatus, school head-
masters assembled their pupils as early as six o'clock in
the morning, and all the municipal corporations were
involved, and as the day marched on through the great
chamber there moved a line of curious participants, the
soldiers put a kind of receiver, the sort telephones have,
on every person's ear, and in that earpiece a crackling
noise was heard and then some brass band music,
which kept on playing the well-known tune *Kolíne,
Kolíne*, but this music wasn't a bit beautiful, it was as if it
was played on a long ago worn-out gramophone record,
but all the same that music was being played in Prague
and it was coming through the air, without wires, it was
being drawn along like a thread and into the eye of the
earpiece far away in our own little town. And everyone
who heard it went out the back entrance of the hotel
totally dazzled by this aural sensation, by the absence of
any wire in bringing them Kmoch's Kolín Brass Band,
and everybody walked past this queue of townspeople,

this queue stretching right across the square as far as the main street, right down to Svoboda the baker's, and people who hadn't yet heard this wireless telegraphy, when they saw what blissful amazed expressions there were on the faces of those who had been granted a taste of this revolutionary new invention, all looked forward to it with greater and greater anticipation, as they approached in this procession winding into the Hotel Na Knížecí.

Mr Knížek, owner of the draper's shop, who liked making speeches, at once ordered his apprentice girl to bring the steps, then he got up on them and explained to the assembled citizenry, "Good people, what you are about to hear is an invention, an appliance which our business party will strive to make available to every household, to every family in a year or two from now, at as reasonable a price as is feasible, so that every one of you can sit at home and receive not only music, but the news as well. I do not wish to anticipate, but this amenity can enable us to hear news not only from Prague, but maybe Brno too, music maybe even from Pilsen, and, to cast modesty completely to the winds, even news and music all the way from Vienna!" Mr Knížek declaimed from his stepladder.

Past that stepladder, with his handbarrow and assistant in tow, came Mr Zálaba, who delivered coal and wood about town, and when he heard Mr Knížek speaking, his assistant had to tip up the barrow, and Mr Zálaba ran up the rungs to the top of it and thundered and pointed at Mr Knížek, "Look at him, the petty bourgeois! He thinks of nothing else but his huckster's decimal scales! Citizens, this invention is capable of establishing mutual understanding not only between towns, but also between nations, we welcome wireless telegraphy as the helpmate of the whole of humanity! For understanding among the peoples of all continents, all races, all nations!" Mr Zálaba declaimed, brandishing his arm in the air, and his assistant stood on the shaft of the barrow, but when he spotted a discarded fag-end on the pavement he couldn't resist and nipped over to pick it up, and the barrow tipped over and Mr Zálaba fell on to the paving stones, I only just avoided him.

And I hurried my bicycle home the minute I heard that foreshortened distance through the earphone between the brass-band music in Prague and my listening ear in the Hotel Na Knížecí. I took off my skirt, laid it on the table, picked up the scissors, and at the point where the knees come in the skirt, I cut short the material, producing so much left-over cloth that I reckoned my dressmaker could make me a bolero out of it, and instantly I took a needle and bound the new edge, and almost feverishly I pulled the skirt on and went straight over to look in the mirror, and there I saw it! Ten years younger I was for that foreshortening of distances. I turned round and knew at once that of course the garters had to be much higher up, and then I saw for an absolute certainty that only now were my legs really beautiful, those beautiful shadows in the tendons under the knees, those brown imprints of God's thumb, were capable of arousing much surprise and delight, but also much civic indignation, especially from Francin, who, when he saw me like this, would blush to the roots of his hair and declare that no decent

woman ever wore a skirt like that. And I ran out into the
yard and jumped on my bike and rode out of the
brewery to the Cross, such a pleasurable draught
wafted round my knees, reaching up to my garters, I
could pedal much more freely in that trimmed skirt, the
only thing that bothered me was, I had to cycle with one
hand on the handlebars, with the other I had to keep
pulling my skirt down all the time, as it rode up my legs
with the motion of my knees. And now out of the
Hořátev turning Mr Kropáček came on his Hendee
'Indian' motorbike, as always he was sitting in the
sidecar and steering the motorcycle with one leg slung
over the handlebars and one hand controlling the gas
on the end of one of the bars, I liked to watch him start
the bike up in the brewery, the minute he got going he
climbed across from the saddle into the sidecar, tossed
out one leg as if out of the bath, and then he drove on
comfortably home. So now, Mr Kropáček, when he
caught sight of my bare knees at the turning in the road,
he clean missed the corner and drove off into the cherry
orchard, and I took that as a good omen and hurried on
across the bridge, only slowing down outside the Hotel
Na Knížecí. Slowly I rode past that queue waiting to
experience the new invention, on the subject of which
Headmaster Kupka had declared, "I don't know, I really
don't know, but it bodes nobody any good," and
everybody sort of stopped focusing on what was
awaiting them in the Hotel Na Knížecí, and concentrated on my knees, and shortened skirt, all of them
stopped looking at the hotel entrance and turned in my
direction. Headmaster Kupka pointed his umbrella at
me and said to the Dean, "And there you have it, the

first results!" But the Dean bowed to me and said, "A lady's full genuflection is another name for the Holy Spirit." And I stopped outside the cake shop, before putting my little shoe on the pavement I drew back my hair so that it wouldn't get tangled in the spokes, I leant the bicycle against the wall, and as I went down the pavement I felt as if I was walking along in a bathing suit.

And in the cake shop I ordered Mr Navrátil to wrap me four cream horns, and I took one right away and leant forward to stop the flaky pastry getting in my blouse. And again, as I crammed the cream horn voraciously into my mouth, at once I heard Francin's voice saying that no decent woman would eat a cream puff like that, and Mr Navrátil smiled guardedly, because he had no teeth, and I paused in front of the window display, just let the women see my silhouetted profile from inside the dark shop, and Mr Navrátil handed me a small parcel done up with blue string. I paid, and Mr Navrátil opened the door for me, and before I rode off, he helped me with my hair, running alongside the bike for a bit, till the hair got into the airstream. I pedalled off with all my might, steering with one hand and holding that delicious parcel on one finger, and my hair welled up behind me, just like those beautiful brass balls in the regulator of a steam traction engine when it's revving up. I went on making as if to look at the middle of the road in front of me, but on both pavements I could see all the various kinds of human eyes, those admiring eyes as well as those glances full of hatred for my bare knees, as they rose up alternately like camshaft joints . . .

And when I reached the brewery I rode at once over to the stables, Mutzek ran to meet me, good little doggie, he wagged his long tail, and when I bent down to him he licked my palm and half-closed his eyes, and I went into the shed and brought an axe and unwrapped the parcel and offered Mutzek a cream puff, and he was distrusting at first, but when I laughed he started eating the cream puff and I considered in my mind how much I ought to take off to shorten Mutzek's tail, and I placed the chopping block behind Mutzek and took his tail and laid it on the block, but Mutzek turned round, so I stroked him and offered him another cream puff, and Mutzek, his paw mucky with whipped cream, licked my hand and the axe-handle too and tucked into the second cream puff, and I laid out Mutzek's tail on the block, and then with one blow I chopped off the greater part of it and Mutzek gasped, he had half of the cream puff inside him, but the pain in his tail was doubtless so great, that Mutzek started to moan and turn around, and with his mouth full of sugary foam he took hold of the stump of his tail, out of which blood was dripping, and Mutzek thought someone else had done it, not me, he licked my hand and the remains of his tail by turns, I stroked him and comforted him, "Mutzy dear, it'll only last a short moment, think how handsome and beautiful you'll be, it's the fashion, it has to be like this, take a look and see!" I straightened up and showed him how my skirt was shortened too, but Mutzek began to lament dreadfully and I could see that I hadn't chopped quite enough off, I ought to chop off just another little piece, but Mutzek wouldn't hear of any continuation, I held his tail down on the block, I promised him all the cream puffs, and said I would buy him some more, but Mutzek broke free and took the chopped off piece of tail into his little mouth and ran off with it to the office, and just as the draymen were coming out, he ran into the counting house.

A moment later Francin rushed out of the office, in one hand he held a number three lettering pen, in the other that piece of tail, and Mutzek stood on the last step and barked in the direction of the shed and stables, out of which I was just wheeling my bike, and when I rode up in front of the office, Doctor Gruntorád came bowling along into the brewery. The chairman's stallion had had its tail cropped and its mane trimmed and the doctor jumped down from the driving seat, tossed the reins to the coachman, and taking a look at my skirt he proclaimed, "Everything is going to have to be shortened and there's no end to what is needed. So, manager, now we're going to shorten the working week, from the first of the month Saturdays will be cut by half, so we'll knock off at twelve. The distances to landlords will be shortened by driving out to them. We'll sell your Orion motorbike and get you a motor-car, which will shorten the time taken up and make scope for a greater turnover of beer. Ivan!" cried Doctor Gruntorád at the coachman. "Hand me my first-aid box, let's put some plasters on the little doggie to stop that bleeding."

That afternoon Francin took the Orion off to Prague. I took the opportunity and after work I went off to the lodgings to see Uncle Pepin. Under a lit bulb Uncle Pepin was brandishing his fist at a great huge maltster, who was kneeling, but even on his knees he was still the same size as Uncle Pepin standing, but Uncle put on a threatening face and roared out, "Suppose I canna hold myself back! Suppose I just fetches you a mighty great Ostrava miner's clout with my fist!"

And the great enormous maltster clasped his hands and begged him, "Oh, Mr Josef, don't make a widow of me wife and orphans of me children!"

And the other maltsters standing round in a circle laughed quietly to themselves, those who couldn't stand it any longer ran out into the corridor and stood there facing the wall and drumming their fists against the plaster and drowning in fits of laughter. And when they had finished choking they ran back into the lodgings.

And Uncle Pepin stood legs astride beneath the light bulb and cried out, "So let's have you the now!"

And he threw himself at the huge maltster, who gave ground, and Uncle Pepin gave him a half-nelson, and tried to put him to the floor, but the maltster reared up and knocked Uncle over and pinned him down and everyone around shouted and clapped, but Uncle Pepin grabbed him round the neck and the maltster allowed himself to be turned just about almost on to his back, but at the last minute he knelt and Uncle gave him a full nelson and the maltster stood up and walked round the room with Uncle, carrying Uncle like a little child, but Uncle Pepin yelled out in his delight, "And it's a stunning victory, just like our own Gustav Frištenský!"

Then the maltster knelt again and did a somersault with Uncle, only now did I notice that the two wrestlers were wearing white long-johns, right down to their ankles and tied at the ankle with laces. And as the huge maltster did the somersault, he pinned Uncle Pepin down, lay on his head, but Uncle shouted out, "Give up, it's no use, I've got ye held fast!"

But the great huge maltster reared up, nabbed Uncle Pepin by the ankles and neck and set him spinning and then fell over with him, but Uncle Pepin roared out, "That's set ye flying, like Fryštenský that time with the negro!"

And then the maltster weakened and Uncle Pepin took him by the shoulders and the maltster subsided into laughter and laughed till the tears ran, and Uncle put him on the floor and the chief maltster knelt down and announced, "Mr Josef, you're the winner again!"

And the wrestlers stood up, Uncle bowed and smiled, bowing at the throngs which only he could see around him.

"And tomorrow it's the return bout," said the chief maltster and dipped his face in his can.

"Uncle Jožin," I said, "could you come over to us for a minute and lend us your saw, please?"

And Uncle Pepin recovered his breath, nodded his head, then he went over and threw the blanket off his bunk, all his underwear and other clothes were at the foot of it, he rolled aside the bolster, which was all grimy at the head, and under the bolster he had all sorts of little boxes and reels of thread and so many funny useless tiny bits and bobs, here Uncle found a key, opened his cupboard and pulled out of it a paper bag, upon which was written: *Alois Šisler, Hatter and Furrier*, and out of that bag he took a beautiful white sailor's cap with golden cords and the gold-embroidered emblem *Viribus Unitis*.

"Old Šisler sewed me this, he wouldn't have done it for anyone else but me!" So saying he planted that beautiful white sailor's cap on his head, and there he stood in his long-johns, behind him the tumbled bed with its kicked underwear and clothing at the foot and its load of useless funny old things at the head.

"Uncle Jožin," I said, "that's a lovely bed you've got there, I'll sew you some covers for it, alright?"

"If ye want," said Uncle, quickly getting dressed.

And the maltsters stood round and watched, they gazed at the floor and couldn't manage to say me a single word, they even seemed sorry that I'd turned up in the middle of all that fun with Uncle Pepin, because it was their fun and I didn't belong in it, between me and them lay a difference like the one between this lodging room, where eight of them sleep together, and my three rooms and kitchen, where I sleep and Francin, the brewery manager, who may even make it one day to brewery director, while they will still only be maltsters, till the day they retire, the day they die. Uncle Pepin closed the cupboard and glowed with joy over that cap, the kind only sea captains wear, or first officers.

"Good night to you, sirs," I said and went out of the lodgings.

Before we had pushed through the gust of wind at the corner of the maltings, the light bulbs began to quaver at the corners of the brewery and stables, as if the draught was draining the electricity out of them. Uncle's cap glowed like the milky shade of a paraffin lamp and Uncle had to hold on to that cap tight with both hands to stop the buffets of wind whipping it away from him. It even seemed to me as if Uncle Pepin was just about to float up in the air like once my bouclé bathtowel did . . . and I knew for a cert that Uncle Pepin wouldn't give up his cap, that he'd rather fly zig-zag up into the darkness towards the brewery chimneys and gyrating weather-vanes. And when I lit the lamps and Uncle brought the saw over from the master cooper, I knocked over a chair and Uncle and I shortened the legs of the chair, not much, by ten centimetres, which each time I measured with a tailor's tape-measure. When we laid the table on its side, Uncle Pepin said, "Sister-in-law, do ye know what? What's the point of measuring it all with that tape-measure? Let's just saw off one leg and then lay the sawn-off block against the next leg, and then we can just saw them off straight without measuring."

I gave a laugh, "Uncle Pepin, you ought to have joined the police force, with such brains!"

And Uncle Pepin shouted, "You leave the police out of this! Uncle Adolf had only been with the force just a month, straight off they took him with them in hot pursuit of one particular character, surrounded the building he was in, and when they entered the kitchen there was his other half sitting all by herself and the chief detective says, 'Where's your old man?' And she says, 'Gone to cut tree stumps,' and the chief kicks in the door to the living-room and there through the open window he sees this character darting up the hillside, so he orders them, 'After him!' And Adolf is first out the window, lands up to his neck in manure, but he scrambles up out of it and off they all scamper into the woods waving a revolver and there they had the character surrounded, and he had a revolver too, so they were persuading him to chuck it away, and the character said if they took one step further he was going to shoot, and so the commander spent an hour persuading the character, saying he'd get mitigating circumstances and guaranteeing him personally only six months, and so the character chucked away his revolver, and triumphantly the commander put the handcuffs on him and they led him off to the bus, and Adolf wanted to get into the police vehicle too, but they said that with all that manure on him he couldn't, so he had to go on foot all the way to the very outskirts of Ostrava, and there they threw him off the tram, so he had to walk all the way home on foot, and at home the landlady wouldn't take his clothes for the wash, so he carted them off to the cleaners and took his ticket, and when he came back a fortnight later to get his clothes, there was heaps of folk around and lots of lassies he knew too, and when Adolf's turn in the queue came the manageress took his ticket, and when she came back, she was all red in the face and she threw the parcel back at Adolf and yelled at him, 'Ye've shat yersel', haven't ye, so ye can just go and wash it yersel'!' And he went home all shamefaced . . ."

And so Uncle went on and I smiled and we sawed the legs off the table according to Pepin's recipe, we shortened the table height by ten centimetres, and Uncle Pepin said, "And so Adolf had no luck in life, once he was passing this pub, and some drunken dentists were there, and they invited Adolf for a drink, and when he'd had some and was glad folks were being nice to him again, all of a sudden one dentist in a drunken stupor pulled out another dentist's front teeth, and seeing as Adolf was drunk too, the one that pulled out the front teeth took Adolf and pulled out all his back teeth, mind you Adolf was dead lucky there was no drunken gelders around that night . . ."

"That would've been pretty mighty sore," I said, laying a sawn-off piece to the last leg and we went on sawing merrily away and Uncle Pepin expatiated, "But then they took Adolf off on military exercises and he was right over in Turčanský Svätý Martin and again, seeing as Uncle Adolf was a qualified engine-driver, they gave him a Sentinel to drive, and one day this bloke, sergeant-major, was reading the army paper and he finds in the circulars, steam-roller needed for road surfacing outside barracks, Cheb, so he gives Adolf his orders and ration allowances, and Uncle Adolf sets off for Cheb in his Sentinel following his map, this was in the spring, and Adolf spent the whole summer just going westwards across Slovakia, and in the autumn he crossed the Moravian border and went on his way, but slower and slower, because each Sunday he went off home, and when he'd spent all autumn getting through Moravia, he went back to make discreet enquiries at the barracks in Turčanský Svätý Martin, but there they told him the sergeant-major had hanged himself, because a gun had been found on the square and nobody knew who put it there, so they had stuck it in the stores and that was one gun too many, and so Adolf went on his way in the Sentinel right across the length of Czechoslovakia, and by spring he'd got as far west as Pilsen, but as he hadn't any coal he had to stoke the boiler up with firewood, begging and borrowing on the road, but he burned up an awful lot of folk's fences too, specially when he was a long way off from the woods, and he was terribly delayed, as in fact he was only driving the Sentinel one day at a time in the end, because it took him three days to get home to Ostrava for the Sunday, and three days travelling back to the Sentinel again, and so finally in the summer Uncle Adolf made it to the garrison in Cheb, and there they locked the pair of them up, Adolf and the Sentinel, and when it was all sorted out and explained, they sent Uncle Adolf as military watch to Košumberk Castle, and as he had nowhere to go now, there out of boredom at Košumberk he fell in love with the daughter of the visitors' guide, and he married her, and all that time he stood there on guard, toting his weapon, but after three years of this he reckoned they'd likely forgotten him, so he just stripped off his uniform, stashed his weapon away in a corner, and there he is to this day, working as a visitors' guide . . .'' and Uncle Pepin straightened himself as the last block of wood dropped off.

I took the lamp and carried it across to the sideboard, to see how this table was going to look shortened by ten centimetres. And when Uncle and I put the overturned table on its side I stared wide-eyed with astonishment and my eyes just popped. I went through to the kitchen, stood for a while on the doorstep and gazed out over the orchard treetops at the brewery chimney stack, then after a bit I went back in.

Uncle Pepin was knitting his fingers.

"What's to be done? Nothing's to be done, Uncle Jožin," I told him, "bring me over those historical novels of Beneš Třebízský from the bookcase, would you?"

And I righted the table, that table off whose legs in half-darkness Uncle Pepin and I had sawn four times ten centimetres, but each time we'd gone and placed the ten-centimetre block against one and the same leg, hadn't we, so that we'd shortened this one leg by forty centimetres . . . and Uncle Pepin brought along those old historical novels and I piled them under the missing leg, but it wasn't enough, so I had to finish it off with Šmilovský's *Parnassia*.

Away in the distance a clatter and thunder resounded, that was Francin on his Orion just coming out of the little woods near Zvěřínek, and that din and clamour grew ever stronger and louder, as if Francin were bulldozing all the Orion's dismantled parts along in front of him. I ran out in front of the office and opened the gates, and Francin rode into the brewery, swaying about on the sidecar was the little lathe which Francin always took with him on longer excursions, and now the motorbike swerved to our front door, and Francin raised his goggles and removed his leather helmet and motioned with his hand for me to go back quick into the house, and I knew he'd brought me another little gift. I ran into the kitchen, and Francin came dragging something in through the back, across the office passage and into the living room, for a while he fiddled with something in there and then he came into the kitchen rubbing his hands and laughing, he patted Uncle Pepin on the shoulder and I threw myself at Francin and as was our custom searched through all his coat pockets and in his trousers, and Francin laughed and was quite charming, till I was altogether tantalised, what could be behind all this? And then I said, "So it's not a little ring or some earrings, and it's not a watch or a little brooch, it's something bigger, isn't it?" And Francin took off his coat and washed his hands and nodded his head, and as he was drying his hands I pointed to the door into the living room and asked, "Is it in there?" Francin nodded that it was . . . and was purposely slow in getting changed and purposely pretended he had to polish his shoes, till I threatened to burst into the room, because I couldn't stand it any longer. Francin raised a finger, asked me to close my eyes, and led me off into the room, and there he let me stand a while, and then I heard music, a tenor began to sing most beautifully . . . "For you my heart is cryin', white flower, my Hawaii . . ." I opened my eyes, turned, and Francin stood holding the burning lamp and shining it on a box gramophone, then he placed the lamp on the table and asked me for a dance, caught me round the waist, squeezing my palm with his other hand, and then Francin paused till the right moment, and finally swam with a long step into . . . "And though he say farewell dear, yet he'll return to you here . . ." and Francin, I was amazed, because he was a poor dancer, he swam into the steps of the tango so well, that I pressed myself to him, he insinuated his leg altogether quite boldly between mine, we were so nicely dovetailed I drew back to get a better look at Francin, then I laid my head on his shoulder, but there came a turn in the dance and Francin slipped out of rhythm. He waited a moment, and when he tried to continue the tango by gliding backwards, he glided correctly, but out of rhythm, and he lost confidence, but when he let the whole thing slide and paused till those first three steps came round, he picked up the thread and swam beautifully across the carpet and avoided twirling about this time, he didn't even want to step away from me, but with long strides, as if his shoes were stuck in hot asphalt, he simply danced from one end of the room to the other, turning awkwardly and stepping out again in rhythm, and yet he couldn't resist trying another turn, he moved away from me and scrutinised his steps on the carpet, I could see those steps were correct, but Francin was lacking one vital thing: the rhythm. He even had a go at flinging me over backwards, it flashed through my head he must have been going to ballroom dancing classes, some private dancing school in Prague, because he even did that trick to perfection, he bent me over backwards till my hair touched the carpet, but when he drew me back towards him, that was correct too, but all the time the thread of the dancing steps was missing the eye of the musical needle . . . and the beautiful tenor stopped singing and the music quietly subsided . . . and Francin stopped smiling and practically collapsed on to a chair, and his inability to get the tango right, his consciousness of failure left him gasping for breath, because at the last masked ball I had danced with young Klečka, a brewster at the brewery, who played the cello beautifully and had four classes of technical school and knew how to dance, and he and I by mutual agreement, when the other dancers had stopped and gathered round us, we two danced together like two true artistes, like two coupled axles, in pure symbiosis, while Francin sat alone behind a pillar and gazed at the floor.

"When I'm with Miss Vlasta at Havrda's," said Uncle

Pepin, "we dance too, only a wee bit different, faster than that, Vlasta pours me a Martell and then she says, 'Well Mr Josef, what can I play for you today?' And I says, 'Give us a good belter!' And Vlasta says, 'You what? Which one?' And I says, 'By the composer Bunda, known as Gobelinek,' so may I have the pleasure also, sister-in-law? Francin, make it go quite a good bit faster! And get a load of this real dancing!"

Uncle Pepin took me by the hands and the jazzy music started to play so fast, with Francin shifting the speed lever forward, like women rushing about in a speeded-up film. And Uncle Pepin began to bow to me and I bowed to him too. Then he touched me with his forehead, and I him, suddenly Uncle turned to the rhythm of the music, and keeping a hold of each other's hands, we turned about to stand back to back to each other, and Uncle lifted a foot and twisted and waggled his shoe and calf, then he spread his arms, clapped his palms and revolved his hands as fast as if he were swiftly winding wool, then he crooked his hands at his waist and cut with his feet this way and that, so that I had to do the same, but the opposite way, so as he wouldn't kick my ankles, then he turned and took me by the waist and tossed me up to the ceiling, till I touched the plaster with my hair, and then Uncle carried me hither and thither to the rhythm of the music, with his nose buried in my navel, then he let me go, turned me round and back to back we touched each other, and Uncle heaved me up on his shoulders like a bundle and I locked myself in his arms too, and we rocked each other to and fro, as if straightening strains in the smalls of our backs, then Uncle let me go, ran round me in a rhythmic trot and started lunging at me, like the Knave of Hearts with his pikestaff, I copied him, and the dance was exact and elusive, but constantly rhythmic, as if the motion filled out the music much more exactly than any other form of dance, then Uncle leapt up and spreadeagled his legs and landed on the carpet and did the splits, and I was afraid I might rupture my groin, so I merely bowed left and right, while Uncle sniffed alternately at his left toecap and his right, then all of a sudden, as if suctioned up to the ceiling, he jumped up, drew his legs together and pulled me so niftily up on to his shoulder, then over his shoulder feet first and down on to the ground again, that I made a stroke mark on the ceiling with the heel of my shoe. Francin watched me smilingly, then he went to the kitchen and came back holding in one hand a mug of warm white coffee and in the other a slice of dry bread, which he nibbled away at, and he watched us, but the speeded-up tango was fading away, the tenor drew to an end . . . "And though he say farewell dear, yet he'll return to you here . . . white flower, my Hawaii, I dream of you . . ." And as Uncle Pepin led me off the dance floor, he kissed my hand and held my arm and bowed deeply on all sides, bowing to some great ballroom and sending kisses out to all corners of the room . . . And just as I walked past the table, I trod on one of the little sawn-off blocks from the leg and sprained my ankle.

"Brother," said Francin, "harmony hibernates within you."

And I fell with a shout and couldn't get up again.

During that night Mutzek took leave of his senses. In

the evening the caretaker had had to chain him up in the shed, and there Mutzek was unable to sort out in his mind the relationship between cream puffs and the pain in his tail, and also he didn't want to be a handsome young fellow in the latest fashion, and so be began to howl dreadfully and foam appeared at his mouth, the foam of insanity mixed with the foam of cream puffs, and at midnight Francin loaded his Browning pistol and went out into the yard, and after a while I heard firing, one shot after another, I hobbled to the window and saw in the light of an electric torch Mutzek straining at his chain, standing on his hind legs and begging with his paws, agreeing to the shortened tail, reconciled to all, as long as his loving master didn't shoot, and Francin fired off a whole round, but Mutzek still did not drop, on the contrary, he was more moving than ever before, he kept standing up on his hind legs and waggling his front paws, and I took it all as a mortal sin which I had inflicted on Mutzek, and I hobbled to the ottoman and burst into tears and jammed up my ears to avoid hearing those shots like accusations . . . And the firing stopped, and I expect Mutzek was dead by now, but surely up to the last moment he had gone on wagging his non-existent tail, because he probably thought someone else was shooting him, since as an animal he surely didn't and couldn't have understood how we could cause him this pain, I and his loving master, Francin, who, when he returned with his Browning, rolled dressed as he was into bed and it seemed to me that he was crying too.

TEN

Now Francin had me the way he wanted me to be, a nice decent woman sitting at home, he knew where this woman was, and where she would be tomorrow, somewhere he would like to make her stay for always, not too ill, but sort of ailing, a woman who would hobble to the stove, to the chair, to the table, but above all a woman who would be some kind of a burden, because for Francin it was the height of matrimonial bliss when I was grateful to him for making me my breakfast in the morning, and going on the motorbike at midday to fetch lunch from the restaurant, but above all it meant he could show me how much he loved me, with what joy he was prepared to care for me, and somehow, just as he took care of me, so ought I to be taking care of him, that was Francin's dream, that every year I might catch angina and flu, and occasionally even get pneumonia. That always made him blissfully happy, nobody else knew how to look after a person like Francin did, that was his religion, his heaven on earth, when he could wrap me in sheets dampened in cold water, when he ran round me with the sheet and wound it on to me as if he were embalming me alive, but then he took me in his arms and laid me carefully in my bed, like little girls do with their dolls. And once an hour he dashed out of the office to take my temperature, every two hours he changed my compresses, praying no doubt in his heart, not that he would wish it, but if Fate would not decree otherwise, that I should never get up from my bed, so that I could be his little child, who needed him just as much as he needed me. And when I was convalescing and starting to get about, when I began inwardly to laugh again, and again that indecent woman in me started to get the upper hand, Francin withdrew into himself and dreamt again about me being paralysed and him pushing me in a wheelchair, in the evening he would read to me from the *National Politics* daily or a novel, and this would assuage his complex about my rude state of health, which loved chance and the unexpected happening and the marvellous encounter, whereas Francin loved order and regularity, repetition indicated to him the right path in life, everything that could be predicted and fixed, that was Francin's existence, a world he believed in and without which he could not have lived.

And now he had me in bed with my ankle bandaged in glowing plaster, immobile for a long time to come, and if and when, at first on crutches and then with a walking stick, now, while Josephine Baker dances the Charleston.

And maybe my ankle came along in the nick of time, because while I was running about Francin was incapable of putting together a single advertising slogan, he covered so many quarter slips of paper with his number three lettering pen, and all that advertising for increased turnover of beer ended up in the stove. Now however, with my white leg resting on its cushion, Francin walked up and down the kitchen and living room, drank lukewarm coffee and nibbled at a piece of dry bread, and suddenly he stopped short with the mug in his hand, as though in a dream, assailed even by a vision, which made him squint. He put aside the mug and the bread, sat himself down, and the number three lettering pen wrote out calligraphic notices for the pubs, and when he had finished, he took a drawing pin and fastened each quarter sheet of paper to the wall, so that I could see it, so that I might get the message, that if only I was healthy but behaved as if I was ill, any day now he would be appointed director of the brewery, that limited-liability company, such zest for work and life my paralysed mobility gave him. In a week Francin must have drunk for inspiration at least half a hundred litres of lukewarm white coffee and across the whole wall he hung out the graphically decorative slogans he had created with his lettering pen. – Drink more ale, for fewer aches and woes. – Our fine ale, reinforcement for flagging constitutions. – Without his glass he sighed alas, after his beer he flushed like a lass and made good cheer. – Without my ale in living death I'd wail. – Our fine ale, reinforcement and fortification of flagging constitutions. – Drink more beer, make better cheer. – Hearty, fresh and hale, you'll find good health in our ale. – If you wish to have good cheer, come along and drink our beer. – They who fraternise the tavern, live a life of double heaven. – Our wholesome beer, the drink

for everyone. – Live a life of better cheer, come along
and drink more beer. – Who shuns the tavern with his
feet, who does not drink and does not eat, his health he
surely will defeat. – At home, on your journey, beer is
always refreshing. – Beer at every time and tide, beer
refreshes your inside. And he was so pleased by his
bout of inspiration, he poured himself a full mug of
coffee, and put on the gramophone ... "Far away
across the sea, lies a magic land, Hawaii ..." and he
tried with creeping steps to dance the tango, and being
so brimful of optimism, and so happy about some event
lying in the near future, in the evening he locked
himself up in the living room, and played *White Flower,
My Hawaii*, over and over again. Every other while he
came out holding a modern dance manual and
laughing, and when he'd expressed his delight, he
returned again to the room, the key hole shone into the
half-darkness just like my leg in plaster, and I knew that
Francin must have drawn all the steps with chalk, in
footprints, not only the basic steps, but also the steps
backward, the turns, a whole itinerary of chalk-marked
outlines of shoe soles, which he patiently paced
through, in the rhythm and melody of *Hawaii*. He was
so happy that he was managing the steps now that even
in the daytime, when I was looking out the window into
the yard and Francin was in a hurry to take instructions
to the brewing house, suddenly he would slow down
and pace out the steps of the tango, then turn around
and backwards, with his arms slightly raised, he would
continue this modern dancing, I saw him looking at his
feet, I saw he was confounded, that if he could, he
would chalk out those dance steps on the road ... but

that didn't put him off, on the contrary, that evening he tried all the more fervently to pinpoint on the chalk-marked carpet that little chink through which he might enter truly into the rhythm of the gramophone, as it performed *Hawaii* for the hundredth time. Every evening Francin removed the electric battery from his Orion motorcycle, brought it in and switched on the high-frequency currents, the case padded with red velvet gleamed dimly with its glassy instruments, and Francin put sparks in my ankle, fulgurational flashes penetrated the plaster bandaging, then he removed my items of clothing one by one, without my realising I was practically naked, the fulgurational currents made me feel good, the massage roller with its tiny sparklets fortified both my legs and reinforced the nerves in my spine, and Francin whispered to me, "The best method, Mary, of enhancing your beauty, using fulgurational currents to conserve the beauty you have now . . ." I looked forward every evening to these violet massagings, with the scent of thunder and short circuits, across the orchard you could hear again the lovely male voice, Mr Jirout in his little satin suit, firing himself with his voice from a cannon, through the wall I could see him fly over the brewery, hands by his sides and smiling a crinkly smile . . . "the love that was, it is gone, 'twas for but a short while . . . golden lassie . . ." and now Mr Jirout began to veer towards the ground, he spread his arms and cast roses and kisses to the watchers below, Francin put a metal electrode in my hand and turned on the machine with a black knob and like a hypnotist he hovered with his palm over my body, wherever Francin's hand moved, there sparks sizzled and crackled from his palm, raining down a shower of purple violet grain, thousands of forget-me-nots and violets from Francin's palm entered me from this appliance, the scent of ozone and lightning striking the building hovered over me, even the ankle dipped in plaster glowed with a blueish sheen . . . "her life is o'er . . . to the deep linn by Nymburk town she's gone . . ." and Mr Jirout landed in the trampoline net and bounced and bowed in his little blue satin suit . . . I felt my body too emitting its own pungent scent of electricity, I was breathing more and more heavily, my whole body radiated its own halo, I looked at myself in the mirror, lying stretched out, the purple violet crackle and sizzle my only camisole, I never had the sense that I was naked, all the time I was encased in a periwinkle coat, and Francin's gutta-percha collar and white shirt cuffs shone just like my plaster leg, he was breathing just like me, lying on my back with my elbow crooked over my eyes. I used to feel all funny from that high-frequency ritual, Francin and I never used to talk about it, we prepared in silence, as if both of us were striving for something forbidden, and when Francin turned back the black knob, each time we avoided each other's eyes, so beautiful it was. If someone had suddenly burst into the room bearing a lamp, Francin would certainly have fainted, and so he preferred to lock the door, draw the blinds and curtain, and for safety's sake he went out and looked in at the windows, to make sure no one could peep in at us and see him unbuttoning my blouse with quivering fingers, drawing the skirt down carefully over the plaster ankle, kneeling down in front of me and reaching out with this cosmetic massage to the cosmos.

ELEVEN

Today Doctor Gruntorád came, he asked me to make him some strong tea, saying he'd caught a chill in the night from attending mothers in labour, he drew his scissors out of his bag, and while he was cutting my plaster bandage he sneezed a couple of times, then fell asleep in the middle of cutting, with the scissors still in his fingers, and he was so deeply asleep, I couldn't resist, I pulled out his gold watch from his waistcoat pocket, looked to see what time it was, and quietly slipped the watch back in its place, so carefully and so thrilled by the precision of my movements, and in that pickpocketing escapade I was once more my old self, the clock on the wall showed me what time it was, but I just wanted to test myself, to see if I hadn't lost my pluck, to see if I was still capable of doing whatever I fancied, and yes, things weren't too bad after all. I used to go to Mr Pollak's drapery shop to buy buttons just because in the afternoon nobody used to be around in the shop, and as Mr Pollak bent down beneath the counter to fetch a box, I would stretch my hand across the counter and take a child's fake watch, and when

Mr Pollak straightened up, I would look all innocent, and in his eyes I could read that he was quite oblivious of my theft, and when I asked to see some more buttons and Mr Pollak bent down, quickly I hung the watch back, and when Mr Pollak straightened up, I smiled, I grew up taller somehow inside, and with that theft and its immediately ensuing effective repentance I released tension, breathed my relief, and on going out of the shop I felt as if I had sprouted wings so great that I was scraping the door frame with them and feathers were fluttering off me, which Mr Pollak had to sweep up kneeling with a shovel ... and Doctor Gruntorád sneezed and woke up and finished cutting my bandage, which split open like a white casing, then the doctor felt my ankle over, declaring, "Now you can get up to your mischief again ..." and he sneezed and I took my crutches and brought a mug of tea, and when I tried to put my weight on my leg it collapsed under me and I said, "It doesn't even feel like my own leg!" and Doctor Gruntorád said, "It's your leg all right, you'll be right as rain in a week ... tishoo!" he sneezed with feeling. "Doctor," I said, "I'm breathing a bit funny too." "Take off your blouse if you would," said the doctor, taking a sip of his tea. Then he laid his ear on my back, and as always that ear was cold, as if he were laying a small glass ashtray on me, the warmer the weather, the colder his ear was, he tapped my back, asked me to breathe deeply, and then his index finger tapped on my back, lightly he touched my back with his ear, like boys putting their ears to telegraph poles, I flicked the current of my hair over, and the doctor fell asleep again, buried in my hair, as if asleep on a bench beneath a weeping willow tree. Once I went past Doctor Gruntorád's villa specially on purpose to see if that willow tree was actually there, overshadowing the whole house, it was such a long time ago I supposed since his wife used to receive visits from a colonel gent who came from Brandejs on horseback, and Doctor Gruntorád, then young and undoubtedly stalwart, unexpectedly returned home in the night, grabbed his gun in passing on the ground floor and went up and kicked open the door to his wife's bedroom, just in time to glimpse the colonel dashing to the open first-floor window. He managed to take aim, and as the colonel propelled himself from the window sill with a clatter and plunged headlong out into the depths of night and down into the faded lilac bushes and flowering jasmines, Dr Gruntorád managed to scatter buckshot at the colonel's vanishing topboots and another load merely at the stars of the blue night filling the empty window frame . . . I would often wake in the night with this image, which kept me awake, I could never properly imagine and associate this wonderful incident with the person of Dr Gruntorád, I kept connecting it in my mind with somebody else, but a quite tangible image connected me with the colonel gent, who with his topboot shot through still managed to hop up on his horse, managed to pull a stem of willow out of his boot, lean from his horse right down to the ground and stick that stem in the ground, a stem which today has become such a huge willow tree, that in stormy and windy nights it taps against the window panes of the whole house like a living memorial. And Doctor Gruntorád continued tapping his index finger on my back, maybe he wasn't even aware he'd previously dropped off, he tapped away like a miner buried in the pit, and when he turned round he took a sip of tea, and while I was dressing, he quietly wrote out his prescription, and again his golden fountain pen suddenly halted, for a few seconds Doctor Gruntorád dropped off, then he woke again and feeling revived finished writing out the prescription of medicine for my chest. I said to him, "Doctor, has my husband boasted to you yet about something he bought for me?" "Show me!" instructed the doctor and sipped his tea. I opened the case lying there on the table. "What kind of junk is that? Where did the fellow buy it?" said the doctor. I said to him, "In Prague, but seeing as you've got a cold, here's a really beautiful attachment, a bit like our national anthem, pines rustle on the rocky slopes." The doctor said, "And do you know how to operate it?" I said, "Doctor, there's nothing to it . . . Look!" and I plugged it in and twisted the black knob and fitted on the tube with bristles for the nerves, and purple violet sawdust sizzled from the bristles, and the doctor ran his fingers down his knuckles and smiled naively and said, "It's poetical, it can't do anybody any harm, and coming from you, it'll be a pleasure . . ." And I took the electrode, the ozone inhalator and atomiser, and I told him, "Doctor, the best thing would be if you could lie down on the ottoman . . ." The doctor sat down on the settee, I drew the beige curtain, and the sprinkled half-darkness and the little purple violet bush of electric discharges sizzling from that special electrode for the nerves, gave a glow to the doctor's bald pate, as he lowered himself gently on to the ottoman. Now he lay on his back, holding in his fingers that constantly sputtering and crackling wand, while I prepared the ozone inhalator with its atomiser. Into the wadding of the ozone inhalator I put some drops of eucalyptus oil with menthol essence, screwed into the tube the forked glass attachment, for sticking into your nose, and then I took the little nerve brush away from the doctor and stuck into the cathode that ozone inhalator with its atomiser and turned the wheel, and the hollow tube filled with neon gas, which percolated through the wadding, soaked in eucalyptus oil. I knelt in front of the settee and put the appliance gently close up to the doctor's nostrils. I told him, "This is bound to cure you, doctor, my husband always inhalates just before he gets a cold, it's really like when the pines rustle on the rocky slopes, don't you scent the smell of ozone, of resin? And that blue fiery discharge of neon, it's a cure in itself, your colour is blue, that eases away all the hurly-burly of life, quietens the nerves, retards the flow . . ." I ran on, holding in one hand that beautiful appliance full of inhalating oil and in my right hand still squeezing the rubber bulb which drove the air through the ozone and oil chamber of the inhalator . . . and everything I said Doctor Gruntorád repeatedly blissfully after me, smiling blissfully too, and I heard the swing door from the office give a clack, then the key turned in the door and Francin came in, ghastly pale, and he cried out softly, "What are you up to in here!" And I took fright and squeezed the rubber bulb, and the doctor never finished repeating after me, ". . .pines rustle on the rocky slopes . . .", he sat bolt upright and yelled out, his whole face was drawn and suddenly he was years younger, he jumped up and jigged his legs about in a funny way and felt for the door-handle and rushed out, and Francin followed after him with clasped hands, "Chairman, forgive me!" But the doctor went on jigging his legs about and ran over to the maltings and into the maltings and down the stairs to the malting floors, there he ploughed through several mounds of barley, the maltsters stood with their shovels astounded, but the chairman left Francin kneeling in the damp malt behind him and ran out still lamenting up the stairs to the lofts, he ran past the dry heaps of malt, but still that pain in his nose drove him on up to the highest floor, there he ran into barley drying on the grids, into that sixty-degree heat, and he ran back down one floor and across the connecting bridge he ran into the brew-house, several times he ran round the vessel and down the stairs he rushed into the fermenting room, Francin still after him, out of the fermenting room Doctor Gruntorád rushed on into the cooling room, the place where the young beer was cooled, he opened the window louvres and ran out on to the roof of the ice room, where the houseleeks were in bloom, Francin knelt down into those beautiful yellow flowers, but Doctor Gruntorád lamented again and ran up the steps back into the brew-house and through the gates he ran into the yard and from the yard he ran over to the stables, the workmen greeted him, "Good day, chairman! Good day, manager!" But the doctor went on jigging his legs up and down on past the orchard, until he ran in again through the open door into our kitchen and back into the living room, where he slumped on to the settee expostulating, "Where did you buy that piece of junk? Show me!" And he inspected carefully the ozone inhalator with its atomiser, then he sniffed it and said, "What did that oil stuff come in, you dratted woman you? Those pines rustling on the rocky slopes and all that?" He put on his pince-nez, I handed him the little flask and when the doctor had read the label he exploded, "You dratted woman you, you forgot to dilute it one in ten! You've burnt my mucous membrane . . . atchoo!" Doctor Gruntorád sneezed, and when he saw Francin kneel and stretch out his hands, imploring him, "Can you forgive me?", the chairman said, "Get up, my good man, I'd much rather be the manager of this brewery than its chairman . . ." and so saying, he glanced at his watch and gave me his hand, then he kissed the top of my hand and said, "My respects." And he left, re-emerging in the yard in the sunshine, trailing behind him a scent of carbolic and disinfectant and eucalyptus, then he hopped on to the box with feudal lightfootedness, as if all that had happened had only given him added strength, and now I could see it! Now I could believe it, it must have happened just as I heard it, that story, the only relic of which was that weeping willow tree, that enveloped the whole house. The doctor sat on the box, the coachman handed him the reins, the doctor lit a cigarette in his amber holder, cocked his soft light-coloured hat over his brow like no other man could, and grew younger somehow with those reins in his hands, he looked as if he'd just arrived in that carriage from Vienna, he straightened himself and drove out of the brewery with his stallion, whose tail and mane were trimmed, while the doctor's coachman lolled behind on the plush upholstery of the landau with the guilty smile of a man who will never understand why his master rides on the box with such zest and pleasure, while he, the coachman, sits guiltily behind on the plush seat . . . And Francin paced about the room and jammed his fingers into his brain.

TWELVE

I glanced at my watch, it was time for Bod'a Červinka to have finished his little round. No doubt he got his vegetables today for a good price, and overjoyed by his bargain he'll have stopped first on the square at Svoboda's, where he'll have had a couple of gills of vermouth and fifty grammes of Hungarian salami, then he'll have stopped at the Grand, where he's sure to have had one small goulash and three Pilsners, then, to start bringing his little round to its conclusion, he'll have stopped at the Mikoláška drugstore, where, lingering in friendly conversation, he'll have drunk three glasses of brandy. It's also possible, however, that Bod'a was so overjoyed at saving two crowns on his bargain purchase of vegetables, that he went on to complete his so-called big round, that is to say, stopping at the Hotel Na Knížecí as well, for a black coffee with Original Jamaican rum, and finally dropping in for a quick one at the special bar of Louis Wantoch and Co., where he had a little noggin of kirsch as a final full stop to his celebration of such a cheap purchase of cauliflower and vegetables for his soup.

After Francin had gone off into his office totally unmollified, I hobbled out into the hall, pulled out my bike and rode off into town, I pedalled lightly with my white and painful foot, but then with each push of the pedals the ankle seemed to gain strength. I leant the bicycle against the wall, and when I peeped into the barber's shop, there on the rotating armchair sat Bod'a in a snooze, I went in and sat down on a free chair. Bod'a must have done the big round today, because he was giving off a smell of cherry stones, he must have ended up at Griotte Inc.'s. "Bod'a," said I. "What? Yes madam?" he said getting up with such a start that he snatched his scissors and started snipping them in the air. I said, "Bod'a, I'd like you to cut my hair." Bod'a started in shock even more. "I beg your pardon?" he stammered. And I said, "Bod'a, I want my hair cut short like Josephine Baker's." Bod'a weighed my hair in his hands and rolled his eyes, "What, this surviving link with the old Austria? This hallmark, which says, 'Here am I, Anna Czilágová, born Karlovice, in Moravia?' Never!" And Bod'a tossed aside the scissors contemptuously and sat down and folded his arms and looked out the window and glowered. And I said to him, "Mister Bod'a, Doctor Gruntorád has trimmed his stallion's mane and tail and he recommended me this modern cut against dandruff." Bod'a was implacable, "Cutting it short would be like spitting on the host after holy communion!" I said to him, "Bod'a, I'll sign you a solemn written undertaking . . ." "Only with that," said Bod'a, bringing his writing things, and I wrote down on a quarter sheet of paper, like before an operation, that I of my own free will and being in full possession of all my faculties requested Mr Bod'a Červinka to cut my long hair short. And Bod'a, having dried this solemn undertaking by waving it in the air, put it carefully away in his wallet, flapped open the white surplice, pulled it under my chin, bent back my head, and took the scissors, he hesitated a moment, it was like that moment when a circus artiste in the big top is about to do a particularly dangerous feat and the drum rolls and rolls . . . and with two big snips Bod'a sheared off my flowing tresses. It took such a load off me, that my head sank forward on to my chest and I felt a draught on my neck. Bod'a laid the hair on the revolving armchair, then he took the trimmer and shaved off tendrils of hair and side locks, then his scissors snipped in the air, Bod'a stepped back and contemplated my hair like a working sculptor, and at once his scissors started working away concentratedly again. Whenever I tried to raise my head and glance stealthily at myself in the mirror, he pushed my chin down between my shoulder blades and carried on working. I saw him starting to perspire, his face gleamed and he smelt of Jamaican rum and kirsch and brandy with a whiff of not terribly pleasant beer about him, he lathered his brush, and every time I tried to look at myself, he pushed my head down, but I saw that a kind of joy was spreading over his face, a kind of delighted smile, indicating that something was going right. Then he soaped the back of my neck and shaved my neck with a razor, then he dampened my hair and trimmed it back with the razor, and suddenly I felt a bitterness in my mouth and my heart began to thump, now, when it was too late, the hair couldn't be fixed back, I saw Francin, sitting in the evening in the office and penning initial letters with his number three lettering pen and round each initial he sets swirling tendrils and my russet hair coursing in the shape of a lyre, I saw Francin having his hands cut from my hair by Bod'a Červinka, having the purple violet glowing neon comb cut away by him, because now Francin will never be able to comb my tresses out there in the darkened room and luxuriate in my hair, which he fell in love with right back in the time of Austria and because of which he married me . . . I closed my eyes and pressed my chin to my chest and sobbed for a moment, Bod'a touched me twice, but I didn't have the strength to lift my eyes up to the mirror, Bod'a took me tenderly by the mouth and lifted my chin, then he stepped back, and was so tactful that he turned away . . . There in the mirror on the revolving chair, up to the neck in a white sheet, sat a fetching young man, but with such an insolent expression on his face, that I raised my own hand against myself. Bod'a unfastened the surplice, I raised myself up, leaned on the marble table top and gazed at myself, astonished, for Bod'a had sculpted out of me my very soul, that Josephine Baker hairdo, that was me, that was my self-portrait, it was bound to stick out a mile at everyone, hit them in the face like a waggon shaft. By now Bod'a had long since dusted the chopped and fragmented hairs off the gown, mercifully allowing me a chance to get my bearings, to get used to myself. I sat down, still unable to take my eyes off myself. Bod'a took the round mirror and held it behind me. In the mirror in front of me I saw in the oval glass the nape of my neck, my boyish neck, which had returned me to my girlish youth, without making me cease to be a woman, still able to tempt herself with that neck of hers trimmed in the shape of a heart. And altogether that new hairdo gave the impression of a helmet, a kind of cap made of hair like Mephistopheles had when the Martin company played Faust in our local theatre, it looked as if it could be removed from my head, just as Doctor Gruntorád a short while back had taken off the plaster bandaging from my ankle, my hairdo fitted close to my scalp like that plaster did to my ankle . . . And I jumped up, but as I was accustomed to my hair pulling my head back, I nearly fell over and broke Bod'a's mirror with my forehead. I paid, promising Bod'a I'd give him a case of lager for good measure, and Bod'a laughed and rubbed his hands, Bod'a too was invigorated by this barber's feat of his. "Bod'a," I said to him, "did you create it all by yourself?" And Bod'a flipped through the series of modern haircuts in his barber's news, from the fringe of Lya de Putti to the bob cut of Josephine Baker . . . I went out, and a gust blew about my head, although there was a dead calm. I jumped on my bike and Bod'a ran out after me, bringing me those chopped-off tresses in a paper bag, he put them in my hand, those tresses weighed a good two kilos, as if I'd gone and bought me two kilos of eel. I said, "Bod'a, put them on the back for me, on the carrier, will you?" And Bod'a lifted up the spring of the carrier and laid the tresses down, and when he let the spring fall back on the tresses, I clutched my head . . . And then I rode off down the main street, looking at the passers-by, I saw de Giorgi the master chimney sweep, but he didn't recognise me, I rode on to the railway station, looked at the departure times, but nobody paid me any attention, people thought I was someone else altogether, even though the bicycle and my body were just the same as they were before my hair was cut short. I pushed on the cycle pedals and returned up the main street, in front of Mr Svoboda the baker's stood Doctor Gruntorád's carriage, only this afternoon had the doctor finally made it to his tubby mug of white coffee and basket of rolls, which would be waiting for him there every morning, for when he got back from his rural deliveries and grumbling gall-bladders, and now the doctor came out, the coachman jumped down from the box where he had been dozing with his hands on the stallion's reins, Doctor Gruntorád looked at me, I bowed and smiled, but the doctor only hesitated a moment, then shook his head firmly to himself and mounted the box and drove off, while his coachman lolled behind on the plush seat. I rode through the square past the plague column, everyone looked at me as if they had never seen me in town before . . . on the parade walk in front of the firm of Katz's, draper's and haberdasher's, a bulldog slept, and a group of ladies dressed in black were standing, with skirts down to the ground, the chairlady of the local civic amenity society was seemingly giving a guided tour to some notable composer, he had a big black hat on like a social democrat. Once I too went round with this amenity society with their skirts brushing up the dust of the paving, in the holy church of St Giles we stood by the closed side entrance and gazed at the floor where not a trace remained, only a memory of how hundreds of years ago there was a dried-up encrustation of blood from that massacre when the Swedes and the Saxons slaughtered all the burghers who had sheltered in there, and then we stood by the only really beautiful, historically valuable Fortna Gate, but we didn't stare at the gate itself, we looked attentively under the arches of the stone bridge, where in the year 1913 the animal-tamer Kludský had bathed his circus elephants, still wallowing there to this day in the waters of the Elbe and squirting water over their backs with their trunks like fire-hoses, just like the photograph in the town museum – for Mrs Krásenská, the chairlady of the amenity society, thanks to her revivifying imagination, sees in this town only that which is no longer visible to the naked eye. Now the lady members of the amenity society took their special visitor across into the arcade in front of Havrda's pub, and they gazed in a moved way at the cement pavement where Frederick the Great had once rested. And then, for the most precious thing in our whole little town, Mrs Krásenská led the famous composer off under her arm to the centre of the square, where on a bench two old-age pensioners were sitting resting their chins on their walking sticks, and the chairlady described and accurately delineated the Renaissance water fountain, which stood there up to the year 1840, when it was demolished, but you would be mistaken if you thought it was the two sitting old-age pensioners that the amenity society members were gazing at, by no means! The chairlady pointed and ran her finger around in front of the pensioners' faces, but what she saw was what she was describing, those wonderful ornaments, sandstone festoons and the two small half-relief angels on that fountain, which used to be and therefore still are one of the adornments of our town. Ah, Mrs Krásenská, who loves everything which is no more, I was filled with affection for her when I discovered her romantic past, thirty years ago she fell in love with a tenor singer at the National Theatre, a Mr Šic, she used to stand after the performance outside the back entrance, and when the tenor singer came out and chucked away a cigarette end, she pierced that butt with a pin and laid it as a precious relic in a little silver casket, and as she was a sempstress, all day she had to sew, in order to make enough for one orchid, and all week she had to sew, in order to buy a seat in the box, where she always threw down that orchid from a day's sewing at Mr Šic's feet, and when she had thrown him that beautiful flower for the twentieth time, she waited for the tenor singer and accosted him and told him that she loved him. And Mr Šic told her that he didn't love her, for the one reason that he didn't like her great long nose. And Mrs Krásenská sewed away for a whole year and for the money she earned she went to Brno and had that great long nose cut off and muscle from her own arm sewn on to the nose cartilage in its stead, out of which in time the doctors shaped a marvellously beautiful small Grecian nose. And so it came about, that Mrs Krásenská stood once more at the rear entrance to the National Theatre, and as she was so beautiful, she could strike up a conversation with the distinguished tenor Mr Šic, but the tenor invited her for a nocturnal stroll and confessed to her that for almost a whole year he had been seeking out a beautiful girl with a tremulous long nose, a nose with which he had fallen in love and without which he was unable to live. And Mrs

Krásenská confessed to him that she was the girl with the great long nose, but that she'd had it cut off for the sake of the famous tenor and replaced by the nose which he saw before him now. And Mr Šic raised his hands in the air and cried out, "What have you done with that beautiful nose! How could you!" And ran away from her . . . And Mrs Krásenská took a look at me alongside the Renaissance water fountain and raised her hands in the air and cried out, "What have you done with that beautiful hair! How could you!" And she pointed me out to our town's precious visitor, and now I knew that my hair belonged to its historical monuments. And I pushed down on the pedals and three lady members of the amenity society borrowed bicycles from outside the Hotel Na Knížecí and pelted off after me, stamping so jealously on the pedals that they easily caught me up, and they pointed fingers at me, "She's cut off her hair!", and several cyclists who recognised me rode off indignantly after me, passed me as well and spat in front of me, and so I rode on through this moving gauntlet of cyclists, all lashing out at me with their angry looks, but that only gave me added strength, I folded my arms and rode on without holding on to the handlebars, and entered the brewery alone. The cyclists stood with their bikes between their legs in front of the office with its sign, Where They Brew Good Beer, There You Find Good Cheer, and now Francin ran out and behind him the three lady members of the amenity society, pointing at me with both hands.

"What have you done with your hair?" said Francin, holding his number three lettering pen in his quivering fingers.

"Here it is," said I, leaning my bicycle on the wall, lifting the carrier and handing him those two heavy plaits. Francin stuck his pen behind his ear and weighed those dead tresses and laid them out on the bench. Then he unfastened the pump from the bicycle frame.

"I'm pumped up enough," I said, expertly feeling the front and back tyres.

But Francin unscrewed the rubber tube inside the pump.

"The pump's all right too," I said, uncomprehending.

All of a sudden Francin leapt at me, he bent me over his knee, tucked up my skirt and whipped me over the backside, and I wondered with a shock, was my underwear clean and had I washed? And was I sufficiently covered? And Francin whipped me and the cyclists nodded in contentment and the three lady members of the amenity society watched me as if they had ordered this rendering of satisfaction.

And Francin stood me back on the ground, I pulled down my skirt, and Francin was handsome there, his nostrils flared and quivered just like when he quelled the run-away horses.

"Right, lass," he said, "we start a new life."

And he bent down and picked up his number three lettering pen from the ground, then he screwed the rubber hose back in the pump and stuck the pump in the clips on my bicycle frame.

I took the pump and showed it to the cyclists and said:

"I bought this cycle pump at Runkas's on Boleslav Road."

The Little Town
Where Time
Stood Still

ONE

On my way home from school I liked to rush down to the landing place by the river where the sand-barges lay, boats with planks running down from them where the sand-diggers carted away loads in barrows from great heaps of wet sand, they loaded the sand up so lightly with their shovels, it looked as if they were scooping up featherweight sprinkly cloud, which glittered in the sun with every tiny nugget of sand flickering in rainbow colours. Once I asked to be allowed to load one barrowful of that sand which came tumbling down from the hills, and if it wasn't dredged up, the Elbe would surely roll it down to Hamburg and out to sea, but when I tried to lift the shovel I thought at first I'd caught it on a plate at the bottom of the boat, I had to plunge the wet shovel into that hill of sand again, and then, slowly and laboriously, as if hauling it out of tar or gum arabic, I lifted the shovel above the plank, but I couldn't get it in the barrow, it fell out of my hands and the sand-diggers laughed at me and I saw them bare from the waist up, each sand-digger had his hands tattooed with anchors and ladies, and one digger had me spellbound, on his chest he had a little boat tattooed, a sailing ship, I looked and the tears welled up in my eyes, not tears of weeping, but with knowledge and certainty, that I too had to have a little boat like that tattooed on my chest, I wouldn't be able to live without it, a boat like that must warm the very cockles of your soul, it's an emblem of the soul, and I'm going to have one too. I said, "That little ship you have, will it wash off?" But the sand-digger lightly took his ten-kilo shovelfuls and hurled them into the barrow, now he slung away the last wet shovelful, leapt on to the plank, chucked away the gleaming empty shovel so tidily it sank into a pile of sand, as he bent over I almost touched the little boat on his chest, he ran merrily along the plank, bare feet sticking out of the blue overalls, he had to shove it up the slope where the plank ended, and there he turned the barrow and ran back with it empty, sat himself down on the plank beside me, lit a cigarette and drew the smoke into his lungs with such force that the cigarette almost burst into flame, its red tip glowed so bright, and I watched as the boat swelled on the sand-digger's chest, as he took in a long deep breath, the boat practically moved, as it got bigger, as if coming into harbour under full sail ... and then the sand-digger breathed out and the boat got smaller and smaller, as if sailing off, and all the time it was swelling like that on the waves and dipping, as the digger breathed out, as his heart thumped, and the effort pumped the blood around the body. "So you're right set on having one, eh?" the sand-digger said, surprised, seeing my tears. "Yes," I said, "I'd like to have one just like that too. How much does a boat like that cost?" And he twisted his arm round and showed me a mermaid and then he said, "They did me that for a bottle of rum in Hamburg." And I said, "Do they only do those boats in Hamburg?" I was stunned, but the sand-digger laughed and shook his head and breathed out consoling words with the smoke, telling me that this anchor here and this pierced heart there were the work of Lojza, who hangs out at the Bridge Inn, he did it for just one shot of rum. "And would he do me one too?" The sand-digger jumped to his feet, tugged at his falling overalls, raised his cap and said, "Aye he would . . ." and he gave his sweaty cap a wringing and I got a shock, the man was sunburnt as an Indian or an ad for suntan oil, but since he always wore his cap to keep the sun off, his whole brow was white, marked off by a rim from the rest of his body, white as the halos worn by the martyrs in the Decanal Church of Our Lord, a brow with rays of light streaming out on all sides, like a convex mirror with the sun reflecting off it into every point of the compass. And I ran, clutching in my palms the straps of my school satchel, with its sea-going ship woven into the blue oilcloth, I ran, my sailor's cap with its black band and its double bow at the back shook, and the collar of my sailor's jacket poked out of the straps of my satchel full of schoolbooks and jotters, and the jacket flapped behind, and the black bow bobbed, zigzagging this way and that to the rhythm of my running like a ship's bell, a ship's buoy, and I knew, that soon I too would have a little indelible vessel tattooed on my chest, a sailing ship to which I would always be true, for never could I be anything but a sailor now.

Dean Spurný, the priest I used to help serve holy mass, was the first person I wanted to tell of my desire, this desire to have a boat tattooed on my chest, because he too, to show his obedience to God, had had his hair trimmed in a special little tonsure on the crown of his head. Moreover Dean Spurný was a marvellous man in every way, still speaking in his original Silesian dialect, in fact to judge by our Dean the Lord God Himself spoke with him in this same dialect, for our Dean used to converse with God, at least so he thundered from the pulpit, He would say on a Sunday, "O Spurný, Spurný, ye hairless old bull, I commit these innocent sheep intae yer care and ye bring 'em tae heaven like pigs sozzled wi' liquor . . ." Now a Dean, I said to myself, that speaks like that, surely he'll give me a blessing when I kneel before him in my acolyte's cassock, spread the palms of my hands out before me like so, bow down my head and tell him about such an innocent little sailing boat. But the Dean was in a rush, he chucked off his mackintosh, sipped at his vermouth, the Dean drank nothing else but vermouth, when we went to administer the rites, I had to take a little basket and in it along with the holy oil and the paten a bottle of vermouth . . . And so the Dean went off, and I removed my cassock, and there I was kneeling before the tabernacle and gazing at the golden figure of Christ poking out of the blooms of peony and guelder rose, and there I saw all of a sudden, that He too had a heart tattooed on His chest, a heart encompassed by a garden thicket of prickly briar roses . . . And so, as I emptied the collection boxes with their offerings for the upkeep of the church, first I took out a five-crown bit, and then I put it right back again, but finally I borrowed it once and for all, totally and unshakably convinced that I was going to return it, as I said myself to the golden Christ in the sacristy, Upon my soul and word of honour, I'm only borrowing it . . . and I showed it to Jesus, so He should know that that was all I was taking. Many's the time I've spoken like that to Christ, because with God the Father I didn't dare, especially since the day one small farmer called Mr Farda, of whom it was said he quarrelled with God for nights on end and shouted up at Him and God back down at him, when this farmer one day, bringing in his last cartload of hay, and me just out of school and a thunderstorm brewing, when Mr Farda was urging the horses on with his whip, to get the dry hay in out of the rain and into the loft, as they got under the bridge it started to drizzle, and then the downpour truly began, a cloudburst, Mr Farda took great handfuls of wet hay and slung them up in the air, skyward, and hollered up to God on high, " 'Ere, 'ave yourself a bellyful!" And God answered him in the lightning, which split the poplar on the towpath in twain, and the horses trembled and so did I, and the onlooking regulars under the eaves of the Bridge Inn public house fell down on their knees, though not before God mind you, it was the scent of the lightning overpowered them, as that bolt of lightning zipped down the road and along the railing of the bridge like a fiery tomcat. Today the Bridge Inn was in a jovial mood. "Who's the little sailor then?" exclaimed Mr Lojza, as I stood before him in my sailor's jacket and white mariner's cap with its double black band, crossed at the back with two bows. "Show me," said Mr Lojza taking my cap and reading its lettering: HAMBURG-BREMEN, he placed it on his head, and I was happy, I laughed and rejoiced at how nice Mr Lojza was being. And Mr Lojza wore the cap and made such terrible faces, that I laughed then absolutely roared with laughter along with the whole table of regulars, and I made up my mind that when I grew up I'd consider it an honour indeed to sit together with such merry gents of the water. For Mr Lojza had teeth missing and so he made his lower lip overlap his upper until the lower lip covered it right up to the tip of his nose, and he walked about and his sand-workers' table clapped their applause, and someone ordered everyone beer and a round of brandy on top of that. I said to myself, if it's merry like this down by the river at the Bridge Inn, how merry it must be and how merry it will be too once I'm a sailor in Hamburg itself. And I said, "Mr Lojza, here's the price of a nice big rum!" And Mr Lojza plonked the cap back playfully over my eyebrows, so that when I stared up with my eyes I was squinting at the brim of the cap itself, and I handed Mr Lojza my five-crown coin. "Where did you get all this lolly?" Mr Lojza said suspiciously. "I borrowed it from the Lord God," I said and nodded, and the cap slipped over my eyes, I blew it back with a puff and the whole table laughed at me and Mr Lojza said, "You been speaking to Him then?" And all of them went quiet. "No," says I, "but His son lent it me, the Lord Jesus Christ himself," I said and added, "but Mr Alois, He lent it me just so as you could do me a tattoo of a beautiful boat, just like the one you did for that man over there . . ." "Korecký," said the sand-digger. "Yes," said I, "for Mr Korecký." "Well now, if the good Lord

Jesus Christ Himself has commanded it, let's get down to business. When shall we do it?" Says I, "Right now, straightaway!" "Blow me," said Mr Lojza, "but I haven't got me tattooing needle and ink." "Then go and fetch it," I said, and Mr Alois dashed out just as he was in his shirt-sleeves, and the customers asked me about the Dean, if he still had the same two cookery maids or was it three now? And to keep the whole table in the mood for the tattooing I answered, "Whad'yamean three? Two, but they're very young you know . . ." and the watermen's table at the Bridge Inn roared with delight and repeated it after me like saying over the litany: "Both of 'em nice and young." "Yes," I said, "and when the Dean's in a good mood, one of the cookery maids sits herself on a chair, while he bends down, takes the leg of the chair and herrup! he lifts the beautiful cookery maid up to the ceiling and her skirt flaps round her cheeks . . ." "O-ho!" cried everyone at the Bridge Inn, "And her skirt flaps round her cheeks . . ." "Yes, and one after the other he lifts them up, and us assistants at mass too, because he's terribly strong, you know, he was one of seven children, and their dad was such a giant, that when they wanted to crack nuts, the Dean's dad put his hand on the table, and the children lifted one of his fingers and under it they put a nut and they let the finger go and crack! It was shattered to smithereens!" And the customers cried, "O-ho! Crack! And it was shattered to smithereens!" "Yes, sirs, but they were so poor, that when they all sat down to table, and their mum put the dish of potatoes down in front of those seven lanky kids, all of them with their spoons at the ready, and their mum put her hand on top of the table with her fingers stretched out and rapped her nails on the table, then all the spoons hurled themselves at the food, and whoever wasn't quick enough, that was the end of his dinner, but the Dean was the weakest of the family, and so they said, 'What's to be done with him? As a miller he'd never manage four sacks, he'd only lift two of those eighty-kilogram flour sacks, so we'll have to make him a priest . . .' " And Mr Lojza came in, bringing a small case, like the one Mr Slavíček the barber carries or Mr Salvet the vet and pig gelder, and Mr Lojza closed the door of the taproom and motioned me over and I pulled the mariner's jacket over my head, and when I came out into the light again, Mr Lojza said, "Now then sonny me lad, I don't know what kind of boat it is you want, a sailing ship? A barque? Or a yawl? A three-master, or a brig, or do you fancy maybe a steamboat?" Says I, "Can you do any ship of any type?" Mr Lojza nodded and suddenly he was no longer drunk, he was solemn and ceremonious, and he motioned, and the sand-worker sitting on the corner of the bench, not the one I'd spoken to but the one who rode in a hat and carted the sand, he took off his hat now in order to strip off his shirt, the top half of his skull shone out so effulgently into the room and light shone from off his brow as from a milky half-spotlight. And when he came over into the light streaking down from above over his tanned torso, there wasn't a single spot without its mermaids and anchors and hearts and initials and ships, and scenes of two naked people, and naked women, I flushed red and the sand-worker turned and on his back I chose myself a really simple one, a kind of fishing boat like little children draw, saying, "Do me one of those!" And Mr Lojza took me and the customers removed their beer-mats and held their beer-glasses and Mr Lojza laid me out on spread sheets of newspaper. "Will it hurt?" I inquired and lay down on my back, quite dazzled by the light bulb. "It won't, it'll only prick you a little teeny bit . . . a little boat you say? . . ." "A little boat," I whispered almost blissfully falling into a doze, and then I felt the light pricking of the needle, then some dabbing with a cool rag or cotton wool, and the customers were around me and I lay in the centre like a ball running on the roulette wheel amidst the players . . . and I heard voices saying, "Aye, that'll make a lovely keel . . . and now for a pair of sails . . . a proper ship's got to have right proper flanks . . . a deep furrow there and a nice rudder on her too . . ." And Mr Lojza whispered to me, "Don't breathe in and out too much, just gently through the nose . . ." And so I lay there on my back, the regular pricking of the tattooing needle roused me, but in the intervals between I blissfully drowsed . . . Then Mr Lojza whispered to me that the little boat was ready, I got up, sat on the table, all round me I saw the rows of beer-glasses, and the customers drank to me, I drooped my chin down on to my chest to get a view of my little boat, but all the glasses clinked against my head, and they all laughed together, and Mr Lojza pulled my little shirt and jacket back over my head, and I remembered that I lived at the other end of town, it was a long way to get home, so I gave a bow to Mr Lojza, and he offered me his hand, and the assembled company at table drank to me and sang, "Hoorah, hoorah, hoorah . . ." and I stood there and saluted with my sailor's cap and ran out into the evening air.

As I ran across the bridge, I found myself in a blizzard, thousands of mayflies were cascading out of the lamps on to the paving of the bridge and walkway, it was slithery, like walking on ice, but the lights of the lanterns on the standards shone away pitilessly and clouds of mayflies soared up from the river into their glow, white-winged moths rose too from the blackness of the river, and winged beetles, only for the light which summoned them up from the river to strike them down to the pavements and roadway, where car tyres skidded and people fell about as if on Hogmanay black ice. I laid my hand on my chest, breathed, and felt my little boat rising up too as if on a swelling sea, and at that moment I wanted nothing else but to show that little boat to the Dean and the two cookery maids, I turned away from the lights, ploutering up to my knees in dying moths, as I picked them up in my palm I felt them moving still, but growing cold and chill just like the dusky river, from whose depths more and more moths ascended in whirling eddies, I slid and fell, crying out, "I've broken my boat!" But the boat wasn't made of paper, or wire, or slivers of wood, it was anchored firmly within, in and upon me, only a knife could gouge it out, like gouging it out of my heart, in which I had vowed my devotion to boats and vessels and ships. Quietly I opened the fastened gate, I had to stick my whole arm through to reach the bolt on the other side, quietly I crept into the vicarage yard, light poured from the two windows of the vicarage, and the mayflies reached as far as here from the river, fluttering in the windows and making a wallpaper covering, a patterning, as if ornamented with white shifting teardrops, creeping vine clambered up the lattices and trellising right up to the roof, sprouting shoots into the light at the window, like tendrils of hair into the faces of the young cookery maids, who freed themselves from the strands and tucked them constantly behind their ears, or under their caps. I said to myself, What's the Dean likely to be doing, mustn't surprise him at a wrong moment, maybe he's lifting the cookery maids on the chair again and carrying them up and down and their hair is drawing lines across the beams of the ceiling and they are shrieking and kicking their little feet in their black shoes, and so I climbed up the laths and lattices like climbing a ladder, brushed aside the latest fresh growth of vine, till I could get a look into the vicarage, and there I saw a scene that put me in ecstasies, I'd never have guessed the Dean had such mighty strength in him, at first I thought the Dean was raising the cookery maids to a higher station, as he tied a towel round them at the waist, knelt before them and diligently bound those little cookery lasses of his at the waist one to another, tied them together with this long towel, and the little cookery lasses like me had no idea of what was going to happen to them, since the chair was a bit far off . . . and first the Dean lifted up those girls, both at once, so that neither even touched the ground and like some little figurines hung there and knocked their foreheads together, joggled themselves apart and laughed, revealing the face of the Dean, who sniffed at their tummies as he lifted them, even sniffed a little bit lower . . . Then he put them back on their feet and laughed one of his joyful laughs that made the hair of just Christians stand on end, as Mr Farda the farmer characterised that laughter of his, then the Dean knelt down before his girls, for a moment I was so stunned that he was sniffing at their backsides, like dogs do or cats, but suddenly the miracle occurred, the Dean straightened up and stood, grasping in his teeth those two cookery maids of his, grasping them in his teeth with that strong towel, and now he carried those girls about the parlour, arms outstretched like a true artiste, and the little cookery maids waggled their little shoes and arms in the air and laughed, they were like Siamese twins joined together by the spinal cord of that towel, and the teeth of the Dean held fast and he moved them with his strength, and I thought to myself, what a surprise it would have been for them in Cana of Galilee, much greater than that miracle with the wine, if Jesus Christ had carried the bride and Mary Magdalene about the wedding hall like that, what a reinforcement it would have been truly for the Catholic faith and for all religious human beings in general, for such loving strength draws towards it not only the hearts of women, but also the hearts of all men, and specially the hearts and souls of sand-workers and sailors. And when the Dean had had his romp, he put them back down on their feet and he keeled over, the whole of him sagged and stretched out in an armchair, and one of his eyes was bloodshot, as though someone had fetched him a blow with his fist, and his hair hung damp over his forehead and his shirt was open, and one little cookery maid stood at each side, one kneeling offered roast pork while the other poured vermouth in his cup . . . And I tapped and the cookery maids ran to the door, and I entered in my little sailor suit and round mariner's cap with its inscription HAMBURG-BREMEN, and the Dean took fright that we were going off somewhere to administer the last rites . . . "What is it?" he said. And he sipped, drank, with his lips fixed to his cup, and I said I'd only come to show him what I had devoted myself to this day. I doffed my sailor's cap, gave it to one of the maids to hold, then I pulled off my jacket and rolled my shirt up to the chin, knelt down and asked him, "Reverend sir, give me a blessing!" And the cookery maids exclaimed aloud, and the Dean pulled himself up and gazed at my chest, then there was a silence, all you could hear were those mayflies and moths pattering on the windows, and after a while he stroked me on the hair and said, "Who did you this?" And I said, "Mr Alois at the Bridge Inn." "And what was this tattoo to be of?" The Dean stroked me on the hair once more. "A little boat with an anchor." The Dean led me off in front of a mirror, took me lightly by the armpits and lifted me up, and there I saw tattooed on my chest a mermaid, its tummy with a full flowing beard, with breasts and eyes as big as round cakes, and that stark naked mermaid was smiling out at me, just like one laughing young Žofín bar girl, before she curled her tongue up into a brazen little tube and stuck it out at me like the devil on St Nicholas' Eve.

TWO

When Dad saw that mermaid tattooed once and for ever on my chest, he gazed at it fixedly for a while, he gazed for a long time, blinking neither one eye nor the other, as if searching back in his mind for the connections which might explain that indelible sign of the sea . . . And I breathed out, my heart thumped so hard that the mermaid closed and narrowed her eyes to the rhythm of my heartbeat, and I shaded that naked woman with my palm, just like Adam and Eve shading their bellies on the altar picture . . . But Dad only gave a wave of his hand, because Uncle's bellowing resounded in the yard, the radiant and penetrating voice of Uncle Pepin, who, as Mum said, had come to us eight years ago for a fortnight's visit and stayed with us right to this very day. And dear Uncle was yelling out, "What's all this impudence? Ninny, nincompoop, what would I be grazing nanny goats for? I'll scrunch you under my heel like a cockchafer! I'll flatten ye to the pavement like hammering in a nail!" And every time Uncle Pepin took him aback with his yelling, every time Dad just stood there by the stove, poured white coffee into a mug, cut himself a slice of bread and drank his coffee, and Uncle carried on yelling away and his shouts cut like a knife through the buttery yellow light of our kitchen: "What crap is it now? Kiddies? I dinna want the goats, so it's no kids either, what's this impudence? Do ye know what it'd cost me if I was to go out grazing goats and Colonel Zawada came and spotted me? He'd holler out, 'Cholera cripple you, you stupid shithead son of a bitch!' And he'd give me a right lashing with his old *Reitpeitsche*, cos no sodger of Austria's gaun to be seen dead towing any old goats on the end of a rope! Another word and I'll squash ye like they'll never scrape ye up off the floor!" And I buttoned up my shirt and sat by the stove on my teeny stool and put my homework out on the little kid's table, dipped my pen in the ink, but I couldn't write, my jotter just stayed open and my pen on the paper, just in case Mum came in, then I'd make out that I was writing . . . And the kitchen sizzled with trials and tribulations, Dad's head constantly emitted a halo of torment, I felt invisible hands pushing me away from Dad, but also just as much from Mum, because I wanted my mum to be just like the other boys' mums, motherly, maternal, but my mum was still like a young lady, always thinking of going out to the theatre and having fun, ever elusive, always slipping from my grasp, so that I could never cuddle up to her properly, it would have taken too much mastery of myself, with Mum I suffered constantly from blushings and flushings, as if I were hidden behind bushes of flowering jasmine at dusk with Lida Kopřivová, sniffing at Liddie's curly locks of hair. And likewise when Mum was pacifying Dad, standing with him under the jingly trinkets of the big lamp, there I sat on the teeny stool, my pen poised on a line in the open page of my jotter, I pretended I was about to write, if someone looked at me, indeed I'd begin to write, but if someone looked to see what I was writing, then that somebody would see it was all a lot of nonsense, because my heart was thumping away with indignation because Mummy was hugging Daddy . . . And I felt as if Mummy was throwing away hundred-crown banknotes on the square, as if she had taken the whole Christmas tree with the presents beneath it and given them away to other children . . . So here I was sitting again on my little seat, and what caused me horror now was that Dad was horrified just like me, that instead of a little boat with an anchor Mr Lojza had gone and tattooed me a naked mermaid lady, and suddenly I felt that the lady with the fishy tail on my chest was as nothing compared to the grief that was streaming through Dad and shooting out of him on all sides of the whole of his body, like the halo in the shape of those golden swords issuing from around the whole body of St Ignatius on the side altar of our church. I felt that Dad was suffering so much that he wished he could just get up and go, not anywhere in particular, but just go and keep on going, on and on right away from this brewery, where he was manager and where he even had his own motor-car, where he had a nice flat to live in and my lovely mother, where I was born too – the brewery, where his brother now worked, Uncle Pepin, whom I loved more than Dad exactly because of all his yelling and dancing, Uncle Pepin, who, when he finished work at the brewery, popped on his sailor's cap, his admiral's sailor's white cap with its black peak and golden cords and embroidered gold anchor in front on a blue backcloth, a cap ornamented with golden buttons, Uncle's cap which no one was allowed even to finger, only the lovely ladies in the bars where he went every day . . . And I wanted so much to go out on to the doorstep and see who Uncle Pepin was shouting with out there, but I thought it better to stay seated, to make Dad just a little happy, with my ink-dipped pen on my jotter, so as to start writing the moment Dad looked at me . . . Oh, how I suffered with this home, how I felt myself shot out through the window, even when it was closed, out through the walls, just out and out and out, where the branches of the old lindens and chestnuts waved at me through the window, where the rain tapped at me, where the wind called out to me, as it rattled in from the brewery through the open window! And just as Dad always wanted Mum to be a decent woman, and just as I always wanted Mum to be a decent ordinary mummy, so Dad and Mum together wanted me to be a proper good little boy, and they often told me off for not washing myself enough, but I cried and swore that the dirt made me feel happy and warm, they showed me how to fold my school primers and counting-books, but I always tore out every page that we'd just finished reading, so that for St Nicholas I always got a new school book and for Christmas a couple more, one to keep for January, Dad wanted to teach me and instil in me a love of gardening, he planted cabbage and lettuce and taught me to dig it and explained how it was necessary to pluck out the weeds, just as it was necessary to root out my bad qualities, so that only the good ones were left, but when Dad went away, I had my little spade and hoe all ready, and I looked about me, the coloured birds embroidered the air and the sun warmed me and the wind flew out of the pine woods right behind the brewery and from the river you heard the shrieking and calling of children and all around me there were so many wonderful things to see and things going on, but there I stood in the middle of the garden, in the middle of the beds overgrown with weeds, I stood, and whenever a window opened somewhere, or I heard footsteps coming along the concrete path, quickly I seized the waiting hoe and dug, but when I could tell it wasn't Daddy or Mummy, I stood again with the hoe ready waiting, but with my head and all its desires distracted far away to any other place but this . . . And so I resolved, no I didn't resolve, but I got an idea, and I pulled up and weeded out all the lettuces and all the cabbage, I chucked it all in a heap, I waited till the greenery wilted and couldn't be planted back again, and then with my hoe over my shoulder I went and reported to Dad that I had finished weeding the whole lot, and Dad was surprised, but I was like Mum in this, I managed to put on such a truthful face, that Dad stroked me and said I could go where I liked, as long as I didn't have any homework still to do. Then in the evening Dad stood over me, holding his belt, but then he fastened the belt on again, went and brought the cycle pump in from the passage and unscrewed the rubber hose, but after thinking about it for a bit he concluded that even this was too little, that giving me a beating, whipping me with the hose, whacking me with the belt, all that was too little, it was fixed inside me just like it was with Mummy, whom he gazed at reproachfully and at such length, even when Mummy laughed and begged him, "Francin, take it like one of those American funny films." But Dad went out into the garden again and had another look at those heaps of wilted greenery like shot green birds, he looked at the nicely hoed fresh weeds ebulliently rising and lining up in the evening dew, and then he lifted up a few seedlings and dropped them listlessly to the ground again and returned to the house, and there I sat on the teeny stool, dipping my nib in the inkpot and writing in my jotter in deep concentration, just as long as Father stared at me and finished contemplating on my behalf what was to become of me, just like tonight, in the early evening, when I had to show him that mermaid of mine, which I would never have shown him off my own bat, but I was forced to show him, because Dad had got to hear about it in town. He looked at me, I felt his eyes on me and so I went on writing all the more beautifully and decoratively, I did my very best all the more, as if that lettering and writing were my only salvation, and I knew Dad was contemplating how he could kill me with one blow of his fist, but I was relieved to find myself turning the page and continuing my piece of homework: All About My Home ... And I went on writing and then I was horrified by the thought that Dad would strangle me, and if Dad had thought of it he would have, only Dad found even this too little, he stood, took a knife, and I wrote on and suddenly I felt it was my last piece of writing, my last piece of homework, that only the writing was saving me from death, that when I stopped writing I would die, that only by writing was I averting death, and even when

Dad cut my head off I wouldn't know a thing about it, since I would just keep writing on and on, longer and longer, and when I stopped writing then I wouldn't know any more that I ever existed, and Dad took a whetstone out of the cupboard, that he kept for sharpening his razor, and carefully he whetted the blade of the knife, whetted it and tried with the cushion of his finger to see if the blade was sharp enough, and I wrote and wrote, and suddenly I thought of a time when I was lying in my cot, and it was such a long long time ago, and Daddy came back with Mummy from a ball, and Dad was wearing a dinner jacket and he was handsome, but Mummy had a pink dress and a fan, and Dad kept shouting something at Mummy, and Mummy was calling out in quite a scared sort of way, "No, no, Francin, it's not true, it isn't!" And Dad was calling, "Shut up, you, a decent woman oughtn't to dance in such positions! You're a married woman, you're a mother!" And I lay there stunned with shock and listened to Dad opening the little drawer in the oval mirror, and Mummy clung close to Daddy, and I was paralysed with terror, it was Daddy's shouting coming as if from a long way off, Dad had a kind of inward way of shouting, quietly, it was a shouting whisper, and Mummy begged on her knees, "Don't shoot me, Francin, will you? For God's sake!" And Dad called out, "What must be must be . . . swear there was nothing between you . . ." and Mummy knelt in that rosy pink robe and the ostrich feather fan was spread on the ground like a rainbow in the sky after rain, and Mummy clasped her hands and Dad with his brandished revolver, in his dinner jacket, was handsome, and

Mummy collapsed in tears and stretched out just as she was on the carpet, her pleated dancing dress spread on the carpet just like that ostrich feather fan, and I was stiff with horror and pretended I was asleep. Later when it had been dark for ages, and I was staring with wide-open eyes into the darkness and listening to Mummy's soft weeping as it faded away, and Daddy was still talking and talking excitedly and whispering, insinuating himself into Mummy's soul in her submissiveness, and then at dawn everything went quiet and I wanted to go and have a pee, but that nocturnal scene after the ball had so benumbed me that I quietly tipped my weenie between the beds and wee-ed and wee-ed, until I'd wee-ed myself out, like crying my eyes out, urinating instead of crying in the crevice between the beds . . . And Dad got up with the whetted knife, laid it on the kid's table, and quietly, like Dean Spurný unlocking the holy tabernacle and drawing apart its golden curtain, he drew apart my shirt and stared at that mermaid, I saw his fingers jumping as my heart palpitated, I dipped the nib of my pen into the ink and went on writing, it flowed out of me, that writing, I didn't even know what I was writing, but I felt that by that writing I was saving my life, but suddenly it struck me that Dad wanted to gouge that lady right out of my skin, my seafaring lady, I felt like Uncle Pepin when they wanted to take away his white sailor's cap, the one Hans Albers wore when he played the ship's captain . . . and I stopped writing, I stared into Dad's eyes like I had never stared into his eyes before, in that look of mine there lurked everything I had ever done to him, everything, I felt like Mummy, when she had lain there and surrendered herself up totally and spread out her dress and her fan on the bedroom carpet . . . "No, Daddy, please, no," I raised my fingers for the first time in my life to utter an oath, like Christ I stood there with my torn-apart shirt and the drawing on my heart and with two raised fingers I swore, "No, Daddy, I swear, I wanted to have a nice little boat with an anchor . . . and Mr Lojza did me this!" And I tapped the sea maiden with a finger of my left hand and with my right I swore and showed Dad the ink-stained cushions of my fingers. And Dad stood, sliced himself some bread, then stroked me, spattering my hair with crumbs of soft crumby bread and said, "I'm in the same boat, we're both in it together." And then angrily, not even angrily, but as if accepting there was nothing else to be done, just like when I was helping the Dean with the last rites, but Mr Kurka died while I was still anointing his feet, and the Dean himself went to open the windows into the summer evening air, to make an easy passage for the soul, so that Mr Kurka's soul would fly up into the sky like vapour to heaven, so this time Dad opened the windows and the fresh air wafted in and past the window came Uncle Pepin's white sailor's cap, hovering, as if floating in the air, as if just slipping along the window breast. And Uncle was hollering, not to anyone in particular, just generally hollering for his own delight into the evening air through which he was walking off into town to see his lovely young ladies, "I've chalked up yet another glorious victory, I've won, I'm the same all over as Colonel Zawada riding into Przemyśl after its capture on Corpus Christi day!" And Dad slid between the dresser and the cupboard, clasped his hands and whispered, "It's just not true, when he was in the army under fire he just lay there in the trench till it all blew over!" But Uncle Pepin ranted on, "Nobody takes any liberties with me, I draws my revolver on him, and bang, bang! there's just pools of blood everywhere!" And Dad carried on clasping his hands, tormented by the truth: "But he was always so timid, I had to go and meet him coming out of work, even at the age of twenty-five, he was so timid, he always had to sit in the corner!" And Uncle Pepin went on roaring away: "Out of my way! In the days of Austria I was the greatest good-looker, lovely women used to shoot themselves for me! My picture hung on the street in the Zeile in Brno and beauties used to nudge around the cabinet saying to one another, 'Which one do you like best?' And each one pointed to this one here. And they tapped through the glass at my picture, and I used to stand at the back and it was like they were rubbing goose fat over my chest, and I sailed along like I was in the money!" Uncle's voice was radiant and Dad carried on clasping his hands between the wall and the closet and raising his eyes to the ceiling and whispering, "But it's just absolutely not true, from his youngest days he was always covered in pustules and at twenty-two his neck was all over boils, with bloody bandages peeling off him!" But Uncle's voice rose jubilantly in the office like the smoke of the sacrifice of Abel to heaven: "I was the one Captain Hovorka liked talking tae best, I was adjutant tae Hetman Tonser, I was the one carried his sword!" And Dad's voice so quiet and shy crept and crawled over the ground like the smoke of the sacrifice of Cain: "But it's absolutely not true, he had absolutely no rank at all in the army, that photograph of his, he borrowed the stuff and had himself taken as a sergeant!" Dad's lamentation rose to heaven, but I knew that the Lord God didn't actually love the truth so much, in fact he loved madmen, crazy exalted enthusiasts, people like my Uncle Pepin, the Lord God loved to hear untruth reiterated in faith, he adored the exalted lie more than the dry unadorned truth, which Dad tried to use to blacken Uncle in my eyes, and in the eyes of my mother, who could get up to such silly tricks with my uncle that the tears would trickle down my cheeks and I would go into fits of laughter, and sometimes there came a kind of crunching in my eyes and my head, when I got the feeling that any moment a miracle would happen in our kitchen and St Hilary from the square would appear unto us, our patron saint of healthy laughter. And our night-watchman Mr Vaňátko came in through the brewery gates, he was invisible, but you could hear the voice of his faithful doggie Trik, you could hear the chink of the flasks and torches and buckles and buttons that glinted and chinked on the uniform of Mr Vaňátko, who always came on duty *feldmässig*, battle-ready, with his Mexican rifle over his shoulder and full of joyful anticipation that surely one day someone would try to rob the safe or at least steal the straps from the little booth between the lifts to the ice chamber. "Halt!" roared Mr Vaňátko, pulling off the Mexican rifle, which was never loaded, because its last owner had lost its breech. *"Wer da?* Who goes there?" cried Mr Vaňátko, anticipating that one day there would be somebody out there in the darkness. But

Uncle Pepin shouted out, "*Ruht, Jozip Pepin meldet sich gehorchsamst!*" And Mr Vaňátko stepped out, stumbled, as Trik gave a painful yelp, Mr Vaňátko had tripped over his doggie, and right away, having had and continuing to have rushes of blood to the head ever since his wartime malaria, he took the doggie and whacked it against the cement, and the dog gave a pitiful whine and whimper, but Mr Vaňátko stepped out in military fashion and went over to Uncle Pepin, now they stood together in the light of the window into our kitchen, they saluted one another, brimful of zeal, and the night-watchman bawled out, "Mister Josef, take over the gate watch, station number one pronto, I have to make my report to the manager." And Uncle saluted on the rim of his sailor's cap, took over the Mexican rifle, and Mr Vaňátko got up on the bench, now he stood there, a terrible sight, with his whiskers and his chauffeur's cap bisected with the tricolour, with his Entente belt upon which his six torches glinted, through the clear window he saluted Dad and reported, "Night-watchman Vaňátko at your service!" And Dad flapped his two hands like elephant's ears, warding off this terrible and, for me, so wonderfully precious scene of the night-watchman, who jumped down, as if he had been limbering up, cast off uniformed ceremony, lifted Trikkie up from the cement and kissed him and stroked him and showed him to us, his own little doggie weeping with pain, of whom Mr Vaňátko declared, "That's my faithful and true animal, I wouldn't give him up for anything," and he gave him a smacker right on the muzzle, and then he took off his back his bandoleer made out of an old rolled-up coat and spread it out on the bench beneath the office. Uncle Pepin called out zealously, "That's the stuff, Austrian army discipline's the finest discipline of the finest army in the whole world." And so, out of the darkness, and even through our closed windows, with the curtains drawn across by Dad, alternate happy commands rang out: *"Zum Gebet! Marsch eins! Hergestellt! Paradenmarsch!"* And over the cement pavement slapped the boots in the parade-ground steps of their parade march, the impact of the Mexican rifle butt crashed against the ground, and the about-turn of the loudly stamping heels. It was no wonder then that towards midnight the yell and roar of Mr Vaňátko made itself heard exclaiming, "Help, robbers!" And the night-watchman blew his bugle and Dad took his revolver, and I too rushed out with Dad into the night, and outside in front of the office Dad with trembling hand aimed his revolver calling out: "Surrender, you rascal!" And Mr Vaňátko shouted, "I've got him, I'm about to put the handcuffs on him . . .!" And he slammed his stick into the gooseberry bushes, twigs flew about as though sliced by the mower, and the chief mechanic ran up and shone his battery torch on it and in the light of the lamp you saw only a smashed, cloven gooseberry bush, and I called out, though like Mr Vaňátko I couldn't see a thing either, "He's running over that way, Mr Vaňátko, run and cut him off!" And Mr Vaňátko ran off into the darkness and came back totally drenched with sweat and happy: "Rapscallion, scoundrel, he won't catch me! I'm on the alert, I'm on guard, I keep good watch over my allotted premises . . ." And Father went off with his revolver and the mechanic with his battery torch, both in their underwear, shivering in the chill of the night. Dad said to the master mechanic, before they went off, "A fixed aim reduces the sense of fatigue." And tired they went off to lie down, and back in bed I suddenly saw myself in my sailor suit, I was looking down from the great church tower, shading my eyes, watching and calling out to ships at sea, I saw myself seeing them, even though no such ships and sea could ever have been seen, just as nobody had actually tried that night to assault the brewery safe or Mr Vaňátko the night-watchman, who in two whole years of duty in the brewery had apprehended with his Mexican rifle and handed over to the police all in all only six young courting couples kissing by the brewery wall, and three nocturnal passers-by, two of them having a pee in the dark at the corner of the brewery and one having a crap, and Mr Vaňátko handed them over just as they were to the police, with a view to investigation by the authorities on suspicion of intent to rob the brewery safe.

THREE

Just like me and Dad, just like Dad and Mum too, and just like the whole of our family, Uncle Pepin disliked staying at home. We got too much on each other's nerves, we caused each other too much suffering and humiliation, we loved each other too much, and so we preferred to shoot ourselves off with this love of ours in different directions, and we preferred being amongst people and things in other surroundings. Dad, as long as we still had the Orion, that dreadful motorbike, which had to go in for general repairs after every ride, used to spend every Saturday stripping it down, but never alone, he even tried to initiate me into this operation, but I only ever did this routine with Dad once, because it wasn't a matter, as Dad had promised, of working on it just for an hour, it took all afternoon and then all evening, and Dad kept enthusiastically explaining to me what all the drawbacks of this Orion model were, and how he was only delving into its innards in order like a skilful surgeon to remove its various faults. But I moaned over the Orion like a dog tied to its kennel, every minute seemed to me like an hour, and every further hour like the whole of eternity, and whenever I later saw so much as a single motorcycle part I felt just like Mr Douša, who couldn't bear seeing innards, the minute he saw any he had to be sick, and me too, at nine o'clock at night, on a Saturday, when Dad with enormous care had reassembled the distributor, carefully wiped it with a cambric cloth, describing to me with enormous affection all those little plates and screws and the function of the distributor, which corresponded to the functions of the glands, the pancreas, and the adrenal gland in the human body, and my brow was tense, with stave lines of creases, and Dad's brow was glowing with pleasure, and when I saw that we still had the engine open before us, its black cylinders and crank shaft protruding, and the carburettor dismantled over the workbench, my stomach churned, and before Dad had time to spring back with the distributor, I sicked up into it, with a generous helping of salami, "tourist" salami, and Dad yelled at me and threatened me with a hammer, saying it was the same for him as if when serving mass I had taken the body of the Lord, the sacred host, and spat it out on the floor, I was horrified by that distributor, piled high like a mess tin at a children's camp, a mess tin with its dollop of food, it always makes me . . . Suddenly it flashed through my head, and it did, I collapsed in horror the very next instant, only to smile at it a moment later, knowing all the more certainly, with every passing while, that what I did was the right thing to have done . . . And Dad ran about with the hammer, and being unable to kill me, he took out his watch, put it on the little anvil and with one blow shattered it to smithereens, the only way to save himself from smashing my head in instead of the watch ... And he opened the gates and drove me with his finger out of my Garden of Eden, and I was out in the starry night, the raised-up stars like tremulous silver daggers menaced me with their blades in the chill heavens, and I went off into the brewery orchard, and I lay down under an ancient avenue of nut trees and nuzzled the earth and osculated the grass with my face and clasped it with my lips and spread-eagled myself out, even writhed, even sweetly whined at intervals. We had a cat at home, his name was Matsik, and one day Mummy decided the cat wasn't going out that night, it was staying at home, it was muddy out and it would jump on the bed in the morning. But at midnight Matsik first of all knocked over a cup with his paw, and when that didn't do the trick, with all his might and main he overturned a heavy old Austrian alarm clock from the dresser, and Dad got cross, he took Matsik and plonked him down on the front doorstep, and since he'd just been woken out of his sleep, first he kicked a chair with his bare toe, and only with a second kick did he managed to kick Matsik out into the night, and so the cat ended up as if for a punishment exactly where it had wanted and longed to be all night long.

And so in the course of two years' tinkering with the motorbike Dad had got through all the brewery workers, then all the neighbours round about the brewery and finally practically half of all our little town. To anyone not in the know Dad, on a Saturday afternoon, would pop the question, "What are we doing then this afternoon?" And anyone unawares would reply honestly that they were doing nothing special, and Dad would take that person tenderly by the elbow and say eagerly with a lovely smile full of mysteriousness, "Well, I tell you what, come up to the brewery and hold a lock-nut for me, just for an hour." And anyone not in the know came along, little suspecting that Dad was dismantling the big end, and the neighbour would hand him the spanners and Dad would delve further and further down towards the rattle in the engine, which was a congenital feature of that engine, a kind of permanent ailment it was, like someone with a hobble on one foot or a stammer. And Dad could describe his descent into the entrails of the Orion with such fervency, that while the wife of Dad's helper raved furiously at home, while his girlfriend swore that if she didn't kill her sweetheart she'd give him the shove or get off with his friend, young men and old neighbours alike took the bike apart with Dad, and time marched on towards midnight, and dawn began to rise, and Dad decided that now was the time to put the engine together again, what joy awaits us when at ten o'clock on a Sunday morning, when the bells begin to ring, let's have a bet on it, Dad proffers his hand, I kick the starter just the once to try it out and the engine peals into life like the Sunday bells. And so it was that everyone repaired the bike with Dad just the once, everyone in the vicinity of the brewery and from our little town took his turn, and anyone who had already repaired the bike with Dad once, holding the lock-nut for him just for an hour on a Saturday, on hearing Dad's sneaky question, anyone who had experienced that horror, shouted back at Dad from afar, "No no! I have to go to the hospital in the afternoon. I have to go to the cemetery. I have to be at home, my sister-in-law's visiting. I have to do the accounts. I promised to help my brother build his family house . . ." And in spite of this Dad would respond sweetly, "But you must admit that engine on the Orion's a terrific thing . . ." And the neighbours agreed, a terrific thing it was, but they didn't have time today and probably never would, because if they'd spent all night in the pub till morning, or if they had gone off on that occasion with other women, it would have amounted to the same thing, because no spouse, no sweetheart ever believed them, even when Dad delivered written confirmation of what had occurred on that Saturday afternoon, evening and Sunday morning, Mr Jarmilka even insisted on having it confirmed by the notary public, but his wife still didn't believe him, so there was nothing for it but to get divorced. So when Dad walked off to town these days, people when they spotted him coming quickly left off their work, sweeping the pavement, or digging their garden, as if in some fairy tale or other, as soon as they saw Dad they were sucked into the doors of their homes and cellars and woodsheds, emerging cautiously only after Dad had passed, looking about them for a long time cautiously and only then continuing in their work, but their peace of mind and mood of contentment were gone. It had got to the point where, even when Dad walked on to the town square, people, seeing him, rushed hurriedly into side streets, ran into the Church of Our Lord and sat down there, and feigning contemplation hid their faces in their hands as they sat in the pews, so that Dad wouldn't recognise them. Some of the locals, having seen Dad on Saturday morning and now even the whole of Friday casting his eyes over people's faces, thought it better to run into someone else's house, where they hung about for a good long while by the door to the cellar or out in the yard, later slinking along the passage and, like sleuths trailing criminals, with the merest twitch of their profile peeping into the street to see if the way was all clear. Burýtek the butcher, who had gone to hold Dad's lock-nut just for a quarter of an hour as Dad had promised, when he'd returned on the Sunday he'd found a whole laundry copper or cauldron of tripe soup totally spoilt, because tripe soup when it's cooling has to be stirred just like soup from a slaughtered pig, until it's absolutely cool, so Mr Burýtek the butcher, when he saw Dad in Palacký Road, he got such a fright that he ran into Mr Šisler the hatter's, and because like all butchers he was terribly shy and timid, Mr Šisler was able to sell him a beautiful hat, and Mr Burýtek spent ages trying it on, and then he bought it, and it worked out cheaper than if he had gone to fix lock-nuts with Dad for half an hour. Uncle Pepin only helped Dad the once. Towards midnight, when Uncle Pepin could see all the beauties in the public houses with ladies' service glancing in vain at their watches and then at the door, expecting to see his white cap enter, there Uncle Pepin was, thumping away with an oak mallet, while Dad held the shaft, on to which, not with a hammer, no sir, with a wooden mallet they were hammering a new bearing, because Dad thought it was this bearing and nothing else that was causing the engine to overheat while going up hills and emit a sort of dry clink, as if you were dropping one little coffee spoon after another into a tin bucket. And so there was Dad gripping the shaft against his midriff and gripping that bearing too, and Uncle thumping away with the mallet, and suddenly Dad could see that one more blow would shift the bearing a bit too far, further than was needed, it was just right as it was, so Dad yelled out, "Hey whoa, enough!" And he should have said no more than just enough, for that "hey whoa" induced Uncle Pepin to fetch it another blow with the mallet, but Dad had pulled away the shaft with the absolutely perfectly positioned bearing, so Uncle with the mallet gave Dad a great clout in the belly, and Dad just keeled over, and just as Uncle Pepin was getting him back on his feet he managed to stand up by himself, and again Dad took the hammer and struck out at Uncle, Dad never hit him, but he had to do something equal to hitting him, so he took Uncle's watch, his Patent Rozkop, that bulbous watch from Austrian times, put it on the anvil, and then, as he struck that watch with the hammer, and its hands and springs and screws splattered over the wall, Dad ceased to feel the pain of that mallet blow to the midriff, and he drove Uncle out, he just had enough time to wash and stick on his mariner's cap, and jump over the fence, because the night-watchman Mr Vaňátko was always so fast asleep after midnight that nobody dared to wake him, he slept with his doggie Trik at his feet, and neither little owls, nor screech owls, nor great barn owls with their tu-whit tu-whooing woke him, our night-watchman wasn't even woken up by those women who tied him up once with a washing line, Mr Vaňátko always slept soundly on.

FOUR

Once a quarter Uncle Pepin got in a revolutionary mood, refused to let Dad put his savings in his savings book, refused to let Dad give him ten crowns a day for cigarettes, refused to let Mum deal with his washing, refused even to eat his hot meal with us once a day ... It always began the same way, Uncle Pepin shouted and shoved away his plate of sirloin and hollered, "What kindae Chinese grub is this? It gives me gripes in the tum!" When Mum gave him some goose and asked Uncle, "How did you find that?" Uncle Pepin waved his hand dismissively and said, "The sauerkraut was okay." And when we were pig-slaughtering and Uncle had eaten his fill of whatever he fancied, on purpose he picked up some pig's tail at the very end, squinted at it and tugged, gripped that tail in his teeth and stretched it out, and when the tail whipped out of his grasp, and Uncle's head banged against the wall where he was sitting, he roared, "I'm no eating yon dish cloths! The stupid wumman reckons I'm some old daft daftie, and all in all the folks say, ye're just diddling me!" And Dad was horrified and wrote out for Uncle on the table just how much he was giving him for his organisation and cigarettes, and how much for laundry, and five crowns for a regular hot evening meal, but Uncle Pepin looked at us coldly, hatefully, all at once he hated the lot of us, for Uncle we were the nobs, we were the lords and masters, all climbing our way up the ladder, while he, being working class, had to walk the flat horizontal ladder, never having had any other option in life but what he had already, and that was till the day he died or took his pension. Every year there was consternation in our house over Uncle's revolution, every year, but this consternation was on a downward trend, for repetition creates its own order and system, and recapitulation weakens the initial shock of astonishment. And so Dad paid out to Uncle Pepin all the money he owed him, handed over his savings books, because Uncle wasn't going to let himself be done out of his hard-earned cash, earned by the sweat of these hands, Uncle solemnly disowned his brother, that lackey of the capitalists, waved away Mum's hand offered in reconciliation, and there he stood in the doorway, as if we'd all done him an injury, as if it was our fault he was staying in the lodgings, while we had three rooms and a kitchen, as if we could help the fact that he was a workman in the brewery where Francin was manager, my dad, my mother's husband. Even once he was outside Uncle still spat with relish, and departed noisily shouting out that "Every nob oughtae be nabbed by the scruff o' the neck and slung tae the floor . . ." That evening we all felt small, and were intimate together, Dad clung to Mum beneath the chandelier, and she caressed him, and Dad caressed

Mum with one hand and me with the other, I squeezed up close to my parents too, for we couldn't sort out in our minds quite what had happened. So, first of all Uncle Pepin spent all his ready cash, the second week he spent the money Dad had saved up for him, and the third week, over the Saturday and Sunday night, he spent his last reserves, borrowing more on tick on the following Monday, Tuesday, Wednesday and Thursday. And yet, as Uncle Pepin went off to town, the gates of houses opened and neighbours came out, and women, and windows opened for Uncle Pepin as he walked beneath them in his sailor's cap, and everyone who could asked after the lovely ladies he was off to pay a visit, and the women asked if Uncle would come and do some play-acting, or when Uncle would make an assignation with them in the dark gloomy woods, or when Uncle would take them on a trip to Vienna and Budapest, the girls asked him when Uncle would take them dancing on the island, and they put his name down for the Ladies' Privilege, which wouldn't be held till the winter, the men asked confidentially about the calves of the women at the public houses with ladies' service, and what the young girls' busts were like, and the feather beds up in their rooms, at the first house Uncle asked for flowers, and he presented them to the women in the houses that followed after, where he requested some more flowers from the garden to give to the beauties in all those windows that opened up for him, all the way to the streets and on to the town square. There came Uncle Pepin marching along, bowing, saluting and distributing kisses, and his replies to all queries reduced every group or individual to fits of laughter, in the aftermath of which Uncle Pepin departed like a moving train trailing wreaths of smoke . . . His very first halt was the Žofín public house with ladies' service, the minute Uncle came in the bored young misses sprang up and strove for the bouquet of flowers which Uncle presented to one of them, they threatened to scratch each other's eyes out, then Uncle sat down and ordered a coffee, and Miss Marta said, "And here's a bumper of champagne, you old goat, from me, to make you pee." And Bobinka put on a record, and the gramophone played "O Graveyard, Graveyard", and Bobinka sat on Uncle's knee, and the customers applauded and called out, everywhere Uncle appeared, he caused delight and mirth, sometimes he took me with him, I sat in the corner and drank lemonade, or the young ladies took me beside them, and I enjoyed being with them, for I loved the scent of cheap perfume and I liked to see the shaded eyebrows and artificially painted cheeks, when they leaned over me I blushed, and for that they stroked my hair and squeezed me to their breasts, and I shut my eyes, while Uncle Pepin went on delightedly: "But ah leddies, my lovely lassies, such a bouquet of flowers as the one I've just brought ye, only the late Emperor Franz would bring the like of that to Baroness Schrat, or the Archduke Karl to the girlies in the officers' casino, in the Red Eagle!" Bobinka sighed sweetly: "Ah, maestro, when you fixes your eyes at me I just swoons like your Baroness Schrat, now if we was to marry, that'd be it! Else I'd just take a knife and snick-snick! That'd be the end! Or I'd take a gun and shoot you!" Marta chucked Bobinka off Uncle's lap, leaned over her and yelled, "I'll scratch your eyes out, he's mine, only I've got rights to old Pippin here, if you don't marry me I'll have to go and poison meself!" Uncle Pepin was delighted by all this talk of shooting and poisoning, he sipped at his coffee, then suddenly he bawled out, "Go on, poison yourself, lassie, with slivovitz!", the place burst into laughter and Miss Marta said, "But what does Mr Batista's handbook have to say on the subject, eh, maestro?" Uncle Pepin pulled out his pince-nez, popped it on, offered a hand to Miss Marta and said decorously, "You can tell right off you're a real lady, gracious as a Mozart, Herr Professor Batista in his handbook on sexual hygiene tells us, that a proper male's got to have a properly developed sexual organ, and this organ must consist of a penis and it's got to have properly developed testicles . . ." Bobinka appended naively, "But what if there's only one testicle?" And she rolled her eyes at Uncle. "That, according to Mr Batista's handbook, is known as a monorchid, and it constitutes a freak." And the ladies began to argue over him, tugging Uncle by his sleeves and arms: "We're not going to buy a pig in a poke, are we! We'll just have to make a quick inspection! It'll all have to be fully and properly inspected, won't it, so you'll just have to come along with us up to our room, right away, sir!" But Uncle Pepin leapt up, broke free from the young ladies and commanded, "Put me on a real belter! And let's have a dance!" And the proprie-tress opened the door, and into the bar came an old St Bernard, called Dedek, and Uncle Pepin took Bobinka off to dance, but the other ladies shoved forward to join in too, so Uncle decided: "Right then, we'll do the

dance for three ladies, known as the trilogy!" And
Uncle took the ladies by the hands, and the ladies did
whatever Uncle did, they ran into opposite corners and
jabbed their fingers into the air at each other to the
rhythm of the music, and then jabbed them again at the
smoky ceiling, and the customers made a circle, and the
proprietress stood by holding a knife, arms folded, and
laughing, she knew it would begin any moment, the
wine and liqueurs would be flowing like water, Uncle
Pepin, master of entertainment, really knew how to get
them going, then Uncle lifted a leg, crooked it, shot it up
and kicked in the air, and the ladies copied him and
died with gales of laughter, squealing to see what they
saw, then Uncle ran up and made lunges, he looked like
a leaping Jack of Diamonds, and the ladies followed
after him, the dust swirled, and Uncle leapt up really
high in the air, parted his legs and landed on the
ground and did the splits. Bobinka cried out, "Hey,
Mister, don't go and split your crotch!" Marta
exclaimed, "Hey, Pepin, don't strain your bag of nuts!"
Only Dáša flushed and said, "What are you saying,
girls? Bag of nuts . . . a hernia, don't rupture yourself,
lad!" And she jumped up and started into the cancan,
and the girls kicked up their knees and legs and danced
the cancan with her, and Uncle bowed as he knelt,
showered with the cloud of dust stirred up by their
skirts. Then Dedek the St Bernard got up, reared and
laid his paws on Uncle's shoulders and knocked him
over, but Uncle rose, offered the next young lady his
arm, took her and tossed her up and lunged forward
with her, flung her arms up and taking the whole of her
by the waist, flung her backwards till her hair swept the

floor to the rhythm of the music, then Dedek the St Bernard knocked Uncle over again, and Uncle lay on his back while the St Bernard growled and dribbled in his face, and the whole place roared with laughter, strangers ordered bottles of wine, and the proprietress brought whole trays of spirit, and Uncle sat up, and the girls lifted him to his feet and seated him on a chair and painted his cheeks with rouge. "You've gone quite pale, Maestro," said Bobinka, while Marta brought her frock, her black frock with a red artificial rose, and so it happened that the young ladies dressed up Uncle in their room in this black frock, and when the music started, Uncle ran into the bar, with the artificial rose in his teeth, he danced Carmen doing her tango argentino, and when he did a somersault and a leap in the air his privates popped out of his underpants, but Uncle took no notice, he grimaced and pouted with his mouth like Carmen . . . And again Dedek the St Bernard got up and knocked Uncle over with his paw, then he lay on top of him growling in his face, till the proprietress, weeping with mirth, took Dedek away, and Uncle bowed, still broadcasting that sweet smile in all directions, with his painted lips and cheeks, not noticing that upstairs the ladies had painted him with enamel paint, which would last a whole week, as he went about doing his barrels and descaling the boiler and descending into the sewer, these days because of the rumpus he made they liked to send him down to the boiler or into the brewery basement . . .

The next morning, during the break, the workmen came to see Dad and told him they hadn't been able to find Uncle Pepin anywhere all morning, not till just

now, when they'd finally found him asleep underneath
his bunk, maybe he was dying. And Dad was
forearmed, he took his bottle of ammonium and went
with the workmen, who were all eyeing Dad
reproachfully, blaming him for starving his own
brother, who was there in a faint, lying in rags under
the bunk in his lodgings. When they got there, two
workmen lifted the bunk and shifted it away. And there
amidst the old musty wellingtons and torn working
boots, amidst the grimy rags and dust, lay Uncle Pepin,
his cheeks resplendent with dried red enamel paint, his
eyes shaded with black, and he seemed not to be
breathing. Dad knelt and listened to his chest, then he
spotted Uncle Pepin breathing through his nose . . . He
stuck the open bottle of ammonium in front of the nose,
but Uncle stopped breathing that way and breathed
with his mouth, so Dad pressed his palm over his
mouth, and Uncle was forced to breathe in some of the
ammonium. He jumped up, spluttering . . . And Dad
drew himself up, pulled the foot-wraps and rags out of
the bed and asked Uncle, "What's this?" And Uncle, his
eyes full of tears, grabbed those rags and exclaimed,
"That's a fine old shirt, given me by that rare beauty
Miss Glancová . . ." And Dad pulled out all the rags and
tatters and dirty underclothes, which, while Uncle was
still coming over to us for his dinner, always used to be
quite clean . . . "And what's this?" And every time,
Uncle shouted out that these were precious gifts from
various ladies and belles of his, and he took those rags
back out of the stove bucket and put them away under
the dirty bolster . . . And Dad looked on, and saw that
the workmen were staring at him, Uncle wasn't the

cause of all this, but the manager of the brewery, the chap's brother, who stayed in a three-room apartment, while his brother Pepin had to sleep here like an animal. Before he went out of the maltings Dad opened his bottle of sal ammoniac, breathed it in a few times, but no tears would come to his eyes, even this ammonium stuff was too weak to deal with all the things his brother had done to him since arriving eight years ago on that fortnight's visit. At dusk I saw Uncle Pepin in his sailor's cap, with his enamel cheeks, walking round to the back, to the outhouses, I saw his cap descend to the ground, I walked round the cart of draff and past the shed quietly up to the door into the small yard. Uncle Pepin was picking out the boiled potatoes covered in groats, wiping the groats off on his trousers, and eating, till he had eaten all the potatoes meant for the hens, then he finished off the discarded peel as well.

FIVE

When the real cold of winter set in, ice formed on the river and it was time for the ice carting to start. Dad used to have some trouble assigning people to work the ice hoists, and deal with the thousands of loads of ice which the smallholders brought on their waggons, because they were well recompensed for every load of ice. Dad couldn't help getting angry, because nobody wanted to do these jobs on the ice, only Pepin was delighted and looked forward to the ice carting, the other workers considered it forced labour and prevaricated, even threatening Dad that one day the time would come when the tables would be turned, the workers would be snug in the office and the masters would work on the ice, all of them, even the new brewery chairman Mr Dimáček. Dad's response to such comments was silence, perhaps he too wished that one day the time would come when the tables would be turned, Dad wasn't fond of the bosses either, especially not the new chairman, who kept pigs and had three pedigree boars, and was so engrossed in his pig rearing, so involved in it life and soul, that he himself resembled a pig, a boar's head, in the way his lower lip drooped and his teeth protruded from his gums, and he'd inaugurated a new regime in the office, such that the clerks now sat with their pens constantly poised, so as whenever the chairman came in they could be busy writing away and counting. And if nobody was actually writing away and counting, the chairman turned pale and straightaway chided Dad as manager and the head accountant for having people idle and said they had one person too many on the staff. And whereas Doctor Gruntorád, as chairman before, would come riding in with his buggy, this chairman would appear out of the blue, grasping the door handle, barging into the offices and fermenting cellars and maltings and workshops and cooperages, pretending not to see a thing, but seeing absolutely everything, so that not only the workmen, but Dad too suffered under him, Mum had to take Dad every evening and hug him under the jingling trinkets of the lamp, and when Dad poured out his troubles to Mum, suddenly his face took on a terrifying expression, and he would point at himself, grasp himself by the chin, but it wasn't his own chin, it was the chin of the new chairman, and then, with a single ripping motion, he wrenched off that chin and chucked it far away from him with disgust, and that wrenching off of the chin made Dad feel good, it was the only way he had of calming himself down.

So Dad assigned the workmen their jobs on the ice carting, and the foreman noted them all down in his book, he who had once been an ordinary brewery worker and had worked his way up to be the gaffer to all of them, who jotted down all the shifts in his notebook and made notes on every worker's clocking-on and behaviour during working hours, the foreman, who was always so pleased with himself that he couldn't believe the luck that had given him this power over the workers, who surely looked forward every morning to looking at himself in the mirror, and dressing and putting on his jacket with the four button-down pockets, sticking into it his notebook with all the names and details of all the brewery workers, and he was always so pleased with himself, that half an hour before the hooter was due to sound he was already standing there in front of the brewery office, legs astride in his topboots and breeches, and staring with prickly eyes to see who was coming to work not only on time, but with what sort of a will, whether still yawning, and so on. The foreman disliked Uncle Pepin for shouting and bawling so much at work, he always used to put him in the boilerhouse, where he had to descale the boiler, chip off the saltpetre, nobody fancied doing this job, because it was dusty in the boiler and the light bulbs glared and two workmen with their hammers like woodpeckers tapped away square centimetre by centimetre, bit by bit, and the saltpetre fragmented into dust, and the workmen had to have scarves and kerchiefs wrapped about their mouths. But Uncle Pepin used to sing and shout away on the job, anyone working alongside Uncle would have despaired otherwise, their only defence against the dust and stifling air of the boiler was being able to have a good laugh at the expense of raucous Uncle, every other moment somebody would come into the boiler-room and shout into the pink dust of the boiler, "Old Řepa says you used to graze goats up at the battle front." And with great hammerblows Uncle would bang away at the boiler, roaring back in rhythm, "What would yer goats be doin' up at the front line, ye great oaf? Goats is sensitive, minute they hears gunfire, off they scarpers. Ach! When there's a battle on, who's goin' tae be messin' about at the front wi' goats an' all?" And the mechanics opened up the ventilation flaps and Uncle's voice thundered through the brewery as though amplified through a megaphone, and the foreman sped up, opened his notebook, and yelled into the boiler, "What do you think you're up to, shouting on the job? Don't you imagine, just because your brother's the manager here, that you can get up to whatever you like, I'm taking a note of this!" And he jotted something down in his book and looked about him triumphantly, smiling brimful of self-contentment and jubilation, that only he, out of all the workers, had worked his way up to be the gaffer, with all this power over the others. And when the business of descaling the boiler was over, the foreman lined up the cleaning of the sewers, and Uncle Pepin vanished again, lowered himself into the ground like entering the turret of a submarine, and one worker stood outside with a sheet-metal wheelbarrow, while Uncle down in the bowels and guts of the brewery shovelled up slime and loaded shovelful after shovelful into a pail, and his companion pulled up the pail, tipped the contents into the barrow, and when he got bored, or when some other worker was coming along past the open sewer, he'd kneel down and yell into the sewer, "Jeannine's been round and she says she's just sewing up her wedding pyjamas." And he'd go on his way, and

Uncle's bellow would come gushing out of the sewer like a huge geyser, coruscating and battering against the walls and rearing up to the heavens: "What, that auld cow? She walks like there's an udder between her legs, and I'm supposed to be weddin' that? Me, that's the darlin' o' the finest beauties aroun'?" And Uncle's voice was so penetrating, it flew across the brewery orchard and over to us, in the open window of Dad's office, and the foreman dashed out, opening his notebook as he ran, and he knelt down over the stink of the sewer and yelled down at him, "Mister Josef, don't you go imagining your brother's got some clout over this . . . I'm the one in charge of the workers here! Get down to work at once and stop dawdling!"

When the time came for the ice carting, the foreman gave Uncle Pepin the hardest job of all. Even before light, in the dark, the ice-workers chopped planks out of the ice sheet, long strips of ice, which a workman near the bank cut up into sections, and into each section he chopped an eyehole, and the workmen on the bank hooked them up by the eyeholes, and then two by two they hauled these sections with the hooks on to the bank, and there again two by two the workmen picked those chunks up in their purple gloves and threw them into the carts, and since the ice was weighed, every smallholder wanted to have a heavy waggon, so they made supports of ice at the side-flaps and flanks, and the loads of glistening ice glowed with iridescent colours in the red and icy dawn sunlight, and the horses strained forward, the hide on their rear haunches creased, the horses always seemed to buckle and squat back, their sharp hooves bit into the icy bank, shattered ice showered from under their hooves and the iron axles stuck, and every waggon grated and groaned beneath the weight, every wheel like a badly greased pump, and then one after another the waggons, like hours on a clock face, rolled along to the brewery weighbridge and onward, sometimes three or four waggons stood together in front of the ice-crushers, the breakers of the ice, which the hoist buckets carried away up the shaft, right up to the roof of the six-storey-high ice store, where the buckets turned out the contents of their pockets, and returned back along the conveyor belt. In the afternoons gramophone music could be heard from the river, punch steamed away on a table, and children and students skated, only I felt this dread, only I saw that toil on the frozen river, only I saw the exhausted horses, their tails and manes grizzled with twining icy hoarfrost, only I saw and felt that weight of lifted ice, I saw the whole crust of the river taken and hurled into waggons, the chain-gang of dreadful labour, where there was nowhere to get yourself warm, or if there was, only in a bothy stuck on to the wall of the boatyard, where several pairs of frost-numbed hands were constantly stretched out over the scorching stove ... And Uncle's singing and shouting rang out from the crusher, his radiant, irate shouting, only the angry fuming of Uncle Pepin could warm the workers, and especially give them zest for work ... Uncle stood by the crusher with a hook, and as soon as a waggon drew up, he shouted, "Sodgers of Austria ever victorious, victors everywhere and for aye!" And he took his hoe, and with two blows he knocked out the catch on the side flap, which opened, and the ice tumbled out into the crusher, and the keen crusher hungrily masticated that translucent, milkily opalescent ice, Uncle Pepin took his hook and squatted down, and, like Don Quixote tackling his windmills in mortal combat, Uncle Pepin took up the bayonet pose, roared, and the workman on the other side adopted the same comic posture, and Uncle commanded, *"Einfacher Stoss! Vorwärts!"* And he attacked the icy log-jam, shouting and yelling and dealing out blows, and the ice hurtled into the crusher, often enough they had to clasp Uncle with two arms, ask him not to fag himself out, toil away so much, they clasped him affectionately, giants a head taller than Uncle . . . but Uncle Pepin wouldn't give in, shouting, "Sodgers of Austria have tae be ever and ever victorious!" And he grappled with the giant of a carter, the other carters rallied round and laughed till the tears ran, for Uncle Pepin knocked down the laughing carter, put him flat on his back and yelled at the others, "Just like Frištenský's win over the black . . . I give 'em all the same medicine!" And he brandished his purple fist over the ruddy nose of this bear of a man, but the noise of the empty crusher alerted Uncle and the workmen to the need to extract the last remnants from the load, and when the bucket hoist had raised and turned out the last remnants of ice into the ice store, Uncle sort of breathed out, happily and emptily, relaxed by the regular pulses, and rested too . . . But sometimes the ice was so hard packed the crusher couldn't get a purchase on it, the ice-workers had to thrash it with clubs, and with hooks and crowbars, but you had to watch that the machine didn't get hold of these tools, which were not only crushed, their blades were ripped off and thrown up and stabbed into the roof of the box surrounding. And Uncle undaunted fought for every haft and handle, while the rest fell to the ground and fled to get behind beams, Uncle laughed and yelled and roared with exultation: "Sodgers of Austria win on every front, even in peacetime!" And one ancillary worker shouted out, "If only Jeannine could see you now!" And Uncle roared, "See? What're ye blabbering on about, ye dimwit! The hussy canna even dance the tango." And not far off the foreman stood unobtrusively, he stepped up with a smile and said, "Jeannine certainly can dance the tango, and how! Right folks?" He said, and turned to the ice-carters and workmen, and then to Uncle, but old Uncle Pepin went all quiet and said softly, "Never ye mind that," and he started sweeping up round the crusher, he knelt down and picked up pieces of shattered ice in his purple glove, and after a minute the workers seemed to take their cue, they knelt down beside Uncle and threw fragments of ice into the hoist, and the carters went off to their waggons, and the foreman was left standing alone, his smile frozen on his face, and he just had to make out he hadn't grasped what had just happened, he pulled out his notebook, jotted down something, and the workmen were even quieter and stared into the empty revolving crusher, as they'd stare into a fire, until the foreman grasped the point, and went off through the brewery gate, for it was a long time since he'd been considered one of the workers. Ah, how differently my grandfather used to vent his anger! During the holidays I would be sitting there with Grandpa in the garden, and my grandfather would be trying to light a cigar, and because there was a wind about, Grandad began to get cross and bawl at the wind for blowing out his matches one after another, until it went and blew out his very last one. And Grandpa called, "Nanny, fetch me some matches, will you?" But no one fetched him any, and Grandpa called out, "Nan, matches!" And he listened, but nobody brought him any matches, so Grandpa shouted, "Nana, for Christ heaven's sake, what are you doing with those matches?" And by now he was gripping the cane chair and sweeping his eyes behind him to scan the open windows, with their billowing curtains. And I said, "Grandad, I'll go and get them!" And Grandad bellowed, "For blithering Christ's sake and all my sainted aunts, why don't you get me my matches, you stupid cows?" So I dashed into the building, where Granny and the maid were scuttling from window to window, constantly unable to disentangle themselves from the curtains, while Grandad yelled in the open window, "You bitches, where's me matches then?" And I took the matches from Grandma and made as if to run, but in the passage I stopped and listened to Grandpa bellowing and smashing now not only the chair but the table too, and roaring, "You bitches, I'll slay the lot of you, where's them matches?" And by this time Gran and Annie had hauled the old closet out of the shed and handed Grandad an axe, and in a couple of minutes Grandpa had smashed the whole cupboard to smithereens, at which point he sank into an armchair, and I handed him the matches, but Grandpa didn't want them any more, he just rested for a moment, as if after a tremendous struggle, like in the films, when the husband finds out his wife has been unfaithful, and whilst Granny and the maid between them gathered up the splinters of the closet into a chaff basket, and took off the solid pieces to the wood-shed, Grandpa glared furiously in front of him and rolled his eyes, but after a quarter of an hour he seemed to come to, he gave a laugh, shook himself, and was his happy and frisky self once more. This was what my mum used to tell me about how her dad used to like letting off steam, he being my grandfather, and I used to think, that was how it once was, but he still liked venting his anger like that even now, in his retirement. Before we set off home after the holidays, he took me on the roundabouts, bought me whatever I wanted, till I felt sick, but, as we were on the way back, Gran was drying her curtains on long laths, curtains showing the four seasons of the year, and on these big curtains the twelve months were embroidered, curtains crocheted by Granny herself, and when I woke up in the morning I used to look in the window and read those curtains like a children's folding picture-book, and Grandpa, as we were returning, got his trousers caught on a nail on those long laths, upon which those curtains were stretched out drying in the sun, and he tore his trousers a little . . . and all at once the laughter was wiped from his face, like the pictures in the "Children's Corner" of *Our Little Reader*, where, if you turn the smiling face upside down, you find on the same head a face that is weeping, likewise it seemed as if Grandpa had torn a hole, not in his trousers, but in his very soul, and the laughter in which we had been living all afternoon had all run out, and Grandpa tugged his finger in that hole and made it even bigger, maybe just so as he could shout and get angry. "Who fixed up those nails there, eh? Who?" he bellowed into the open windows of the house. "Where's Annie? Nan, where are you all?" he bawled, but the curtains just billowed, and the building was quiet. "You lot there, what stupid bitch did that? Will you own up or won't you?" Says I, "Grandad, I'm just going to go and look for Grandma . . ." And I went into the building and looked through the curtains into the garden, there stood Grandpa looking into the windows, staring full of anger, as if the windows were eyes, and he roared and stamped: "Come on, you lot! So you won't answer? Those are my new trousers, you stupid bitches! Come and get them sewn up, right away!" But nobody moved inside the house, all was silent, the curtains drifted, and Grandad glinted amongst the flowers beside the green lawn, where the gleaming, starch-impregnated, drying curtains hung, with their four seasons of the year and twelve months, all the figures on them were figures of little angels, even for winter the wee angels had wings just as Granny had sewed them in her youth for her trousseau. "So, you lot there," Grandad bellowed, and he jumped into the curtains and stamped on them, and the curtains were torn from their frames of laths and nails, and Grandpa wound the little angels up on to his shoes and twisted his feet in them, and, being half a century old, the curtains tore, as Grandpa parted his legs, I heard the ripping sound, but that still wasn't enough to satisfy Grandpa, once he'd torn his way out of the curtains, he issued a final challenge, shouting out, "Annie, fetch the thread, Nanny, get the thread, you pair of silly bitches, and fix up this ruddy snag!'' But the house was quiet, and Grandad stuck his finger and then his whole hand into the tear, and ripped the trousers right down, and then, bending over, he took the untouched leg and in trying to rip it he tripped and fell, the fabric was so strong, but once on the ground he undressed down to his long-johns and tore up the discarded trousers, then jumped and stamped on them, but that was still too little, he ran into the laundry with them, and stuck them under the boiler, but even that was too little, he took the matches from the boiler, struck one and set the trousers alight ... At that moment the maid came in with Grandma, they wrung their hands and put down the baskets of washing from the mangle, and first Grandma and the maid hauled out the cupboard, then Grandpa knocked the cupboard over and bashed it in with his hands and the weight of his body, then with his axe he chopped up the doors, while Granny pulled the burning trousers out from under the boiler and ran outside with them, removing his wallet and identity card from the pockets, for Grandpa, when something got on his wick, was dreadfully sensitive and touchy, but when he sobered up again, he was the nicest and kindest grandfather in the world, and he himself used to blame it all on race, declaring, ''The Slavs are a terribly sensitive race.''

So there I stood with my skates over my shoulder, the light bulbs were already lit, far away you could hear the trains, and the ice men said a thaw was in the offing, in the next two days, and I watched the carts of ice arriving out of the darkness, those great lumps of ice loaded slantwise on the waggons made mountains like the Tatras, the drivers and ice-men were swathed in blankets, with drenched sacking wrapped about with ropes on their feet, some waved their arms in the air and their purple gloves were like the heavy wings of birds which can never fly up in the air, so they waved their arms about at least, to get warm, and Uncle Pepin shouted and sang, "A nightingale on the lake shore warbles," attacking with his hook the bergs of ice billowing from the side flaps of the waggons, like St George with his lance doing battle with the ice dragon, gramophone music sounded from the river, and in the glow of the coloured light bulbs student couples danced, and beneath the light bulbs you could see the vapour rise from the pan out of which ladles of steaming hot water were taken to make hot punch, and I watched Uncle, who wasn't coming to see us any more, because he was having one of his rebellions again, and I was unhappy, I used to spread slices of bread and take them to him on the pretext that I was spreading them for myself, I couldn't bear to see how Uncle Pepin, after spending his entire pay packet in two days with his little pretties, by Wednesday was taking stale bread from the hens and eating their potatoes. When I remembered I was supposed to go home, I didn't feel like going, I preferred to go on standing there in the corner in semi-darkness, just like the picture of the Orphan Child we had in our school reader, there I stood and didn't feel like going home, even though I had everything I could want at home and warmth and the gramophone, there's bound to be another smart gathering of people there again tonight, people from town who come visiting in the evening and talk about the theatre and culture and drink beer, three times the next morning Mum would curse, because one of the guests had mistaken the larder for the lavatory, and instead of peeing into the bowl of the WC had gone and done it into a pot of lard . . . And Mum poured it off the next morning, and in the evening, when the company gathered, I saw her bring that pot and hand the guests a knife and some fresh bread and ask each of them to spread some lard on his bread as they fancied . . . and the guests spread the lard on their bread and tasted it and proclaimed, ''Well now, that's some lard, you can really tell the brewery feed in it . . .'' And I stood and watched them just like Mum, and Mum was only returning to them what they had done to her, but I was glad for the sake of our guests, because I hated the lot of them, they were just too perfect, they gave me a complex and I didn't know what to say to them, I blushed and said nothing, and nobody got a word out of me. I found those guests of ours a bit of a joke now as I watched those dozen or more heavy wet boots come past me, wrapped in sacking and ropes, and I saw all our guests quite close by, just over there across the orchard, how all their shoes meanwhile fitted so closely, it was even fashionable then for men to have small feet, often I saw our guests after walking this great distance from town past the river and across the fields, how they would lean against the brewery wall, lift one foot and bend down and rub and massage the toe of their shoe to get the blood flowing, their toes hurting simply because they were wearing shoes one size too small, in order to look elegant . . . And I said to Uncle, ''Uncle, please come back to us . . .'' But Uncle waved his hand: ''Work takes precedence, and what of it!'' And he showed how neatly he could knock out the catches, and how his arm with undiminished energy, as if he were drunk, tore away with the hook and dragged the platelets of ice into the crusher. And I walked through the open gate, the lanterns shone on the corners, a sweet-smelling breeze blew from the river bringing the thaw, trains clattered in the distance, as if they were just the other side of the brewery wall . . . And a gust sprang up by the maltings as always, whooshing against my back, so that I had to lie back into it, if I'd been leaning forward even a tiny bit more I'd have gone flying and stumbled till I fell, so strong was this wind, now it whooshed round my ears, and the ice-skates hanging over my shoulders were seized by this gust and swung away from me . . . But after a few metres the wind ebbed abruptly, and the skates jingled beside each other, and I saw the lit-up windows of the tied lodgings, I glanced into the kitchen, but Dad was standing there by the kitchen stove, lost in thought, slowly and absent-mindedly sipping coffee, I saw how the range was full of various pots and pans, then the primary school head came in, laughing, and Mum was standing in the doorway leading through to the living rooms, laughing too, and then I saw these rags lying on the table cut up into squares, Mum and the head teacher were picking up these rags by the middle and flapping them and then fastening them together with thread, and soaking them in the saucepans on the stove, next the counsellor-at-law and the pharmacist came out of the other room too, and all of them in a happy mood, even Dad was smiling, then they gave him those rags and Dad bound them up together, they were all relishing this work enormously, and I couldn't work out for the life of me, what was this all about? What was it going to be? And then I saw it . . . Mum untied those strings and threads, and when she unfurled those rags, they were beautiful as the wings of a butterfly, as a peacock eye, for every rag shimmered with blue and green and red metallic colours . . . And our guests carried those cambric hankies off into the other room, where I couldn't see them . . . So I went round the tied lodgings and quietly through the garden, I heard the ice hoists crushing a new load of ice, the glow of the light bulbs running up by the ice store delineated sharply the angles of the roof, as if there were a fire over there at the back of the brewery, as if it were some kind of holy picture of the Last Judgment, such an ominous sign burning with sulphur and mercury did those light bulbs send out there into the night, that the outlines of the brewery and the shadows seemed to me green . . . But through the window I could see into our flat, where hundreds of cambric kerchiefs were drying on long clothes-lines, and Mum and the guests kept bringing more and more of them in from the kitchen, this was such a marvellous sight to see in our house that I felt like going in to help too, but when I remembered my Uncle Pepin muffled up in scarves and with his boots wrapped up in sackcloth and string, and remembered the other participants in the ice hauling, I began to smile unpleasantly, as if I had started to understand something quite different from what I saw over here and over there, I practically shook with that sense of another different world, a world which is cut in two like St Martin's cloak with his sword, but continues nonetheless, adjacent to itself, just like the cambric handkerchiefs, which the teacher started ironing, after putting on Mum's apron, and the soaked boots and clothes out there behind the brewery and the ice store, where the bucket hoist constantly hauled away upward the noise of crushed ice and the light of the light bulbs running up into the livid dark sky. And Mum pushed in the sewing-machine and measured Dad's trousers, when she took his measure at the crotch the company roared with delight and choked itself laughing, only Dad looked solemn and embarrassed . . . And Mum assembled those dry ironed cambric kerchiefs, and the sewing-machine hummed as the company watched and conversed, laughing and sipping their beer, and in a trice Mum had plugged away at the pedals and produced a beautiful pair of trousers, and then she took Dad's measurements, chest and arms, and she sewed and sewed, while the head teacher sat on a chair and fastened the sleeve to the body with a swift needle and sewed on bobbles instead of buttons, like black viburnum berries, and after an hour Dad went off to change, and when he returned, he was a harlequin, a black close-fitting beret was added with a tall ostrich plume, Mum put new black patent leather shoes on him with the same kind of bobble instead of a buckle, and then she also cut out a tiny square from a black band and stuck it on Dad's face and powdered it with white talcum, till Dad choked . . . And everyone marvelled, so did I, at how handsome Dad was, not just handsome, but the most handsome of all men, in spite of being convinced that he was ugly, a puny slave to infinity. And the head teacher with the counsellor-at-law brought the oval mirror in from the bedroom, and Dad, when he looked at himself, I could see it, it was just like me all over, Dad was equally mistrustful, I too was afraid to look at myself in the mirror, and now Dad had to see it, and he did, he looked at himself for a long time, then he stretched out a hand, probably he didn't believe his eyes, that it was really him, I was rooting for him there outside the window, just take a proper look at yourself, Daddy! And take a look at the rest of our guests! And Dad struck a pose like a true harlequin, laughed a hearty laugh, for the first time in his life, in spite of being dressed up like a clown in the circus, he recognised himself, he found his own self. And he lifted his foot with its ribbon and laid it on a stool, leant his elbow on his bent knee, cupped his face in his palm and so created the melancholy figure of the harlequin, the melody of "Harlequin's Millions" . . . And Mum brought in a pail from the passage and put it down on the carpet under Dad's mouth, it looked like at the ball, when Harlequin feels so ill, like being sick . . . I saw it all and understood . . . And I saw the company go on ironing and sewing, and the sewing-machine went on humming away, while out there behind the ice store the bucket hoist hummed away relaxed and free, not a single fragment of ice was being carried up any more, and now the sewing-machine, too, joyfully produced its rattle of belts and jolting parts . . . And I too relaxed and felt free, my tension vanished, I empathised so much with the machine that today I had embodied it for the whole afternoon, but then the lights went out . . . And the driving belts cooled down, and Mr Vaňátko, the night-watchman, pulled off his Mexican gun and loosened the catch on his revolver, both weapons were incapable of firing, and slowly, flitting between the trees, with his little doggie in tow, he went off to guard all night in fear and dread those genuine driving belts, because they cost fifty thousand crowns, and Mr Vaňátko had given Dad his signature, that he'd have to pay for any loss. Then, at the corner of the maltings, Uncle's white cap appeared, the kind worn by Mr Hans Albers, Uncle held on to it with both hands and struggled with the wind, but finally he managed to bring his cap safely through into calm waters, I saw Uncle leap the gate and rush off, to be in time for the lovely Žofín bar girls, to dance with them and make them a gift of the last two ten-crown notes he had, which he'd stuffed into his shoe on the Saturday, so that the ladies wouldn't take them on the Sunday. And then I slipped back home, I waited till the coast was clear, undressed and lay down in bed, nobody had been looking for me, and then as if to fulfil my wish the door opened by itself and I gazed out from under the quilt, out of the darkness into the lit-up series of rooms, and saw how hour after hour more and more pairs of cambric trousers and sleeves and long jackets flowed off the sewing-machine beneath Mum's fingers, I saw the men's nimble hands indefatigably sewing on black bobbles, and more and more crates of beer and undiminished fatigue . . . and towards midnight I saw how there was no end to the cumulative enthusiasm of the company . . . And I felt old, I suddenly had the feeling I was terribly old, much older than my mother's companions, they were like little children, sewing dresses for their dolls . . . But, when the company dressed up in the harlequins' costumes and they all put on their tight-fitting black berets and their plumes and had a good look at themselves in the mirror and in the mirrors of their companions' eyes, and when they had finished praising each other, saying how well each costume went with the next and all with each other, and really they all did, then the head teacher clapped his hands and gave the signal, and the company put their black masks on over their noses, and when they had powdered themselves, the head teacher announced they would start rehearsing the midnight scene of harlequins for the Sokol association's masked ball.

SIX

Later, when Uncle Pepin had lost five kilos in weight, and when he'd stopped taking a bath, and so one week he would wash one hand, the next week one leg, the third week the other hand, and the fourth week the remaining leg, and the week after his neck, and the following week his chest, and so on, when he'd begun to get all messed up physically, his rebelliousness and revolutionary spirit evaporated. He returned to us all contrite, bearing his sailor's cap in a translucent paper bag as a demonstration of humble subjection, and he sat himself down in the kitchen, just as he had done three months ago. And Mum gave him horseradish sauce and a dumpling, and Uncle ravenously devoured it, exclaiming vociferously in the intervals, "This food is just fit for an archbishop!" And then when Mum heated up the dumplings and sauerkraut from yesterday's lunch, Uncle Pepin's enthusiasm and praise knew no bounds, before tucking into the whole pan of food he shouted, "Now this was the favourite dish o' the late lamented Emperor Franz himself!" And then he kissed

Mother's hand, leaving an imprint of horseradish sauce on the back of her little hand, and a bit of sauerkraut, and he said Mum was built on the selfsame lines as Baroness Schrat, the Emperor's mistress, otherwise an actress and at the time the greatest beauty not only in Vienna itself, but in all Austria, not excluding Transylvania, which used to have the loveliest whores in the whole of Cisleithania. And then he requested Dad to look after his accounts again and give him a daily allowance for spending money, and for his cigarettes and laundry and organisation. And Dad, seeing his brother so meek and humble, felt tears come to his eyes and said, "D'you know what, Pepin? I'll teach you how to maintain a Škoda 430!" Uncle Pepin said, "So long as I've got the criminal talent needed, it's the same sort o' business as a safe-breaker cracking open a safe." But Dad said, "Where there's a will, there's a way," adding, "And where is it written you have to spend the rest of your days as a maltster and assistant labourer? I mean, you could become a driver for us, we've sold the horses and acquired two delivery lorries!" And it was true, as he said this, even Mum looked dreamy, Bubik, the enormous gelding, when they trimmed him bare and led him off to the slaughterhouse early one evening, he untethered himself at the slaughterhouse, opened the gate, and came stepping along through the whole town, and across the bridge, he knew all the roads off by heart over the whole district, and sometime after midnight he neighed at the gate, and Vaňátko, the night-watchman, was fast asleep, but Dad recognised Bubik's neighing, so he got up, unfastened the gate, and the stable door, and Bubik neighed and went straight to his place, in the morning he neighed at the workmen, to say he'd come back to them, to his friends, but the drayman wasn't there, the drayman had three days off, because when you've been riding eighteen years with the same horses, and these horses are sent to the slaughterhouse, Dad had resolved, it's like a death in the family, and the three days were for that, for weeping and drinking to drown your sorrow at losing your horses, just as if your mother or brother had died, in short a close member of the family ... And so Bubik was led off again to the slaughterhouse, this time he went humbly, without neighing, the way he looked you could tell he knew there was nothing to be done, that it was likely the end of him, because at the slaughterhouse his sense of smell had told him that this was a place where your life was in jeopardy. And so Dad stepped out along with Uncle Pepin, Dad even took his brother by the shoulder, as they went off that Saturday in a mood of warm intimacy, and Dad enthusiastically explained to Uncle Pepin how the Orion motor-bike always had to be taken apart and put together again because it had a certain technical fault, but this Škoda 430 worked to such perfection that Dad took it apart simply to find out why the machine performed so flawlessly, why it started and drove so perfectly, for that perfection kept Dad awake in his bed at night. "You just have to understand these things," roared Uncle Pepin. And Dad nodded contentedly: "Aye, and not only do I understand, but I long, like a philosopher, to discover the reason for the perfection of its mechanical order, for, Pepin, remember that the engine of the likes of a Škoda 430 is just as perfect as nature, and the Universe." And Dad laid coats and sacks on the ground, laid Pepin down on top of them, and backed the car on to Pepin, then he climbed under it himself, inching himself under the chassis, and hauling the wrenches and spanners after him. When he had settled down beside Pepin, Dad said, "Now, these cables lead to the brakes, and we're going to have a look to see why those brakes are so good at doing their job . . ." And Dad set to work and handed Uncle a spanner and asked him to tap off the dried-on mud gently. And Pepin shouted, "We human beings can know just too much, ye ken, and look what can happen! There was this chappie Johnny Sachr in the army on military service, he asked the sarge what exactly an artillery gun was. So the sarge spent a whole Saturday morning and afternoon making it all clear to him, and finally Johnny asked, 'And how do you release the carriage?' And the sarge said Johnny was a fine example to all the lads and taught him how to release the carriage. And one Sunday afternoon Johnny took the gun, as it stood there in the Jičín barracks, released it, and the gun crashed through the sentry bar, ran through the gate and went careering down the hill to Jičín along the avenue. Folks only just managed to jump behind the trees as it went, and in the end the gun bounced off into the municipal recreation garden. Aye, people can know just too much," Uncle appended, and as the mud was stuck fast, he struck the dried-up undercarriage of the Škoda 430 three times with his spanner, and Dad wasn't expecting it, and the mud spattered in his eyes, and Dad cried out, "Pepin, you hairy swine, what're you doing?" And he lay there on

his back, blinking and wiping his eyelashes with his
dirty hands, then he had to turn on to his tummy, to let
all the muck get washed out with his tears. And then
they found that the brakes were in order, and Dad was
amazed that he couldn't find anything special to see,
because the brakes on the Orion used to fail, and when
he took them apart and put them together again, just as
carefully as the brakes on this Škoda, they went wrong
just the same as they did before. "Don't you find this
car maintenance business a lot more fun than going off
after your bar girls?" Dad remarked, raising the bonnet
and showing Uncle where the spark-plugs were, and
the big end, and the air cleaner, and then he removed
the various parts, and the big end, clasping his hands
and explaining it all devotedly to Uncle and pointing
out which were the cylinders, and the pistons, and
where the crankpin on the crankshaft was. And Uncle
exclaimed loudly, "Brother, you're right there, take that
Vlasta girl over at Havrda's for instance, now you tell
me, brother, the lads were playing cards, a game of
'God Bless', and Vlasta says: 'Come on you old goat,
pay me a bit of attention!' But auld Švec had me looking
after thousands o' crowns, there I was sitting next tae
him like some Rothschild, who else would've had the
honour, right? And Vlasta took off her blouse and stuck
her arm round my back and says, 'Tell me about the
European Renaissance, d'you hear?' And there I was,
holding those thousands and no paying attention, and
all of a sudden the lassie undoes the fastening on her
bra, and out pops her bosoms, like two half-kegs of
beer, and one o' they breasts thumps me on the head
and the other just floored me, and auld Švec fell doon as

204

well, swept the cloth off, and all the players were swept away by that Vlasta lassie's pair of bosoms, and there she stood over us, it was like a holy picture, Jesus arising from the dead, there we were felled and lying on the ground like the sodgers in the picture ... And Vlasta stood there putting her boobs back in her brassière, and auld Švec says, 'Time for the kits to go back in their basket ...' and he orders two Martells and tells me, 'Now you've to sit next to me, you Catholic son of a gun, you bring me luck, you do.' " And Dad said: "Hold this lock-nut for me, so that's your fine fun, is it?" "Aye," said Uncle beaming back at him, "right enough it is!" "Well," said Dad in disapproval, "but today for the very first time we're going to take out the sump as well, all right?" "Oh aye," said Uncle, "so you agree it's gey good fun over at Havrda's! Now if only you could meet Vlasta! Before she went to work as a barmaid, she was a theatrical hairdresser, and she was famous in that theatre, Francin, as well, she worked as a wig-maker, and one day, she told me, they forgot the wee box with the make-up and whiskers, and as they were on tour and playing some Spanish comedy or other – Sid or Kid it was called – do you know how Vlasta got hold of the beards and moustaches?" But Dad just said simply, "Now we come to one of the most magnificent parts of the operation, we get down under the car again and loosen the sump!" And then he inched himself under the Škoda again on his tummy, while Uncle continued, "Well, dear wee Vlasta, she just tucks up her skirt and then she takes her scissors, and snip, snip, she snips off her pubes, trims it all off, and as there wasnae enough for the moustaches, she half-trimmed off the pubes of the hairdresser's assistant as well . . . they stuck 'em on wi' strips o' elastoplast or sticking-plaster, and there was ten chevaliers strutting about the theatre twisting their moustaches, and Vlasta got a certificate of commendation from the director after . . ." "Ugh," expostulated Dad, "they could have got the pox or the crabs or something, but for goodness' sake, concentrate for a moment, these screws I'm about to hand you, put them on the board, and this last one too, and I'll support the sump on my chest while you climb out and bring over the old gherkin tin and I'll pour the oil out into it." "I know," said Uncle Pepin, "that's the oil from the gearbox, right?" "Gearbox my auntie, that goes with the differential, we'll take a look at that next Saturday, or tomorrow morning if you like, the gearbox and differential are towards the back, this is the sump, from the engine there, as I've just been telling you, the oil drops down and the pump pumps it round and up again, do you see?" "Now I see," said Uncle, even though he'd seen nothing, "so the oil goes back up to the distributor, right?" "Up your arse it does!" shouted Dad, "Up your arse and not the distributor, up your stupid arse!" he yelled, as oil started slopping down over his chest. "Now for the love of God concentrate, will you, and I'll just lower the sump down on to my chest." And Uncle called out delightedly, "Right you are then, Caruso used to have books piled on his chest to give him a better voice, and he could sing like a right-hand ox, pure joy to hear, a throat like a fine Swiss heifer, but d'you know what Vlasta said, that as a barmaid she has to pay tax on her artistic earnings? And maybe literary too? As an author or painter?" But Dad was engrossed body and soul in the engine and only wheezed back in excitement, "Hold up the sump, one more screw, hold it up with both hands like this . . ." "I know," said Uncle, "to stop the carburettor falling out." "For Jesus Christ's sake, don't torment me, the carburettor's way up on top . . ." "I know," said Uncle confidingly, "that's the cam that drives the petrol into the distributor." "What d'you mean, the distributor?" Dad mewled. "Well, so as to get sparks into the cauldron, one of the folks in the City Bar told me, Jarunka, he's the one that works as a station assistant, looks terrific in uniform, just like General Gajda, d'you know what happened to him? Once, when he fell asleep on the job, the lassie on the telegraph took out his privates, and the dispatcher coloured 'em with the ink for the stamps, and when Jarunka got home that morning, he wanted his missus' strongest and highest proof of love and affection while still in his uniform, and his lady said yes, but when Mr Jarunka took out his privates to carry out, in the words of Mr Batista's handbook, this marital cohabitation, alias coition, his missus was horrified by his purple-painted privates and she flew off to ask the stationmaster what sort of swinish behaviour alias misdemeanours were going on there during working hours, and as she burst into the stationmaster's office, she caught the stationmaster bald-headed, with his toupée sitting on the table on a false head, he was just combing it ready for duty, and so the missus just had to take some soap and scrub Mr Jarunka's genitalia on the washboard, but it wouldn't come off, so she took some acid liquid she kept for cleaning the WC, but Mr Jarunka started bellowing and rushed off with his genitalia through the workers' estate all the way to the railway station and back, and people were shocked, partly because he was in uniform, partly because of his purple private parts, and partly because he was bellowing so loud . . ." And Dad removed the last screw, and the sump settled down on his chest, and Dad roared out, "Stop roaring in my ear like that, or I'll start roaring too, go and fetch some staves and prop up this sump for me, it's blessed heavy." Uncle Pepin lay on his tummy and proffered advice: "Try singing, brother, like Jára Pospíšil, a tenor has to be trained to be a tenor, has to be trained by a trainer . . ." he rambled on and then he climbed out, but then, while still kneeling there, he thought again and bent down his head and enquired, "Oughtn't I to go and pay my organisation?" But Dad roared, "You're not going anywhere, bring me those props, it's dripping in my eyes!" "What where?" inquired Uncle. "In my eyes, oil!" And Uncle expressed wonder: "Your eyes, oil? But to finish my story, that Jarunka chappie, that worked the barrier poles on the level-crossing, he also sent a report to the Academy once, backed up by his own observations and those of the engine-drivers and stationmasters, saying that sparrows were taking free rides in groups and alighting on empty waggons and going on train trips to Southern Bohemia, or the spa town of Bohdaneč, once they even set off on an outing from Kostomlaty to Vienna, with no permits, just to see what Vienna looked like from the top of Steffi, alias St Stephen's Cathedral, and back they came in empty waggons to Vršovice, switched to the milk train, and returned to Kostomlaty in the waggons, except that when in Prague while they were at it they nipped off to have a quick peép at the Castle . . . but they're going to be closing soon, oughtn't I to pop over and fetch my laundry?" And Dad couldn't stand it any more, he poured off half of the oil from the sump and lifted it with his last ounce of strength and placed it down carefully beside him, it couldn't be done straightfor- wardly, it was as if he was buried by a mine slip, he had to worm his way out, for the sump and Dad were squeezed together like two sandwiched slices of bread . . . And Dad clambered out into the light of day, greasy and soaked with oil, then he turned round and hauled the sump carefully out, straightened up and carried it off in his arms and tenderly, like putting a child to bed, he laid it down on an old honey extractor. "So this is the sump," rejoiced Uncle Pepin, seeing that Dad was now fuming. "This is the sump," said Francin, growing mollified, "and now come and see what beauty awaits us underneath the vehicle!" He knelt down and invited Pepin to creep in after him beneath the Škoda chassis. "Oughtn't I to go and buy some bread and milk instead?" said Uncle with sudden trepidation. "You're feeding with us again," said Dad, crawling on his elbows into the puddles of oil with Pepin following after, then they turned on to their backs and lay in the oil, while Dad pointed his screwdriver and reeled off in a soft and ardent voice as if in prayer all the various parts of the car which hung there fastened to the shafts and joints above, here and there a fat drop of oil plopped in their faces, but Dad went on talking and teaching away, while Uncle Pepin longed with regret for the golden times only yesterday when he was eating the hens' own groats and spuds, but by now he would've been off, stepping along in his sailor's cap to visit his lovely ladies, and before he got there, on the way over, the windows would open and the garden gates of the town too, people would rush out, and Uncle would salute them like he was Hans Albers. At that moment a pair of white trouser-legs stopped in front of the Škoda 430, then a pair of shoes with divided uppers went up and down a couple of times, and after that a figure squatted down in a white spa suit. Mr Burýtek, the butcher, dressed up spa-fashion, his ruddy and full face redolent of "tea", for Mr Burýtek called rum "tea", he'd finished work, it was all the same at the slaughterhouse, every week when two waggonloads of Hungarian piglets came in, with his assistant he put the narrow gangway in place, then he and his helper positioned themselves each on one side with their knives, and as the piglets rushed out into the light of day, so they each slit their throats with the knives, and then the piglets ran about hither and thither amidst blood and dying rattles until they fell, and when the last piglet sidled out, they stabbed its throat too, for, as Mr Burýtek said, this running about was the only way of bleeding them properly. Mr Burýtek wasn't just any old butcher, he would go for a big pig, a four-hundredweight hog, single-handed with his knife, he'd struggle with it willy-nilly, make a fight of it, and when he got one on its back at a private slaughtering, he plunged his knife into its throat and held it there and held down that pig's last mortal tremor. This butcher could master anything, except his own wife, though she stayed at home in the shop, she was partial to the bottle, sometimes when she got drunk, she stripped naked and didn't know what she was doing, and the neighbours poured water over her, and when that didn't do any good, slops or liquid manure. And now Mr Burýtek, squatting down, begged Dad, "Manager Sir, it's getting to be a crying outrage, please please could you drop in at our house during the evening and persuade that wife of mine to quit the bottle, do you understand?" said Mr Burýtek sadly. "I'm going off to Hošt'ka Spa to recuperate, I'll take a walk in the colonnade, I won't be at home in the evening, for pity's sake, have a word with her . . ." He lit himself a cigar and rose slowly and ponderously, for his legs were sore, as with every butcher at his time of life. And he looked about him, Dad's head was just showing from under the Škoda chassis, like a tortoise's poking out of its shell, next to him Uncle Pepin emerged too, and Mr Burýtek looked about him, and before Dad could prevent him, Mr Burýtek sat himself down in that sump full of oil, comfortably and contentedly he hooked his white trouser-leg over his knee, lit his cigar and looked at Dad, saying insistently, "We're friends after all, twice I've spent two whole days working with you on your Orion, it was you that made my wife take to the drink, because she thought I was off somewhere playing cards with somebody for two days in a row, off spending two days with other women, while all the time we were here working on the bike . . . It's just a little bit your fault that she took to the bottle, and if you had a word with her, she'll listen to an intellectual type like you, she'd even be willing to come and work with you on this car of yours . . ." And Dad, when he saw the butcher's quizzical face, when he saw the oil soaking into the trousers and the butcher still sitting there in his comfy posture in the sump as if in an armchair, the sump even fitted him neatly as though made to measure, Dad said, "Don't fret yourself, my good man, I promise you, I'll drop in at your place, I'll make an attempt . . ." And he wormed back under the car, and Uncle crawled in after him, they thought it better to lie there in the huge puddles of oil beneath the car, watching from the half-darkness, as if from under a roof or a hat pulled down over your eyes, as Mr Burýtek reached round to touch his backside, then put his black palm up to his eyes, then slowly got to his feet, took hold of the cloth on his bottom, prised off the clinging·trousers, then stood on one foot and shook the other about, then turned round, leaned over and placed both hands in the sump and watched the oil close gently over his wedding ring. Uncle Pepin went on: "Once I was travelling wi' a real beauty from Bruck and I was busy staring at her, and she, all embarrassed, was reading away at her novel and flushing red with it, opposite us a colonel was sitting, reading Prager Tagblatt, and I watched, and down from the rack came slowly dripping a thin plaited strand, a streamlet, a slender golden snake, and this slender snake curled itself on to the colonel's epaulettes, but the colonel smiled, probably he was on the humour section, and that slender snake coiled and trickled on further and ever more thickly, and I looked, and it was honey, running out of the tipped-over bag of the young lady, who, when she saw it, just wrapped herself up tighter in her coat and pretended she was asleep . . . And all at once the colonel scratched himself on the shoulder and his fingers stuck, then he jumped up, and at that moment the guard came in, and it ended up with two other passengers sticky with honey too, and I still had honey in my hair when I got home, I was going home on furlough . . ." Mr Burýtek whipped round and shook his fist at the Škoda 430 and cried out, "Armageddon! Armageddon!"

Then he disappeared off round the corner of the maltings, in order to be in time for his train to Hošt'ka Spa, to take a turn on the promenade, as he said, yes, on the promenade, but also to meet up with a friend and fellow butcher, for the two of them were members of a preaching society, while Mr Burýtek was busy slitting the throats of the squeaking piglets, in their dying rattles he heard the voice of God, smearing and anointing him with pig's blood, and so Mr Burýtek got involved in peripatetic preaching, he preached the word of God according to "God's Messenger", a programme with booklets sent to him from America, and Mr Burýtek's mission was to preach the word that the final battle of Armageddon was nigh, the butchers laughed at him, but when Mr Burýtek went home from the slaughter-house he used to preach about that last battle, and that's why he'd been going every Saturday over to Hošt'ka, to the spa, so that he and his friend could test out each other's preaching technique. But a week ago Mr Burýtek had received a gramophone with some records from America, and on those records the message of God was inscribed in Czech, all you had to do was wind up the gramophone and put on the record and out came the voice crying out about the preparations for the final battle of Armageddon, which was imminent . . . And Mr Burýtek, being a cyclist, had the rear carrier on his bicycle strengthened and on it he lashed that gramophone, and in the evenings he went round the villages and pubs on the edge of town to proclaim Armageddon with his gramophone and the trained voice which issued from it.

So then Dad and Uncle Pepin halted outside the butcher's shop on the edge of town, there in the lamplight shaded with pinned-together newspapers sat the butcher's wife Mrs Burýtková, gnawing her lower lip and sticking out the point of her tongue and trying to touch the tip of her nose with it. When she failed, she got up and took a long wreath of sausages and set about counting them, as if she were praying the rosary. When she finished counting, she thought for a bit and started counting them over again, more concentratedly, but in the middle of the wreath she must have lost count, for she chucked the sausages aside, took a knife, and carefully started scraping splinters of bone and fat which had stuck from the chopping block. Then she sat down, slowly unwrapped a throat lozenge, and absent-mindedly put the paper in her mouth, threw the sweetie into the basket and felt for the doorhandle on the wall, eventually she found it and gripped it and went into the kitchen and brought the gramophone, she wound up the spring and put on the needle, but the gramophone didn't work properly, it played, but off the groove. The butcher's wife took the cleaver and first lightly, and then with a powerful sideways blow, she caused the needle to jump straight into the music, choral church music: "Love divine's sweet angel

flameth in the blue stars' holy glow . . ." And Uncle
Pepin, scrubbed and wearing his sailor's cap, came into
the butcher's premises, saluted, the butcher's wife
laughed, clasped her hands and exclaimed, "Maestro,
you've come at the right moment, shall we dance? What
about a bit of theatricals?" But Uncle Pepin pointed to
the gramophone and said, "Is it some sort of canonical
hours or what? Let's make it faster," and he lifted the
lid, shifted the speed lever forwards, and sure enough,
love's sweet angel revolved to the rhythm of the polka
in the stars' holy glow. And the lady butcher extended
her arms round Uncle's shoulders, Uncle kissed her
greasy hand and danced with her, watching so as not to
get grease on his sailor's cap, for every other minute the
butcher's wife swept and brushed him up against some
pig's lights or tough old cow's boot. And the butcher's
wife sighed and wiped the perspiration from her brow
with her palm. Then she left Uncle standing and went
into the kitchen, and when she returned, there she
stood in the shop doorway naked. Only her hair was
tied around with a large kerchief. A moment later Dad
stepped in with a little case, carefully he closed the door
behind him and bowed to Mrs Burýtková and said,
"Dean Spurný's sent me to see you," and when he saw
the nakedness of the butcher's wife he grew all uneasy.
Then he lifted the gramophone lid, slowed down the
speed, and put the needle on again, and through the
butcher's shop fluttering off the floor tiles and wall tiles
the choral church singing resounded again: "Love
divine's sweet angel flames . . ." "Come along in both of
you," invited the butcher's wife, "come on, come on,"
she nodded her head and sat herself down on a chair.

"Wouldn't you like to put on an apron?" Dad proposed. "No I wouldn't, it's too hot, take off your clothes too, make yourselves cosy, gentlemen," she declared and laid her hand in her lap. "What's that you're bringing me?" she asked suspiciously. "Take a look, dear lady, the church is really not so much against gluttony as against drunkenness, the Dean . . ." "What about the Dean?" cried the butcher's wife raising her arm. "He drinks seven pints of vermouth a day, and when he's pissed, the mastiff takes him back to the parsonage or Trávníček the butcher." "True enough," observed Dad, "but one minute before the stroke of midnight he drinks up, and then he touches not a drop till it's time for morning mass, whereas you, as we well know, sit up boozing spirits here, shame on you. Why do you drink so much?" asked Dad, opening the box he'd brought and sticking the plug of the fulgurational currents into the wall socket, then he rose and put out the light, closed up the shop, and when he returned to the kitchen, the purple violet air was sweet-smelling and sizzling, and Dad attached the anodes for epileptics and menstrual disorders, aimed at his forehead that purple, sizzling, glassy, hollow, blue-vapour-filled plate, then he raised it up high, touched Pepin's forehead, then slid it round Uncle's face, right round it, and then he placed the appliance close to Mrs Burýtková's forehead, and a crackling issued forth from her kerchief and hair, and tiny sparks flew and sizzled, then Dad touched the woman's shoulder and Uncle murmured blissfully, "Well, you'll have to lend me this next time I go to see my little beauties, they'll be wetting their knickers . . ." "You've got to see it," said Dad, and like a magician and hypnotist he continued with this instrument, drawing a purple violet cloud and perfume round the chest and heart of the butcher's wife, her breasts heaved not with indignation, but with delight, with astonishment. "So," Dad remarked softly, "if you stop drinking, I'll be along to give you an electric massage like this every Saturday . . ." and the lady butcher got up, tugged a string at the back of her head, and her kerchief dropped, and then her russet long hair fell tumbling down almost to the ground, and Francin, when he saw those tresses, the appliance began to tremble in his fingers . . . Then he gave the butcher's wife the instrument to hold, took the butcher's apron and covered the naked woman with it, he fastened it for her himself with a white tape, and the butcher's wife was dressed as well in her long tresses, and Dad drew those tresses to him and twisted them round the butcher's wife, her hair was like a bathrobe round her . . . And Dad sat the butcher's wife down on a chair and fixed the neon comb and started combing through those tempestuous old-fashioned tresses, and the butcher's wife lowered her head and closed her eyes, and you could hear the erotic cooing warble of the comb and the luxuriant cooing gurgle of the ultraviolet rays . . . "Where do you keep the alcohol?" enquired Dad tenderly in the ear of the lady. She took a key from her bosom and handed it to him, and Dad let her hold the appliance with its fragrance of thunderstorms and violets and pointed to the cupboard: "Here?" But the butcher's wife shook her head. "Here? Not here. Here then?" Dad knelt down, inserted the key and undid the lock, and there on a little shelf stood jars of thyme and marjoram and pepper and paprika . . . "Here?" Dad shifted aside the jars and behind them were three bottles, one of Nuncius, one of Sagavir and a third with cherry brandy. Dad put the bottles out on the table and said, "It's a sin to get drunk, mark you, but when you only taste it, it can't do any harm," and as he said it the butcher's wife handed him the instrument and fetched some glasses. "But not you, you mustn't ever again!" said Dad indignantly, but again he was charmed by the butcher's wife's tresses, hair like Mum used to have, hair she had cut off, without asking Dad's by your leave. "Gie it here," said Uncle Pepin, "and I'll pour out just a wee drop, old Holub, when I took him his rolls, he used to give me a dram of this as well." And he poured some Nuncius into a glass, and he and Dad drank some and declared the drink fortifying for the stomach and medicinal for all liver and digestive troubles. "You say you'll come and give me the treatment every Saturday?" the butcher's wife inquired in tremulous tones. "Every Saturday, I'm your obedient lamb, bringing you a new life," said Dad, "the treatment is absolutely simple, all I have to do is run through your hair with this comb," said Dad and, unable to restrain himself, he took her hair and sniffed it, it had that same never-to-be-forgotten smell, the smell of his mother's apron, where he used to run and hide when he was small . . . And now, in the drunk butcher's wife, he found that from which he had been severed these eight years past, the long hair of his wife, which she had brought back from Bod'a Červinka the barber's on the rear carrier of her bicycle, like an oblong Christmas cake, or four kilos of wine-flavoured sausages. Uncle Pepin remarked, "Well, Vlasta likes drinking this, she

says, you have a drink of this too, lad, get something
decent in your tummy . . ." And the butcher's wife
turned round and looked at Dad with eyes full of
gratitude, and then, unable to restrain herself, she
stroked the back of his hand, in which Dad was still
gripping that effulgent comb. "But I reckon," she said
tenderly, "that some of that Sagavir, that bottle with the
young swain on it, will be better for you, the Nuncius
has an insidious flavour about it like its monk's
Franciscan habit, it seems medicinal, but like all
medicines, the minute you take a little bit too much,
that's the end of you, and believe me, I know, but as for
the Sagavir? It has a lovely lightish greenish yellowish-
tinged colour, as if you were drinking the iridescence of
the spheres, and its flavour is spicy, with an upper tone
resembling the best dessert wine, and a lower tone
suggesting the laundered skirt of a shepherdess who's
been sitting in the pasture on banks of thyme, and then
peppermint and pimpernel." And Dad and Uncle were
about to pour some out, but the butcher's wife
expostulated, "You pair of barbarians!" and she got up,
carefully winding herself in her hair, and she went and
rinsed out the glasses in a pail, and when she brought
them back, she poured the glasses, took the comb
tenderly out of Dad's hand and put its glow close up to
the glasses and bottle, and the liquid glinted and
glistened and seduced one to drink. They sipped, and
drank up. Then there was silence, only flies buzzed
round the shop and banged into the maddened
windows. The gramophone stopped playing, and Dad
went into the shop with his glass, instead of the handle
of the gramophone he turned the handle of the old safe,

which opened with a clinking sound. Then Dad felt for the gramophone, cranked it up, put on the needle, and when the church choir began again – "Love divine's sweet angel flameth in the blue stars' holy glow" – Dad shifted the speed lever, and the church music turned into a blaring galop . . . Dad came back and took another drink, the butcher's wife was lying back in her chair, her hair swept back away from her shoulders, she was struck by something, her hair lay on the ground, as if flowing off the back of the chair. Then Dad had just one more glass, and when he'd drunk it, the butcher's wife stroked him on the back of his hand and said to him with incredible tenderness, "Not like that." And she was walking straight now, she went into the shop proud and august, as if the neon comb had imbued her with sanctity, she reached into the gramophone and slowed down the music, and now the church music was church-like, it floated with grandeur through the butcher's premises as if in some old Romanesque chapel. When she sat down, she touched Dad again, and Dad plunged his face into her hair and couldn't restrain himself, for so many years it had been denied him, for eight years he'd been deprived of sniffing at these long female tresses, he plunged and took that hair lightly in his lips, and it tasted identical, and the butcher's wife felt the trembling male lips and pressed herself to him, pressed herself until she moaned out loud, for eight years or more she had never moaned like this to the touch of male lips, for so many years she had been apparently without feeling, never again, she had thought, never again will I be a saint to someone, embodying something more than myself . . .

"Gentlemen," said the butcher's wife, when Dad stood up straight and said they really had to go, "all good things come in threes, now this cherry brandy, gentlemen, is quite a drink, every European house stocks this brand, every restaurant in the whole world marked with the sign of a cock, every world-class restaurant has this cherry brandy, six hundred cherry trees Mr Wantoch grows exclusively for its manufacture, and the recipe is a secret, it's a drink as famous as Becher's Becher Liqueur, Jelínek's or Gargulák's slivovitz, or Pilsner beer. When you take it in your mouth, one tone reminds you of the scent of bitter almonds," but Dad sniffed at the butcher's wife's hair and repeated after her, "Yes, the scent of bitter almonds," and the butcher's wife continued: "Yes, bitter almonds, the second tone of cherry brandy is the high, July tone of ripening cherries, cherries swollen ready to burst, and the third tone is the scent left behind by summer lightning, when it splits a lime tree in half and all its leaves bristle ... Gentlemen, excuse my manners, I went to a *lycée*, did you know, and from such a fine start in life here I have come to such an end ..." The butcher's wife bowed herself, and Dad took her by the shoulders and raised her up and said, "It's unworthy of you, you are and you will be a good woman, only you must agree to be treated with these fulgurational currents, and," he whispered to her in a voice fragrant with the blend of Sagavir and Nuncius, "only by me ..." And the butcher's wife nodded solemnly: "Yes, only by you," and she opened her eyes, which had been permanently half-shut all the time, for years they had stayed half-shut, she used to look out at the world like a savage from a thicket, like an animal, like a fugitive . . . She opened her eyes and looked into Dad's, then Dad lifted the brilliant comb and shone it into her eyes and saw that they were lovely and full of fiery sparks and that not even his wife had ever shown him such eyes, such eyes had only been shown to him many years ago by his own mother. And Francin poured a glass of cherry brandy, and the butcher's wife jumped up, took him tenderly by the hand and said, "You're barbarians . . ." and she put the glass into the cupboard and took out clean ones and filled them with cherry brandy, that heavy, syrupy, darkly passionate liqueur. Dad said, "You could just have a little one along with us, one glass won't do you any harm . . ." But the butcher's wife shook her head: "I've been tasting a stronger liqueur than all this." And Dad inquired, "A lot stronger than this?" She sipped and nodded. "Much, much stronger, stronger than anything else."

Uncle Pepin just drank, silently, he poured for himself, and saw that the butcher's wife and his brother were looking at each other, Dad drank, the butcher's wife sighed sweetly, and as they were leaving, the butcher's wife burst sweetly into tears. And there in the shop, amongst the huge beef lungs and hearts hanging on hooks, Dad extracted an oath from the butcher's wife, that he could come and treat her alcoholism again the following week. As the brothers left and turned the corner, a wind blew, and the gust made both of them stagger. First Dad fell on one knee under a street lantern, then all of a sudden he uttered a shout, such a kind of joyful shout, not a human voice, but a happy blurred roaring, whose fundamental tone was joy. And Uncle Pepin went back over the bridge, into town, and he fetched the local policeman Mr Holoubek, who'd just come out of the Gypsy Inn, he was taking off his helmet, which the dealers had mercilessly rammed down on to his skull, he'd been sent by Procházka the chief of police, who, seeing they were about to start a brawl over in the Gypsy Inn, had run off and said to the first policeman he met, "Holoubek, can't you hear it? I've got a feeling something's about to happen at the Gypsy Inn . . ." By the time Holoubek burst in, it was too late, they squashed his helmet down in the doorway and hammered it with a stick till his ears rang with the blows. "Mr Holoubek," Uncle Pepin said, "there's a drunkard lying over there roaring his head off, go and fine him, he's making a terrible hullabaloo." And so Dad was taken in a drunken state to the brewery by that giant Mr Holoubek, while Uncle Pepin took the case and sped off to the bar to his beauties, to try out the radiation on them and treat them, as the handbook instructed him, for interrupted monthly cycles.

SEVEN

It was in the middle of the War, Mr Burýtek's name was added to the list of those in prison, the Gestapo arrested him along with his gramophone. They loaded him up with his bicycle, and Mr Burýtek was radiant with delight, and called out, "Armageddon! Armegeddon!" but then they knocked him down, and people remembered that this butcher had actually been telling them for years that the final battle had begun, the battle of Armageddon, and they had laughed at him, calling after him as he rode along on his bicycle, "Armageddon!" And he only nodded his head and repeated it after them, but in a different sense, "Armageddon! Armageddon!" And a military commission came to the brewery and decreed that it was confiscating the malting floors and the brewery would have to buy its malt elsewhere, a munitions factory was going to be put in there, but the munitions factory never turned up, only a man from Vienna, an engineer called Mr Friedrich, who billeted himself in the lodgings and spent all day drawing up plans, showing where the various machines would be put, and at nightfall he went out on the town, he visited the Žofín bar, and chatted up the girls in broken Czech, but Vlasta, the one with perfect German, ever since the time the Germans entered the little town where time stood still, she spoke only Czech. And Friedrich, when he walked round the brewery with the bosses, he greeted each workman respectfully, but the workmen looked right through him as if he wasn't there, as if he was transparent, they didn't respond to his greetings, but Mr Friedrich went on greeting them persistently time and time again. And when dusk fell, the black-outs were drawn, and when nightfall came, the street lamps went out, but Uncle Pepin went on doing his rounds of the public houses with ladies' service, he continued persistently taking flowers to the lovely ladies, he went on wearing his white sailor's cap, and when he came into the Žofín bar, he yelled out, "What're you sitting around here like toadstools for? Put us on a real good belter!" And he handed Marta some fading roses and Marta had a sniff at them. "Those are specially for you," said Uncle Pepin, ordering a black coffee. "My, you're all dolled up tonight, maestro!" said Bobinka, "Not going a-courting are we?" she asked searchingly, running her palm down Uncle's calf and ascertaining by feel that Uncle Pepin was wearing three pairs of underpants and warm leggings over them. "Got a touch of the shivers, have we?" said Marta, "And you leave him to me, Bobinka, this is my visit, right?" and Uncle twisted his fingers, and into the bar came an old fellow, his hair was curly like a lambskin cap, he was carrying a parcel and immediately he called out jubilantly in the doorway,

"Life's just marvellous, folks, it's just so marvellous, I'm going to buy you all a dram!" And he sat down straightaway beside Uncle Pepin, tore open the parcel and showed Uncle the contents, one light-coloured fabric and one dark. Then he said, "I can't see too well these days, but I can see sure enough you're a man of the world, what kind of suit should I have made for me out of this?" Bobinka brought in a tray with large glasses of spirits, passed them round, and the old fellow lifted his glass and said, "Cheers, to the end of the War! I'm eighty-three years old, folks, and I'm looking forward to peace! And I'm going to have two suits of clothes sewn for me in honour of that peace! So, mister, what am I going to have?" Uncle Pepin said, "Use the light-coloured stuff for a casual outfit with patch pockets, and a hunting hat to go with it with a chamois tuft or coloured feather, like the Emperor Franz used to wear when he went out in the landau to Ischl to hunt chamois." "He must've been a handsome figure of a man, just like you, eh?" said Bobinka. "Not at all, I'm a handsome figure of a man, right enough, but the handsomest figure of a man in those days not only amongst civilians in general, but amongst the ruling families of the whole world, was the Emperor Franz, with his fine bald head, muttonchop whiskers like a tiger, and splendid nose, just like that of a little child. Marvellous!" Bobinka stroked Uncle's thinning hair and said in a voice full of admiration, "My, your hair's grown so thick, maestro, when you comb yourself, I suppose you can't get the comb into it? You have to put oil on it, don't you!" "Never you mind that," said Uncle waving his hand, and as he recoiled from the lady's hand he overbalanced and fell on to his back, chair and all, the girls lifted him up and dusted him off, they cleaned his trousers for him solicitously at the flies, and Bobinka kneeling raised her eyes to him and said, "Feeling any electricity yet?" But Uncle Pepin raised his finger in front of the old gent's nose and said, "And to match the white suit you wear a blue shirt and a white spotty tie, like Hans Albers sported in La Paloma, and out of this blue material here you make a double-breasted suit, like the one Jára Pospíšil wears in 'I Have Nine Canaries', and a white shirt and metallic blue tie to go with it . . ." The old fellow banged the parcel several times on the table, laid his head on the tablecloth and shouted and laughed: "Folks, I'm happy, I'm so happy, all the drinks are on me!" And the proprietress came in with a knife, wringing her hands, then she turned the wireless knob and a solemn voice was heard announcing that the Herr Reichsprotektor Heydrich had been shot, and all theatre and cinema performances were prohibited, all dance entertainments and parties . . . And Uncle Pepin jumped up and cried, "Christ, what kind of order is this? Can we Czechs never do anything? Christ almighty! In 1920 we occupied a chunk of Hungary, and then they told us we weren't allowed! We occupied a chunk of Teschen, and again we weren't allowed to take it from the Poles. And not long back we wanted to have a fight with the Germans, and again we weren't allowed! England and France again! Christ, catch me being woken up at midnight by the ambassadors, saying we weren't allowed to have a go at the Germans! If only I was President! I'd soon tell those doormen and lackeys: 'Kick the ambassadors up the arse, kick 'em right on out till they hit the pavement!' And then I'd surround myself with ensigns and sergeant-majors from the old Austria and I'd wage war and we'd soon defeat those Germans! And now, coz they've done for Heydrich, we're not allowed to dance, is that it? Come on, Bobinka, put on a real belter!" And Bobinka put on the record of "I Have Nine Canaries", and Uncle asked her to dance, and the old chap thumped the parcel of material he'd bought for the clothes he was going to wear as soon as the War ended and peace began, and all the time that curly-haired little old gent yelled out, "Folks, life is beautiful! Bring on the drinks, I'm sticking around till I'm ninety! Do you hear?" And Uncle danced at speed with Bobinka, first he drew her on to his back, then he took her, threw her up high and planted her on his shoulders, and carried her through the bar with dancing steps, and the proprietress locked the main entrance and wrung her hands, and the old fellow shouted out, "My old Dad, though he'd lost both his legs, had the advantage of being the oldest one in the whole Invalidenhaus, so that every year, on Count Strozzi's birthday – he was the one that founded the Invalidenhaus for the veterans – every year he laid a wreath on his monument! – Folks, I'm happy today! – The soldiers pushed Dad along in his wheelchair up to the memorial, put the wreath in his hands, lifted him up, and carried Dad over to the monument, and all around a guard of honour made up of veterans and soldiers from the garrison! Only Infantryman Valášek envied Dad his position, but what could he do, Dad was ninety-two and Valášek was only ninety! That Valášek fellow, whenever Dad was laying that wreath, he'd whisper to him, 'Time you snuffed it, you knackered old jade.' And every day, when Valášek went out into the corridor, first thing in the morning, and him in a wheelchair too, all of the veterans were, first thing Valášek did was go and have a look, open the door to the room where Dad's bed was, and ask him, 'Still not snuffed it yet, eh?' And Dad hollered over from the bed, 'Aye, Valášek, I'm alive and I'm going to live to be a hundred, another ten years yet I'm going to be laying wreaths at Count Strozzi's memorial, and meanwhile you'll kick the bucket furious as hell!' " And the old fellow stood up, suddenly he was all handsome, with his smooth face and his lambskin cap of stiff bristling curly hair tremulous like the horsehair on a Roman helmet, Marta took him by the hands, and they danced a kind of childish dance, "She watched her sheep in the woods so deep", and Uncle lifted Bobinka and lowered her from his neck, and they danced a foursome, "I to her went clippy clippy clap, she to me went tippy tippy tap", and as they held hands their feet went darting about, and the gramophone record started up again with "I Have Nine Canaries". And the door opened and in came Dedek the Saint Bernard from the passage, the one who couldn't stand dancing, but he no longer had it in him even to knock over Uncle Pepin, so he just ambled through the bar gnashing his toothless gums, he had a go at gnawing Uncle's long drawers, which were peeping out from under his trousers, but Uncle jerked back, and finally the two girls and the old man left off dancing, and Uncle was left to dance with Dedek the Saint Bernard, but it wasn't a dance any more, it was a defence, because Dedek was trying to knock Uncle over, but Uncle kept prancing away, prancing up in the air, still to the rhythm of the foxtrot, and Misses Marta and Bobinka applauded and wept and roared with laughter, while the old buffer went thoughtful for a moment, then banged his fabric a few times on the table, rested his head on the tablecloth, and roared with laughter: "Folks, life is just beautiful!" And in through the door the Saint Bernard had entered came Friedrich the engineer, quietly, wearing his Reichs uniform, tired, but suddenly irritable, he sat down and surveyed the company, Bobinka took Uncle and danced with him, and Mr Friedrich all of a sudden banged his fist on the table and said, "Enough!" And Bobinka went and sat down, while Uncle Pepin pointed at the soldier figure and said, "Is that him?" And he sat down and breathed out, Marta wiped his brow and combed his hair with the palm of her hand. "Didn't you hear the radio?" said Friedrich, "A man of such nobility falls, and you carry on dancing?" Bobinka said, "Hansi, remember, if you make a scene, I don't want to have anything to do with you ever again." And Friedrich went on, "The German Reich is fighting also for you." Bobinka said, "But we're not Germans. Hansi, you wouldn't inform on us!" Friedrich got up, lifted the gramophone lid and stopped the music. Uncle Pepin shouted, "If only we had a hundred Austrian divisions, my God, we'd soon have you lot beat! Old Freiher von Wucherer would give the order: *'Vorwärts! Nach Berlin!'* and we'd beat the lot of you!" Bobinka took Mr Friedrich by the sleeve and said, "The guv'nor means the Imperial armies, don't you, Pepin duck?" But Uncle bellowed right out, "Rubbish, I mean the bunch with the swastikas, we'd drive 'em right back tae Berlin, if only we had a hundred good Austrian divisions and the Archduke Karl in charge of 'em!" Bobinka changed the subject: "Hey, guv'nor, let's be having some softer stuff, let's hear some more from you about that sexual hygiene, let's have something for the ladies. What's the most important thing, maestro, according to Mr Batista's handbook?" And Uncle breathed out and darted his eyes at Mr Friedrich, but Bobinka stroked him and made him look her straight in the eye and coaxed him: "And then I'll let you see our nice new quilt covers, what about that, eh?" And Uncle Pepin gave her a smile and said, "Do you like to hear about it, eh? Well now, as ye ken, the main and most important thing is a right proper fully grown male organ, testes and a penis." "That's more like it," Marta commented, blissfully inhaling the smoke from her cigarette. Uncle carried on: "Auld Havránek, he went and tried to get himself run over due to his state of cohabitation alias conjugal relations, his wife used to eat apples the whole time they were at it, so auld Havránek, he took some sleeping powders and lay down on the line and fell asleep, and in the morning he woke up with all the trains going right past him, they'd been mending the line, and it was single-track working, so they never ran auld Havránek over at all, now you see according to Mr Batista's handbook intercourse should be executed properly in bed, in quiet peace and concentration, not with your auld wife crunching apples all the while ... But a hundred Austrian divisions would soon," said Uncle pointing at Mr Friedrich, "finish that lot." Mr Friedrich sipped his liqueur, crossed one leg over the other and said, "No they wouldn't." Uncle barked out, "Yes they would." Bobinka rushed to intervene: "So how could me and Marta here get ourselves in a bad kind of situation then?" And Uncle Pepin said, "How? Is there so little crime and calamity about? The newspapers are just stuffed with it! Now your proper respectable male organ's got to have a penis and a scrotum, then there's your testes and your decent epididymis as well, according to Mr Batista's handbook the penis has to have a foreskin, so-called, and the end alias beginning of the penis is termed the glans penis, then you need a nice fraenulum, and the scrotum's important as well, that's a kind of bag, that holds in the male glands . . ." Marta breathed: "The shy – I mean thyroid . . ." "What're ye babbling on about like young magpies? Those're somewhere in the chest, I'm talking about the glands alias balls or as Mr Batista crudely puts it, bollocks, now by feeling them you can tell according to Mr Batista's manual that there's an epididymis as well, but sometimes even the testes are missing, I mean to say they're there, but they've vanished up through the groin and into your abdominal cavity, or else they've got into your inguinal canal, now the special term for that is cryptorchidism." "You what?" said Bobinka taken aback, bringing in some glasses of coffee, "Cryptorchidism, cryptobollocks you mean?" And she gave a laugh in the direction of Mr Friedrich, who ordered a cup of hot chocolate and added, "No they wouldn't." Uncle Pepin rose up and brandished his elbow at Mr Friedrich: "Yes they would! They'd win hands down! Over these Germans!" But Mr Friedrich shook his head and said, "No they wouldn't!" And

Marta knelt in front of Uncle Pepin and clasped her hands: "So I'd really have to take a proper look and size it up beforehand like, would I?" And Uncle Pepin roared on: "You would, you wouldna be laughing if instead of a high-strung youth ye was to get a poofter or a pansy, or end up like it says in Mr Batista's handbook wi' a bisexual, there was one chap Gotlisch, now his scrotum according to Mr Batista's handbook was composed of two testicles, but instead of a penis he had a clitoris alias clitty, now if you was to end up with a chappy like that, that'd soon make ye weep . . ." Bobinka, when she saw that Uncle was about to shout "We'd beat 'em!" at Mr Friedrich again, she laid her hand over his mouth and said tenderly, "Where did you get those lovely speckly ears from, maestro?" And Uncle laughed happily: "That's right, it's paint, it's when I was painting a fence along with a certain lovely lady that sewed me a lovely pair of pants after by way of gratitude." "Made to measure, I bet, you faithless swine!" Marta said furiously and bustled about the bar stumbling over the blissfully snoozing old man, hugging his parcel of material and fast asleep on the floor. "What's this going on between you and that lovely lady what sews you them underpants?" Bobinka exclaimed as she carried in a steaming cup, a mug of hot chocolate. "You'll just have to make up your mind, it's either her or me, or nobody," she stamped her little shoe, "and if anything happens, if I go and do something to myself, then you!" she prodded Uncle in the chest till he felt a shock, "You've got me on your conscience!" "Wouldn't!" said Mr Friedrich after due consideration. "What are you on about? We'd win and we'd win hands down!'' roared Uncle, but Bobinka shook her finger in front of his face, ''Wait, it's me you have to be winning, but tell me now, when's the wedding to be?'' And Uncle Pepin melted, knitted his fingers and said, ''Once I've got my new wardrobe, and then you have to go and see the doctor, Mr Batista's handbook says, once you're up in years and unmarried for so long, you might have tendencies towards onanism alias self-defilement . . .'' ''What's all this? What's this he's accusing me of?'' Bobinka clasped her hands. ''That's when, instead of a proper decent male organ you uses your fingers, or in Mr Batista's book even a beer bottle or other objects that simulate this male member and substitute for the real sensation o' pleasure, just like now in wartime, when instead of coffee beans we drink this Perola stuff or your Caro Franckovka from Pardubice, and so the best thing would be if ye got married, coz you've got the prime pre-requisite, which is a decent upstanding physique . . .'' ''What really?'' said Bobinka, colouring. ''You've struck it lucky this time!'' Marta exclaimed. ''Aye she has that, only mind that for proper co-habitation as in Mr Batista's handbook there should be no railway traffic beneath our window, and no blacksmith's shop either, it's awful disturbing,'' Uncle Pepin rattled on eruditely, glowing radiant with delight. ''You wouldn't!'' said Mr Friedrich. ''What?'' bellowed Uncle, but Bobinka said, ''Stop it! Now you tell me, and me a silly goose and all, my only schooling's been this here bar, what's it like to possess a proper male organ. Eh?'' ''Well ye see, some have it like when they get in the bath, first they have to toss in their member and only then can they get in the water themselves, others have to use a pair of tweezers if they want to have a pee, but the main thing is you have to watch not to catch them veneral diseases like typhus, cholera, dysentery and influenza – what was that? Yes we would!" said Uncle, rising to his feet, as did Mr Friedrich, they stood facing one another and shouted thirty times into each other's face, "Yes we would!" "No you wouldn't!" "Would!" "Wouldn't!" and the bar girls ran about and separated the vociferating German and Uncle Pepin, they stuffed up their mouths, but Uncle always jerked himself free and roared, "Oh yes we would!" And suddenly Mr Friedrich was all ablaze with wrath, he pointed his finger and yelled and dictated with his finger: "And here you were, dancing, while our Herr Reichsprotektor, Heydrich, was fiendishly shot, when an assault was made, on his life! One more word out of you and I'm handing you in! Victory is ours!" And Uncle Pepin was silent, he knitted his fingers and stared at the ground, and Bobinka said softly, "No it's not!" and Friedrich threw his money on the table and walked out, and as he unfastened the door and went out into the dark, Bobinka called out after his disappearing back, "Hansi, don't you report a word of this, remember, if you do that's the end of you and me!" And Mr Friedrich did make a report, that Pepin had been dancing to celebrate the assassination of the Herr Reichsprotektor, but not to the Gestapo. He simply told Dad, and Dad was aghast, but Mr Friedrich waved his hand and said nobody else knew about it anyway, only he alone and the Žofín bar girls, so Dad devised a plan and confided in our police constable Mr Klohn, and Mr Klohn came up to the

brewery and that evening Dad had Pepin summoned to
the brewery office, and into the boardroom, and the
police constable took his seat and lit a candle and
interrogated Uncle on when he was born and what his
name was, and then he informed him that a report had
been made saying that Uncle Pepin had been dancing,
thereby expressing approval of the assassination of the
Herr Reichsprotektor, and he posed Uncle various
questions, and Uncle responded, and when he read out
the statement to Uncle, Uncle Pepin knitted his fingers
and felt all embarrassed, especially when the constable
stated that by this act he had harmed his brother, the
manager of the brewery, above all else, for the Germans
were ruthless and dragged the whole family into these
affairs, and hence Uncle Pepin by his dancing had
thwarted his brother's promotion, for it had been
expected he might be appointed managing director.
And then the police constable inquired if Uncle had
ever been wounded in the Great War. And Uncle Pepin
said, yes, in the head, the back of the neck, he'd lost a
whole bootful of blood. And the constable said, that
since he'd been wounded like that, the consequences of
the wound might have caused Uncle's mental state to
be impeded, and hence he had been dancing without
knowing what he was doing, and so the police
constable would consent to append an addition to the
written statement, stating that Uncle had been wounded
in the head when the Austrian armies proudly entered
Przemyśl on Corpus Christi day, 1916, and that the
consequences of the said wound still remained with him
to the present day, and he recommended further to
Uncle that he obtain a medical certificate stating that his

state of health was very poor, that he did things of which he was not himself aware, and that therefore he was not responsible for his own acts, he ought to go tomorrow right away to see Doctor Vojtěšek, who would issue him this certificate absolving Uncle Pepin of all awareness and associated responsibility for his actions. And Uncle went with Dad the very next morning and obtained just such a certificate, and when they brought it in the evening, the police constable read the whole statement out to Uncle again, requested him to append his signature, and finally he issued this appeal to him: "But if you promise me that never again will you go dancing in the public houses, bars and hostelries with ladies' service, then I shall regard this present statement as duly null and void . . ." And Uncle Pepin wept, while Dad slapped him on the back, and Uncle Pepin gave the police constable his hand, and the constable took the statement and tore it in two pieces, and each half he tore again in two, and once again, then he dropped the pieces of paper on to the floor of the boardroom and departed from the office. Dad then gathered the papers together, so that nothing would be lost, or found by an unauthorised person, and he threw the lot in the stove and burnt it, and when the paper had burnt up, Dad went out on his bicycle and caught up the police constable by the boundary wall and thanked him, squeezing his hand and pressing into it a thousand-crown note "for the official transaction". "And not before time," said the police constable, "that dancing of his would have landed the lot of you in a concentration camp." And so Mr Friedrich carried on seeing Bobinka in the Žofín bar, and when he and Uncle

Pepin met, they continued to shout at each other until
they were both hoarse and nobody had a clue why or
what they were shouting about to one another. Uncle
went on calling "Would! Would!" And Mr Friedrich
would call "Wouldn't!" And so they passed on their
way, still shouting at one another from a distance in
faint tones, like the dim lines of a number four writing
pencil, just to convince themselves that theirs was the
final trump call . . . But later on Mr Friedrich stopped
his shouting, and when the battle front started to shift,
Mr Friedrich found himself a corner beside the brewery
maltings, between an overhanging roof and two old
plum trees, and there he used to go every day, in the
early evening or even afternoon with a hacksaw, and
out of assorted poles and boughs he shaped and
fashioned a lovely bench, a sort of children's bench,
then he spent a whole Saturday and Sunday working
on a little table, and then with his saw and pocket knife
out of various staves and sticks and branches he made
chairs and seats, whenever it rained, he sat beneath the
overhanging roof and read and worked away, here in
this little child-size room of twigs and branches he even
made little wardrobes, which looked like birds' cages,
they opened and closed, you could fit a coat and a shirt
inside, then for a whole month Mr Friedrich worked on
a rocking horse, he even made a chandelier, and
whenever Mr Friedrich rode off to the garrison or to see
officials about where that machinery was for manufac-
turing munitions on the malting floors, the brewery
workers went to take a look, they were all amazed by
the work, they just stood there and marvelled and
wondered why the fellow was beavering away like this,

why he spent whole days and evenings playing with these toys ... And then the brewery workmen were seized by horror at this little child-size room, which was so absurd, but Uncle Pepin said, "Just take a good look at what that German's doing, just to stop himself thinking about how the allied armies are gloriously beating those German armies, the bitter end is nigh," he appended, "and that old gent can have his two suits of clothes sewn up now, because peace won't be long in coming ..." And so it was, Mr Friedrich was sad now, he was insecure, he could see that he would soon be going off somewhere else, but even there it would all be just the same, until the end finally came and other armies engulfed not only the country where he was now, but also his home, and the retribution would be proportionate to what his own armies had done in the countries they had entered uninvited ... And so he sat out there on the rocking horse and rocked himself up and down, evening in and evening out, till one day the order came and Mr Friedrich was summoned elsewhere. Dad said goodbye to him, but when he offered the workmen the things he was leaving behind, his sweaters and work coats and shoes hanging up in those see-through cupboards in the little nursery room made of twigs and sticks, nobody would take a thing, and it was as if Mr Friedrich was kind of see-through, transparent as well, he went and nobody bade him farewell, only Uncle Pepin shouted out after him, "We'd win! A glorious victory!" And Mr Friedrich departed with his suitcase to the station, softly observing, "Yes you win ..." and then nobody heard any more of him ever again ... The very next day the coopers took a canister of spirits and brought pails and buckets of water, and there behind the maltings they poured the spirits over that little nursery room, over the chairs and the wicker horse and the closets with the coats and sweaters, and they set it alight. The little room blazed up and burned away, but right up to the last moment that room defied the fire, it stood there still, and the stakes were wrapped in a fiery mane of flame, once again that room was there to be seen, but fiery throughout, until all at once the chairs and bench began to collapse all together, they fell to the ground, and then as if to a command blazed up even more strongly, the sticks twisted and dropped to the ground, as if they were burning only within the groundplan of those triple-storeyed things ... Only the rocking-horse carried on burning for a long time, it reared up with the fire and leaped, as if it wanted to leap over the flames, but as it reared it collapsed on its side, its hooves slackened and its mouth opened and its buckles twisted up from its mouth and smelt pungently of smoked meat, then the whole wicker horse stretched itself out, and the head cooper spattered more spirit on to the chandelier of twigs and lit it and it flared up, like some kind of heavenly portent, swiftly, and blazing feathers kept fluttering down from it, like feathers from the fiery phoenix bird, and finally the coopers with great showerings of water from their pitchers and buckets doused that little nursery room, which from the very start had been a better barometer and indicator of developments at the battle front than all the military despatches in the world.

EIGHT

Towards the end of the War, when petrol was running short, so that the brewery vehicles could still deliver the beer, our two lorries were altered to run on gas produced from burning wood. Dad, who used to drive round the villages to see the landlords, also had his Škoda 430 converted to this gas. And Uncle Pepin, who always got the jobs nobody else wanted to do, was appointed stoker on the lorry, and Dad appointed him stoker of the Škoda 430 to boot. Mr Fuks, a bookseller with a shop on the square, had a big Lancia, a sixteen-cylinder model, eight metres long, which he also converted to gas, the mechanics had to attach not just one, but two boilers to that splendid piece of bodywork. Every Saturday, first thing in the morning, two men stoked up the Lancia with oak chips, so that the car would be properly heated up by afternoon and have enough gas to last it out. Then in the afternoon Mr Fuks put on his white spa suit and got into his Lancia, the two mechanics stood behind on the running-board beside the boilers, and Mr Fuks drove out of his narrow yard, but he was always getting stuck fast in the entrance in such a way that the mechanics had to call in workmen with jacks and crowbars to lever the car off the side walls. So the mechanics had to put whitewash marks on the ground in the passage showing him where to drive in order to get out. But the minute he got out the fire in the boilers was always low again, so the mechanics had to stand there poking away with their hooks and piling on more oak chips, and the locals hung around ogling and staring, a lovely sight it was, this outing in his car, smoke rose up from the boilers at the rear, and the mechanics stood there poised to toss on more blocks of oak, and Mr Fuks drove off, through the square he went in his smart white clothes, and once they'd made a single circuit of the square, back he drove straight into his home yard, and again as he went in, like a piston thrusting into a cylinder, he kept getting the Lancia jammed in the passage, so that labourers had to come with jacks and crowbars and prise the vehicle off the wall, and straighten it up, so the mechanics put down more whitewash marks, showing which way the front tyres had to go, to help get the car back in the garage. The beer lorry which Uncle Pepin had to stoke was no better. Either Uncle Pepin stoked it up too much, or else too little, when they loaded the beer, Uncle Pepin bellowed away and engaged its one great boiler in battle with long hooks and pokers, cursing and apostrophising the boiler as if it were a horse or an ox or a stupid, obstreperous person. And so when the beer lorries came out of the brewery, the driver, who loved all this, spent the whole time in fits of laughter, and when there were lots of people on the square, he stopped, though nothing was holding him back, and said, "Josef, something's up with the engine, there doesn't seem to be enough gas, you'll have to go and take a look!" And Uncle Pepin got out of the cabin, bellowing, "Honestly – if Captain Tonser, whose sword I used to carry for him, was to see this Austrian sodger now, he'd he horrified!" And he jumped on the running-board, climbed over the side and put his ear to the boiler, then he gripped it with both hands and felt it over to test just how hot it was, then he raised the lid, every time it seemed as if the fire had gone out, but that was only for lack of air, suddenly the gas ignited and soot exploded into the air, a detonation rang out across the square, and a five-metre-high column of black smoke puffed up, with sparks flying all over the place, and when the smoke cleared, there was Uncle Pepin standing gripping on to the edge of the boiler, with the lid of it bowling over the square, Uncle black in the face with singed eyebrows stood there roaring, "Your Austrian sodger shows his worth in the tightest of situations. Victory is mine again!" And he took his hook and raked in the boiler and put on more chunks of oak, attached and closed the lid, which one of the braver onlookers brought back, because after the explosion all the townspeople had fled . . . And Pepin sat down in the delivery-man's cabin and yelled with enthusiasm. And so it was with every topping up and stoking of the boiler: Uncle Pepin failed to size up the situation properly, each time he thought it was all right to look in the boiler, because it had almost gone out, but when he lifted the lid to get a proper look, every time a loud report followed and fiery smoke belched upward, like a rocket going off, and always Uncle Pepin failed to get his face away in time and each time the smoke lashed his cheeks. And so it happened once, when a funeral was passing, and Uncle was raking about in the boiler, the horses took fright, they bolted and ran, and another time a platoon of German soldiers were passing on their way back from drill all singing "*In der Heimat, in der Heimat*", and after the detonation from the boiler all the soldiers dropped to the ground and took cover, and nearly smashed up the beer lorry, because they thought it was an attempted ambush. On Corpus Christi day the driver said, being a free-thinker, just as the line of girls came past scattering flowers and he was unloading beer for the Catholic Hall, with its altar of birch boughs out in front, the driver said to Uncle Pepin, "The boiler's going out, we won't be able to get started ..." And Uncle Pepin just lifted the lid up a little, and the soot caught fire and the gas ignited and the smuts exploded in the air, and the soot solemnly showered the procession of children in their white and blue, as they scattered flower petals out of their baskets, and though the gust failed to seize the monstrance out of the reverend priest's hands, no one was able to stop the portable canopy from soaring up, breaking free from their grasp and floating off over the square like a red, gold-lined sail, like a flying Persian carpet ... Another time during the annual market fair, just as they were delivering beer at Beránek's on the corner, Uncle was stoking up, just about to put some more on, and him already so black from these explosions, it didn't wash off, like a true boilerman, swarthy as an Italian or a Gypsy, with singed eyebrows and bald-headed, because his hair or cap always caught fire as well, and again the driver expressed doubts as to whether it was really burning in there, suggested he rake it with the poker, but leave the top well alone, however Uncle, after listening with his ear pressed against the boiler to hear if there was any roaring sound, thought it had really gone out this time, so he lifted the lid and again a loud report rang out in the middle of the fair, and after the detonation and concomitant smoke the villagers scattered and fled, tripping over the trestles, the guy-ropes of the stalls and the canvas awnings, and the stalls collapsed, children screamed and screeched, stallholders cursed and swore, but the onlookers and customers, as they scattered and radiated out from the centre of the vehicle, they stumbled over the raised trestles and tumbled planks, entangled themselves in the fabric and sheeting, and worst of all, on open ground they ran into piles of earthenware pots, and it took hours for the fair to get going again ... But towards the end of the War Dad no longer used the car even to fetch lumps of beech-wood, he didn't even go out and tinker with the car either. Uncle Pepin went on going into town though, and he met with ever greater acclaim, especially after people found out that Uncle Pepin had danced on that night to celebrate the assassination of the Reichsprotektor Heydrich, then the gates and windows opened for him all the more, and more and more people wanted, if not to speak to Uncle Pepin, then at least to see this hero, who went on sallying forth to visit his lovely ladies in his corvette captain's seafaring cap, as if nothing had happened. No one in town was willing to come and tinker with the car with Dad any more, partly because there was a company of Reichs soldiers stationed in the brewery, and partly because they had all taken their turn tinkering with Dad one Saturday and Sunday already. Then came the mobilisation of all means of transport, Dad jacked his car up on blocks, and one night he woke Uncle Pepin up, Dad removed the wheels and put all the pieces in sacks, and then they took the tyres, and the spare tyre as well, went up on to the brewery roof, and Dad opened the top of an old chimney and first he let down a rope, then he lowered Uncle Pepin down the shaft with a torch, and whispered, "What's it like down there?" And Uncle Pepin reported back merrily that the soot was right up to his chest . . . And Dad was content: "That's the best preservative, just like putting it in a bath of oil, better than storing the parts in graphite or plumbago or covering them with tallow or pork fat . . ." Then Dad lowered all the parts to the bottom, and Uncle untied them and stowed them away for better times, at the bottom of that chimney which hadn't been used for twenty years or more. Then Dad passed down one tyre after another, but as he was lowering the last one, the spare tyre, it broke loose and fell, Dad yelled out, "Jožka, watch out!" There was a dull thud, and soot carried on billowing out of the chimney for ages, Dad leaned forward into that cloud of soot and called, "Jožka, are you all right?" And Uncle Pepin's merry yell resounded from below: "Nothing happens to a proper Austrian sodger, I'm victorious again! How d'ye like that!" But the hiding place was no longer necessary. The front had shifted so far that now even the trains had stopped, wounded German soldiers made their way through town on their own, on foot, those who couldn't walk were carted along in barrows, they stood by the ferry in the first village along the Elbe, asking the ferryman to take them across, they stood wretchedly, the white colour of plaster predominant, they resembled pieces of modern art, the bits left over when the plaster wraps are taken off, all along the verdant river bank in the fresh grass and yellow buttercups, legs and arms with gunshot wounds and broken collarbones and bandaged heads, they felt themselves over and stood, stretching out their arms and offering coins, chains and watches in their palms, and the ferryman scratched himself behind the ears, but finally he took all the wounded Germans across in groups, the wounded soldiers thought that over there on the other side of the river they might still find their fleeing armies, they reckoned they still had a chance of getting home, but the ferryman knew there were partisans lying in wait at blockades of felled timber, drains and gullies and roadside ditches, with their machine-guns and rifles at the ready, he knew they'd all had it, but he ferried them across all the same, because, though he had no liking for Germans, nor could he, when he saw that hope in their eyes, that moment of joy at the prospect of being saved, when he saw how pleased they would be to haul their shining bandages and plaster out on to the far bank, then why should he begrudge them their little bit of happiness? Just like those condemned to death, when they have their last realisable wish fulfilled on their last night. And the Germans stuck white pieces of clothing on poles, and set off on their march to the Promised Land. That was the last detachment of Germans, after that a few britzkas still came ricketing about this way and that with their bolting horses and frightened Germans, and in the evening the Russians came, and the Soviet Army. That night Grandad, Mum's father, stole off to pick some fresh lilac blossom, the Russian soldiers were occupying his yard and they lay down in the beds and fell asleep with their weapons in their hands, they slept like logs, outside the room where the colonel was sleeping a soldier lay across the threshold with his gun and slept and simultaneously kept watch and guarded the colonel, and towards dawn Grandad came with that fresh lilac and tried to put it in a vase, but the vase was in the kitchen, and Grandpa, when he wanted something, he always had to have it, as usual he was so blinded by his desire that he didn't even notice that the big vase in the sideboard was only there because along with a couple of books it was acting as a vertical support for one side of the dresser, so, holding the plucked lilac in one hand, with the other he tore at that vase, which was holding up a number of plates and sauce-boats and assorted crockery, he tore at it, yelling away, "Nan, where the heck are you, come and give us a hand!" And he went on tearing away at that vase, full of joy over the lovely bouquet of flowers he was going to put on the colonel's table . . . And then he shouted again: "Girls, where have you got to, for Pete's sake! Nana!" But Grandma and the maid were holding a pitcher, into which a Soviet butcher was tossing the liver from a disembowelled cow, so Grandad roared out, "Come here, you fucking bitches, why don't you help me? Damn and blast you!" And he roared it out, because he wanted to give the Soviet soldiers this lovely surprise of lilac blossom . . . And Grandma came scurrying up, just as Grandpa had succeeded in ripping out the vase, and at that very moment the sideboard caved in with a crash, Grandpa stamped on the crockery and yelled, "You bitches, why didn't you come when I called?" And Grandma rushed to close the windows, but Grandpa opened them again and yelled out of the window to the neighbours, "Stupid idle bitches, won't even come and get you a fucking vase!" And Grandma shouted out the window, "It's not true!" and shut the windows again, but Grandpa opened some more and yelled out, "Stupid bitches, I'll slay the lot of you!" Then he stamped on the crockery, pulled down the whole dresser including the remaining unbroken plates, he stamped and cursed, but then he started stamping a bit less and more slowly, even quit shouting, he sat down, laid the lilac blossoms in his lap; he was shuffling his feet and trying to say something. When Grandma bent over him, he just whispered, "Nan, God bless . . . I'm passing on . . ." And shortly after, Grandma took Grandpa's pulse, and seeing Anka opening the shed to drag an old cupboard out into the yard, she opened the window and said, "We shan't be needing none of them wardrobes no more," nipped on her bike to fetch the doctor and called in at the undertaker's to have them come over during the afternoon . . . Later that day Dad and Mum put a black band on their coat lapels and got out their black clothes, while Uncle Pepin in his white sailor's cap went to join in the celebrations, down at the landing place by the river the Russians brought along their accordions, they passed round chunks of roast meat and bottles of vodka, by nightfall they were drunk, a number of the locals couldn't take this bout of enormous toasts to good health and this drinking to the end of the war, toasts of vodka drunk out of mustard glasses, they vomited in the half-light over by the fence, and the alcohol was so powerful, they were ripping off the planks they clutched on to in the half-light and careering backwards through the yard illuminated with fires and lights, someone even threw up at home in a washbasin set into the wall, and he ripped that porcelain basin right out and went careering backwards over the front doorstep, on to the street, and backwards he went, still gripping on to that basin, he careered right through the dancers and landed on the river bank with the basin on top of him. Only Uncle Pepin drank and clinked glasses with all and sundry, and the more he drank, the soberer he was, he let himself be lured into dancing with the foremost dancer in the army, responding to his little Cossack dance with one of his own, but he embellished it with an extra leap in the air concluded by the splits, then Uncle was enticed by another soldier into some kind of Savoy medley, incorporating a quick Armenian number, a dance with variations a bit like the Moravian Slovaks do, with intricate footwork, Uncle Pepin cottoned on straight away and embellished the footwork to the rhythm of the accordion, with lunging leaps in the air, a flying knave of diamonds, who, before landing, twisted about in the air, then did a forward and a backward somersault on the ground, and the Russian soldiers were crazy about him and clapped and cheered, "*Bravo, papashka! Bravo, papashka!*" Then another soldier tried Uncle Pepin with a sword dance, he fussed like a cockerel, leaping over an imaginary sword, avoiding its sharp cutting edge, while Uncle Pepin got his breath back, surrounded by his lovely barmaids and beauties, and went on drinking toasts with all and sundry, getting himself ready for his next dance, which he embellished just as he had seen the pair Fuks and Košťálová do, as if he had a dancing partner as well, he leapt up and did a handstand, just like he used to do with Miss Vlasta on the billiard table, it seemed as if Uncle Pepin's lifelong dancing experience had all been building up to this one encounter, where for the first time in his life he found himself with real partners to match, who danced like this, not as a laugh or a joke, but because this was the habitual way for them to dance back home, and so here for the first time Uncle was dancing not just to entertain and give people a bit of a laugh, but for the sake of the dance itself, he could see that the soldiers too were making the dance a contest, they were consulting amongst each other to see who to send up to win a victory over this *papashka*, since they couldn't defeat him with alcohol, which they were accustomed to, but which Uncle Pepin drank just like they did, clinking glasses with his neighbours and drinking for those who couldn't take it, or couldn't take any more. And everybody could see that of all the locals round the landing place, the Russians respected and admired Uncle Pepin most, they accorded him the honour of a seat next to the bandmaster, and finally the bandmaster even gave Uncle Pepin a stick of willow and requested him to conduct the brass band, which had come to play in honour of victory. After the dances were over, and the soldiers were slapping Uncle on the back and calling him *papashka*, and he'd conducted the band, the best Russian dancer agreed that Uncle was as fine a dancer as he himself was, and declared, "I'm taking this *papashka* back with me to Moscow." But Uncle Pepin said he couldn't, he had to pitch barrels at the brewery the next day, he wouldn't have time till Saturday afternoon, when he could come over to Moscow in an aeroplane if they had any dancing contest for him. For, he added, "Your Austrian soldier is always victorious, wherever he may be." That night Dad wore his black mourning clothes to wait for Uncle Pepin as he returned at crack of dawn from seeing his barmaids, he took Uncle Pepin up to the roof of the maltings, took off the lid on top of the blocked-off old chimney, lowered Uncle Pepin on the end of a rope and pulled up one part after another, finally the car tyres . . . When everything was safely up, Dad listened, but he couldn't hear a peep out of Uncle down at the bottom of the chimney. "Jožka, Jožka!" Dad called down the chimney, he shone his torch down, but all that came straying up from the depths of this black gullet were plumes of soot, one after the other. "Jožka, say something!" Dad cried out in despair, then he ran down to the office, where Mr Vaňátko the watchman was fast asleep under the crane wrapped in his bandoleer, he woke him up, but the watchman was so drowsy that at first he thought robbers were after the safe, and he was delighted, but Dad explained that Uncle Pepin was in the chimney and making not a sound, so Mr Vaňátko said, "Just a minute!", clicked his heels, saluted and reported: "Night-watchman Vaňátko reporting for duty, action stations . . ." And he untied Trik his faithful little doggie, and climbed up with Dad on to the roof of the maltings, then he shone his torch and both called down one after the other, then they tried it both together in chorus, but there was complete silence down below . . . Watchman Vaňátko was full of delight, he took off his Entente belt, laid aside his Mexican rifle and his revolver, Dad put a rope round his chest, and Mr Vaňátko saluted, clicked to attention and reported, "Night-watchman ready for action, sir!" Then he stood easy and Dad lowered him slowly down the chimney . . . And Mr Vaňátko called up, "Reporting, Mr Josef's here, but he's asleep! Taking a nap!" And Dad cried, "Tie him to the rope!" And Mr Vaňátko called up, "He's tied, haul away!" And Dad laboriously hauled Uncle Pepin up, the rope scraped against the edge of the chimney, but slowly yard by yard Uncle ascended out of the seven-metre-high chimney. When Uncle's head finally appeared, totally black, Dad didn't have the strength to grasp Uncle by the hand or hold him by the armpits, because he had to hold on to the rope from which Uncle was hanging. When it seemed at last as if he was going to have to let Uncle back down again, Mr Vaňátko called up from below, "Go and tie the rope to the lightning conductor!" . . . And for the first time ever Dad was truly glad that Mr Vaňátko had come to the brewery all those years ago, because for the first time he found that what the watchman was proposing was good advice. He fastened the rope, tied it firmly round the cramp-iron on the lightning conductor, took Uncle by the armpits and pulled him out, then, totally exhausted and wiped out, he slumped right over with his brother into the yellow bed of houseleeks, and there

Uncle went on slumbering, sound asleep, lying on his back crowned with a coronet of cold stars. And Dad pulled out Mr Vaňátko as well, fervently squeezing his hand in gratitude at first, but that was too little, he embraced him, and Mr Vaňátko gave him a military kiss with his blackened mouth. Then, with a shock, they both had the same thought: Where was that sailor's cap? They shone a light down, but the pool of soot had closed over again, and of the white cap there remained not a trace . . .

NINE

The foreman stood inside the gate as usual holding a notebook in his hand, the workmen went on coming to work just as before, but that was only a superficial semblance. They avoided greeting the foreman, all deliberately turned up a quarter of an hour late, and the foreman was transparent, non-existent, a non-person. He jotted things down, noted down late arrivals in his book with sarcastic comments, but when he was sorting out the work for the day the assistant cooper said, "We don't need you as a bailiff over us any more, and we don't need Mr Frantz acting as king of the castle either, we're going to sort out things for ourselves from now on." And the foreman said, "As long as I'm your appointed superior and the brewery management board which appointed me remains in charge, you're going to have to go on taking your orders from me." But the assistant cooper declared, "Only from now on, this brewery is a national enterprise, and there's no more bosses any more, we're the masters now, and from now on a factory council is in operation, and I'm the chairman . . ." And off he went and the foreman stood there in a sudden state of shock, and when he came back from the office, he suddenly looked quite small. He went to find the assistant cooper and he said tearfully, "But I'm one of you, I was employed for years in the fermenting cellar as an ordinary workman." But the assistant cooper retorted, "You were against us all along the line, you always wanted whatever the boss wanted, a boss's love is a pain in the back, moreover you used to play the boss and lord it over us, and we can't forgive you that, it was unforgiveable . . ." The foreman remonstrated further, "But you didn't accept me . . ." But the assistant cooper said, "No we didn't, but now we're telling you to quit, we've decided to do without you . . . Anyway, your letter of notice is in the post, and the best thing for you is just to get along home now . . ." And the foreman went away, then he came back again, and just as before it had always seemed like a dream, to have reached the position of foreman, and he couldn't believe it all those years ago, now he had to return to the brewery yard once more, because he just couldn't believe what had happened, he thought he was dreaming, it was impossible for him to get the sack like this, but nobody noticed him, nobody paid him any more attention, he was see-through, transparent, because he'd lost his authority, he could no longer sack a worker and take on somebody else in his stead, workmen no longer crumpled their caps in their hands in front of him, asking humbly for a job, for they were the masters now. And so it happened, that when Mum started picking the apples that autumn, and when the foreman came too to pick the apples from his own perquisite trees, bringing his own containers and ladders, standing there on the ladder and handing down basketfuls of apples for his tearful wife to pour into big laundry baskets, while Mum and two other women were picking apples for their own baskets, suddenly his wife burst into tears, saying that Mum was picking apples from her tree, picking those Tubby Rattlers that had always belonged to her . . . But Mum said the foreman had no say in the matter any more, these trees were hers now, Dad was still employed and, according to long-standing agreements, as brewery manager he had the right to one half, and the halfway mark ran through the orchard, taking in the row that the foreman had taken wrongly in the first place, so the foreman's wife climbed up the ladder behind Mum and started picking those Tubby Rattlers, and Mum deliberately started scraping the mud off her boots, and the dried mud spattered the wife's face and hair, but she carried on all the same, so Mum came back down the ladder, treading on the wife's knuckles gripping the ladder rungs, and forcing her to come down too, so the foreman's wife took Mum's basket of apples and poured it into her own, and then the two women turned face to face, it looked as if they would go for each other, they started their run-up, all ready to grab the other's hair and rip the other's blouse and give vent to their long-standing hatred, roused by this autumn apple-picking, when at that moment three workmen came over from the maltings led by the assistant cooper, and when they arrived the cooper said, "The perks are finished, over and done with, the fruit garden is ours. The whole of it – take your ladders away, from now on we're the ones who are going to pick the fruit, we've got children and grandchildren, and even if we didn't, the orchard belongs to all of us now, it doesn't belong to the bosses any more ..." And Dad came through the garden, dodging the branches, and when he overheard the end of the conversation, he observed in a quiet voice, "But I never acted the boss." The assistant cooper replied affably, "No, sir, you didn't, you were kind and decent to us, but the fact you were decent just makes it worse now, because you were serving the bosses then, but now we are the bosses, and since you're here, you might as well know that you're not going to stay on as manager, we're going to appoint a new manager from the ranks of the workers, the unions are going to give us a workers' manager, because from tomorrow all the nationalised shares are to be sold only to the workers, and we are the shareholders of the brewery, so it's our right to appoint the people in charge, just as the bourgeois limited-liability company had the right to appoint its own people to run the firm in the past ... You, missus, take the apples you've already picked, and you too, lady, take the apples you've picked as well, and go home now, manager, sir, you've got three months' notice, you needn't come in to the office on Monday, because we've already got our own director. You were decent to us, and that has to count against you, because it meant that you blunted the edge of the class struggle, do you see?" Dad shook his head and said, "Not entirely, but I get the message, I'll go and fix my things ..." And as he went off with the three members of the factory council the cooper turned again and then, with an effort, but all the same, he said, "We're also going to start clearing out the garage today, right away, take away your car, and all the canisters and spare parts too, we'll put all the stuff beside the wall for you . . .' And Mum went red to the roots of her hair, taking the baskets full of apples she turned them out on to the trampled grass, she piled the smaller baskets inside the bigger ones, laughed, and said to Dad, "Now we'll begin a new life," she stroked him and gave him a laughing smile and he stared her right in the eye, he hadn't expected this from Mum, then he took the handles of the baskets and off they went, looking round as if for the last, or the first time at this beautiful brewery orchard, where together they had lived for a quarter of a century, and the garden they saw was beautiful as it had never been before, the apples on the boughs offered colours and scents made for a final journey through this garden where they used to hang out the washing on lines, where Mum used to pick daisies and other meadow flowers, but all they had to do was close their eyes and in their minds they were back in this garden once more, when Mum closed her eyes not only could she count all the trees from beneath her closed eyelids, but she could tell each tree apart just like remembering people, their faces and movements, and their tiny flaws . . . And when Dad had carted off the spare parts to the new shed beside their own house which they had bought a few years back, when he had hauled the Škoda over, he returned to the office for the last time, emptied his drawers, and took his pens, while the new director opened his mail, drinking beer first thing in the morning as he was accustomed, he opened the post and distributed it and waited for Dad to go, and Dad waited, lingered, went out to the brewery again, he'd left some empty canisters deliberately by the wall, he lingered there too, but none of the workmen came up to him, nobody said goodbye to him, nobody said he was sorry, not a single word, they walked straight past as if he wasn't there, as if never in his life had he given their wives a lift in his Škoda and on his motorbike when they were about to give birth, or taken their children off to holiday camp, as if he'd never only recently lent them the lorries and cars for transporting new furniture or material for buildings and houses they were putting up, and so Dad went off, as if guilty of something, he departed like the foreman. When Dad had carted off the last box of pens and tiny calendars and notebooks, he opened the cupboard and took out the two portly lamps, the light of which he had used to write by all those years ago, and which were ready and waiting, in case the electricity failed, the portly lamps with green shades, and as he was carrying them off, the workers' director remarked, "But those lamps are listed in the brewery inventory . . ." and he took them out of Dad's hands. "I'll buy them," said Dad quietly. But the workers' director shook his head and said in an alien voice, "You've bagged enough already, and you've built yourself a villa . . ." And when Dad left the office, this was what the workers' director had been waiting for, he took both lamps with their green shades and he threw them out of the window on to a heap of lumber and scrap, and the green shades and cylinders smashed to pieces and Dad clutched his head and there was a crumpling sound inside, as if his brain had been smashed. "The new era's beginning here too," said the workers' director, and he went into his office. And on that same day, when Dad and Mum moved house, after they had hung up the last curtains, when Dad had fixed his name on the little wall with a screwdriver, just when he had screwed the green letter-box carefully on to four blocks of wood, Uncle Pepin came over from the brewery with two suitcases, a swallow-tailed butterfly was fluttering round his head, and wherever he went, after him this brown butterfly with peacock-feather eyes on its wings came fluttering, hovering over him. When Uncle Pepin put the suitcases down to get his breath back, the swallow-tail rose up above him like a dove announcing the Immaculate Conception, Dad looked at Uncle, and Mum came out, and when she saw the butterfly she said, "Uncle Jožin, where are you off to, and what's that butterfly doing over your head?" And Uncle Pepin gave a wave of the hand and said, "Silly thing's been following me a' the way from the brewery, the moment I left the lodgings, it started off after me . . . I keep drivin' it off, but it willna go." And Mum asked, "And where are you going, Uncle? On your holidays, is it? On a trip, to visit your lovely ladies? Which one's invited you?" And Uncle Pepin said, "No, no, I'm a pensioner ye see, I'm just coming to ye for a wee visit. All I've got is here in my hands." And Mum took fright, she made a motion with both hands as if she was warding off a black storm and her hair bristled in horror. But Dad smiled and said, "Come on in then, brother." And Mum whispered to Dad, "He'll stay till the day he dies now, you'll see . . ." But Dad just smiled again and said, "So what?"

And so Uncle Pepin moved into the basement flat, and some kind of other time began, Dad got started on the garden, and as he worked he started to change, he that had always drunk coffee and a piece of dry bread with it now began to eat meat, and liked a good beer, he that had once loathed onion now just loved it. And as he ate, his voice grew stronger too, he liked to rail and shout, and the more he shouted, the stronger his voice grew, and the shouting began to give him a real appetite, and when they slaughtered a pig, Dad not only ate up all the soup from it, but he even ate the cold boiled pig's head and neck, and he ate the sausages without any bread and drank beer with it. But Uncle Pepin, who'd been so fond of his food, and wherever he was invited would eat six dinners and drink up whatever he was offered, Uncle Pepin began to go back to his beginings, becoming what Francin had used to be like in terms of food, and he would leave his meat and ask for just a mug of milk or coffee and a piece of bread. "There's no helping it, sister-in-law," he said, "if ye're no working ye dinna want to eat." But as he reduced his intake and ate only staples, potatoes and soup, so he stopped shouting too, stopped railing and carrying on, he no longer had any reason to roar away with his tirades at the whole town, he just waved his hand, and when Francin railed and shouted and carried on, Uncle Pepin pacified him, clasped his hands, stuffed up his ears and begged Francin to be quieter. And so the brothers worked together during the day in the garden, but Uncle claimed his eyesight was starting to get poor, so Francin gave him the hoe, fixed up strings, and Pepin hoed the vegetables, but when he hoed up the cabbages along with the weeds Francin shouted, and Pepin could only dig the paths. He dug out those paths so much, however, that he made them into ditches, but Francin was just glad that Uncle was getting a bit of exercise, so Uncle went on digging, but gradually less and less, he sat around, and learnt to walk with the careful step of the blind or poor-sighted, fumbling in front of himself with outstretched hands, as if some obstacle were constantly about to cross his path, "Like walking in water," he used to say, and then he couldn't even find the path, and when Dad led him on to it, again he couldn't feel to find the hoe, and when Dad put it in his hand, he dug helplessly and couldn't keep his direction and dug the path out into the beds, and Francin yelled and roared. And so the neighbours, knowing Uncle Pepin of old, started to proffer advice at the fence: "Mr Josef, what about just getting two steam engines in and ploughing up the whole garden?" But Uncle Pepin just felt for the edge of the path, sat down, and Francin shouted back, "What d'you mean, you great idiot, d'you think we can just haul some great threshing-machine in here between these trees? A monster like that, how'd we ever get it in here? It'd knock down the fence! Who did you get that from?" And the neighbours held on to the wire fence with their fingers and said, "Mr Josef, Captain Meldík suggested it, the fellow that's chairman of the gardeners' organisation." And Uncle Pepin gaped into the distance, and was far away, while Francin shouted, "What's a chap like Meldík doing being chairman of the gardeners' organisation? He was never a captain in the army anyway." And the neighbour insisted, "He was, sir, and he's been saying, 'Know those two lads at the villa, I need to show them a bit of gardening. Pipsy now . . .'" And Dad shouted,

"How can a cretin like that teach anyone gardening? Pipsy, eh? I'll give him Pipsy! He's got about as much grey matter in his noddle as my brother and me have up our arses!" Dad exclaimed pungently. And the neighbour said, "Meldík reckoned he'd teach you how to cultivate clover, you see, and then you could have a few goats, but you'd have to dig up the garden really deep with a coulter ..." "What d'you mean cultivate goats, it's not that simple," shouted Dad brandishing the hoe. "Goats are bloody guzzlers, once one swallowed three gulden from Mum's purse, and another time we put out a bucket of pork fat to cool and the goat drank the lot, leave goats out of this, you cretin!" And Mum opened the window and said: "We could put the goat-shed next to the garage, we'd make something from it." And Dad cleared his throat and shouted back at Mum, "You're all cretins, you always lose money on goats!" But Mum stuck to her guns: "Not at all, I'd like to have a nice quiet pair of goats, it'd wake you up in the morning, and it'd be nice to take them out to pasture, in the fresh air ..." But Francin shouted that they could keep their fresh air, and he started shouting at his brother, who wasn't fighting back any more, he was somewhere else now, he didn't feel the need to shout, nothing he heard riled him now, nothing gave him cause to get angry, he just sat there on the edge of the path, sat on a board and felt the sunlight, as if he were in a warm bath, and he needed nothing more to complete his happiness, just what was around him, that warm silence. "I can't see any more," said Pepin, and Francin started shouting, "What d'ye mean, 'can't see'? You don't want to see, that's what it is!" And Uncle Pepin said quietly, "I wouldn't be able to feel my way to find the goats, except in the shed." And Mum said from the window, "Then I'd take you out to the pasture, I'd tether the goats to your arm, Uncle Jožin, out in the pasture," she went on happily, glad to have inveigled Uncle into the game, but Uncle Pepin looked in through the window, where the pale curtains were glistening, and waved his hand and said, "Oh never mind . . ." "But there'd be the milk, and goat's milk goes to the blood!" the neighbour said with hope in his voice, but instead of Uncle Pepin, who had drifted off into definitive silence with that wave of the hand, Francin shouted back, "What's that you say? My brother Pepin, what got cognac and champagne from his lieutenants and entertained the young ladies and conducted sociable conversation till the police rolled him up and brought him home like linoleum, my Pepin's supposed to start drinking goat's milk, is that it?" The neighbour spread his two palms in a fan and said, "But this brilliant man, who enjoyed so much to sing and dance, if he was to sing to these goats they'd produce lots more milk, Michurin writes that when you sing and play music to the cows it improves their milk yield . . ." But instead of Pepin it was Dad who angrily remonstrated in reply: "What's all this? Michurin tells us you can grow apples on willow trees, by grafting them on, but what can he know about raising goats? How dare you?" Dad shouted and adopted a bayonet pose and called out, "Come on, Pepin, let's give him your *einfacher Stoss*, give him one right in the nose, like good Austrian soldiers, come on, hit him!" And Dad lunged out straightaway with the blade, with the end of the hoe through the wires, adding joyfully, "And your Austrian soldier wins again . . ." and he looked across at his brother, but Uncle Pepin was quiet and silent, looking another way, he just waved his hand as though what had been said was no longer worth a single exclamation, a single motion, all was vanity of vanities. Yet still there was one more occasion on which Uncle allowed himself to be swept along by Francin, they started going out picking mushrooms and other edible fungi. But there again Francin had to employ cunning, the first time they went out to the woods near Dymokury, Francin bought three boletuses beforehand to take with him, and as they rode off in the train that morning they could see there were another hundred mushroom-pickers travelling with them, when they got to Rožd'alovice, they all poured out, a whole herd of mushroom-pickers all livid with one another, and all the woods re-echoed to their cries and calls and summonings. But Francin knew how to dispose of the pickers who constantly got in their way and crossed their path, he let them pass and right at the edge of the wood he took out one of the boletuses he'd bought and lifted it up to show one of the pickers hurrying by and said, "So you're just going to leave these ones behind are you?" And he lifted up this bought boletus, and the mushroom picker stood there lightning-struck, and Dad cleaned up this nice boletus and put it in Uncle's basket, and Uncle handled it and sniffed it and was blissfully ecstatic, and so in this way Dad made use of all three of the bought boletuses to remove the other pickers from their path, each time he lifted the second, and then the third boletus to a passing picker, and any picker behind whom Dad had found a mushroom was so devastated with jealousy, that it put him off his hunting. And so the two brothers walked on through the woods, Francin led the way for Uncle across ditches, and then they sat, Uncle took the boletuses, sniffed them, and Dad shouted with happiness. But then so many pickers started taking the train out from their little town where time had stood still, that Dad said they'd better start going in the afternoon, but the rest of the mushroom-pickers must have started saying the same, and so they all met again at the railway station in the afternoon, then they decided to go by bus, but again all the mushroom-pickers who used to go by train turned up for the bus, so Dad said the best thing would be if they started taking the car, but in the morning at crack of dawn, out of this little town where time had stood still, a whole great long column of cars and motorbikes and cycles set off, all again in the same direction, so that there they all were again in the woods with everyone within eyeshot and at arm's reach. So Dad made up his mind, and following the legacy of Professor Smotlach, they started collecting both inedible and suspect fungi and toadstools. Dad took with him a saucepan and a pat of butter and he and Uncle Pepin began to practise some experimental mycology. This way they always had fungi almost from late spring up to the end of autumn. They started by picking grey tall amanita and bunches of sulphur tuft, they kindled a fire, softened onion in butter, and added a pinch of common earthball and panther cap. Dad handed the fried concoction of fungi to Uncle Pepin first, waited half an hour and asked Uncle, "Jožka, you don't fancy you hear any ringing sounds, do you?" And then, since Uncle wasn't hearing any ringing sounds, or rather he was, but it was only the clanging of the bell from the church or the tinkling of a bicycle bell, Dad ate some of the mixture too and pronounced it quite excellent. Once however they stayed in the woods for a whole five hours, Dad had added a bit more earthball or truffle, and when they'd eaten some there they stayed stuck in the woods for hours, because their legs had gone numb. Uncle Pepin rejoiced that he wouldn't ever have to walk again, he'd be an invalid, they'd have to push him about in a wheelchair. But a couple of hours later Uncle Pepin was to be disappointed. The strength returned to their limbs and they got to the station and returned safely home. By that time Francin was starting to feel enormously fit after all those suspect toadstools and fungi, and they took Mum along with them as well, but by now they were both so far gone that they fried up a mixture of bitter boletus, and lurid boletus, and sulphur tricholoma or gas tar fungus, as well as a few common white helvella, which according to Professor Smotlach contains helvellic acid . . . And first of all they gave this tasty concoction to Mum to try, and when after half an hour Mum still couldn't hear any ringing sounds in her ears, they had some too, and subsequently Mum pickled the helvella they had collected in vinegar and pronounced it really excellent, far better than ordinary edible boletuses. Then Francin got the idea that if you took this pickled helvella, put it in tarragon vinegar with chanterelle, hydnum, known as urchin of the woods, and a tree fungus called chicken of the woods, then it could be served in a cocktail, sprinkled with lemon juice and a spot of Worcester and Tabasco sauce, for such a combination tasted just like the finest shellfish and lobsters. And one day it happened that they got off the train at Třebestovice, and after Francin had led Pepin by the hand across the football ground near a little wood, Francin said, "What's that red patch over there?" And they went back, and were amazed, they knelt down and filled a basket piled high with beautiful orange birch boletuses. And then they sat in the sandy ground by the woods and warmed themselves, and later back at the station the other mushroom-pickers, who'd been out looking all day and had only a couple of edible mushrooms to show for it at the bottom of their baskets, shouted at them and said they must have bought them somewhere, that Francin and Pepin were just out to provoke them. And so it happened that same evening, when Mum for the first time in ages cooked up those classic edible mushrooms, all three of them were horribly sick and Uncle Pepin had fainting fits and diarrhoea, then he got a dreadful thirst and vomited again, and this was followed by a dull headache, cramps in the calves and intermittent double vision as well as continuous ringing sounds in the ears. When they took them all off to hospital, because their legs had been numb for six hours, the consultant said they'd all been poisoned by edible fungi, the last person that had happened to was Professor Smotlach himself, found in a deep coma after partaking of edible mushrooms.

TEN

One day Dad came back with Uncle and no fungi, but full of enormous enthusiasm. The next day Dad bought the biggest size of lorry tyres, loaded them in his Škoda 430, removed the back seats and put in his tool kit and stuff, as well as his treadle lathe, and Uncle Pepin too, they took several days' worth of food with them and blankets and drove out to the woods. The day before, when they'd been out searching for mushrooms, Dad had discovered a lorry in the bushes, it was a White, and it totally enchanted him, the lorry had no tyres, it was all overgrown with brambles and raspberry bushes, there was even a birch sapling poking through the cabin, but when Dad lifted the bonnet, he was dumbstruck. The engine was intact, because it was chrome-plated or made of some special steel, it wasn't just an engine, it was a whole engine-room, and when he took a look at the chassis he found that this lorry had drives on every wheel, and so he and Uncle Pepin jacked up each wheel in turn, fixed tyres on the hubs, and when the lorry was back on its feet, Dad dismantled the carburettor, and then the distributor,

Uncle's vision was as if he were swimming under water again, so Dad gave him every part to touch, and Uncle nodded away contentedly. Then Dad took out the big end as well and he was jubilant, the engine hadn't seized at all, it was still lubricated as if it had stopped only yesterday . . . So Dad inspected the level of petrol in the tank, topped it up from his canisters, fixed the starting handle, and turned it over once, slowly turning the engine over to get the right mixture and put it at the top, dead centre, then he cranked and the engine sprang into life, and Dad hopped about the woods and shouted and sang, and Uncle Pepin cleared his throat, he wanted to sing a high C as well, but his voice failed, he wanted to dance with his brother, just for his brother's sake, but he stumbled and fell into the raspberry bushes and brambles. And Dad climbed into the cabin, stepped on the gas, and the engine roared, emitting a jubilant voice, a merry white singing noise, then Dad cut off some birch stems, and adjusted the engine revolutions with more gas . . . Then he got up into the driving seat, revved up the engine, carefully, anxiously pushed down the clutch, put it in gear, and when he released the clutch there were drops of moisture on his brow, but the White not only started, not only moved, but took all that little forest growth along with it, mercilessly tearing it, snapping effortlessly all those hundreds of sprigs and roots which had overgrown it with great vigour, and the engine didn't blink an eyelid when it came to boggy ground, Dad shouted and Uncle, whom he had seated beside him, wanted to shout out something joyful too, to make his brother happy, but he couldn't utter a single note. And Dad was so overjoyed, that he sat Pepin close beside him and gave him the steering-wheel, then he opened the door and jumped out of the cabin, Uncle Pepin just gripped on to the steering-wheel for grim death, dumb with horror and with the responsibility entrusted to him by his brother in letting him drive this vehicle, but in fact nothing could really happen, because the White was heaving its way through a clearing, quite slowly, almost at a walking pace . . . And Dad took a look at the flaps from the back, then he ran forward and gazed at the White from in front as if it were a complete novelty, as if he'd never seen this lorry before, and each time he looked at the White, from whatever side or angle, every time he could see that this lorry was a really fine vehicle, especially if he were just to give it some new oak side flaps. And now he felt that the rest of his life had all just been leading up to this point, the fact that he'd been an accountant, then a manager, and finally just about director of the brewery, was really all a mistake, he felt that right from the very start he was actually made to be a lorry driver by profession, now his amateur love for engines had turned professional, just like someone who spends thirty years writing poems and stories after work for his desk drawer, and then decides to quit work, get away from it all and do nothing else but what he reckons to be his real calling. And so Dad drove the White out on to the road, stopped, returned for the Škoda 430 and drove it back to the White, where Uncle Pepin sat feverishly gripping the steering wheel, then Dad drove on half a mile or so in the White and returned for the Škoda, and bit by bit Dad drove on until they arrived home to the yard . . . And that night he couldn't sleep, he woke up constantly and went out with the torch to look at the lorry, he lifted the bonnet and inspected the engine again, and couldn't get over the wondrousness of it all. In the morning he went straight to the National Committee to report what he had found, and he bought that lorry from the National Renewal Fund for ten thousand crowns out of his restricted account. And straightaway he set about giving it new side flaps, and after a month Dad announced he was going to start using the White to deliver vegetables, he needed to augment his pension. So Dad started delivering vegetables, Uncle Pepin went with him as his delivery boy, every time they reached the field or the vegetable store people asked, "Where's your assistant?" And Dad would ask them to help him get Uncle Pepin down out of the cabin, and when they saw Uncle trying to carry cases of vegetables, but every so often going astray with a case and missing the lorry completely, they put Uncle back in the cabin and helped to load it themselves, and so after that whenever they saw Dad's vehicle coming and Uncle Pepin as delivery boy the workmen in the store would say, "We want to get it done quicker, better leave Uncle where he is . . ." So then Dad closed up the flaps, they threw a few more cases up on top for him, Dad carefully lashed the whole load down with ropes and took the steering-wheel with a great happy laugh, he stuffed the delivery chits in his side pocket, and nothing gave him greater delight than the prospect of driving along in his lorry to other towns, over hills and dales, listening to the White's engine eating away the miles, and all the way Dad sang aloud and Uncle Pepin bleated away with him. And again when they reached their destination, Dad backed up on to the ramp or against the warehouse, and when they asked Dad if he had an assistant with him, Dad said yes, but could they help him get his assistant down, and when they got Uncle Pepin down and saw what a wretched state he was in, either they put him back in the lorry or they sat him in a chair and loaded the boxes themselves, because they all wanted to get the load done a bit quicker. So Dad went about delivering vegetables, then he started delivering stoves over to Moravia, nothing was too much for Dad, somehow or other the era which had gone against him had now put him back on his feet. It seemed, as the years advanced, as if they were being discounted, for Dad now acquired again the strength he'd had in his youth, and his muscles and back grew stout, and his arms were like shovels, and his fingers splayed out, and when he closed his hand it became a working-class fist, just like the ones on the posters. And now Dad, like Pepin once, began to tell grotesque yarns about his youth, he shouted and raved ecstatically as he spoke, just as Uncle Pepin had shouted too as he told his yarns, but now he was in such a wretched state that he only smiled, in fact Dad eventually spotted that in order to avoid shouting and raving ecstatically, instead Uncle Pepin would excite and aggravate Dad with questions and purposely ill-put remarks, so that Dad would shout just like Uncle Pepin had used to do a quarter of a century ago, when he first came to the brewery on that fortnight's visit. And his vision wasn't really all that hopeless either, many a time Dad said, "What's that passing over there, Jožka?" And Uncle Pepin said, "Old woman on a bike.'' And Dad said, ''What's she got on the handlebars, a horse-collar?'' And Uncle quietly exploded: ''What're you on about, it's a wreath.'' And Dad said, ''And what's that writing on the ribbon? R.I.P.?'' But Uncle Pepin looked and said, ''What d'ye mean, you're as daft as in a test afore noon! It says One Last Farewell . . .'' Then Dad would sigh, and Uncle Pepin would clasp his fingers, because, you see, he knew he was not incapable of seeing, but now he'd proved that actually he could, he could see only too well. But Uncle Pepin had resolved that his eyesight was bad, and so it was. Dad gave him a birthday card to sign for his female cousin, but Uncle signed it in the wrong place, on the table, on the oil-cloth covering. And so spring came round again, and Dad started delivering fizzy drinks and lemonade. In May they went out taking refreshments to a nearby small town where there was to be a solemn unveiling of a memorial to a famous general, but as they were leaving Dad had to change a tyre, so they were a bit late. When he and Uncle Pepin reached the town they were stopped by a lieutenant of artillery who instructed Dad to wait – in ten minutes' time there was to be a gun salute from the ditch to inaugurate the unveiling of the memorial. But Dad said it would only take him a couple of minutes to drive past the artillery battery, he was coming with refreshments for the ceremony and it was nearly noon already, the schoolchildren assembled for the opening were bound to be thirsty, like all young people the whole world over. So the lieutenant of artillery made radio contact once more with the town square, and he was told that the lorry with refreshments might pass, because there was sufficient time. And Dad saluted and the White drove on, slowly it drove along and Dad could see the artillery strung out in the ditch, 122 mm guns, serviced by seven gunners, and so he passed the first gun, and as he passed the second he saw the gunner in the sunlight with his ammunition standing right beside the gun, at the third Dad observed how the men were kneeling by the gun-carriage anchoring it more firmly to the ground . . . And for the first time in its whole life the White began to sputter, a speck of soot in the carburettor, no doubt, Dad took fright and Uncle Pepin said, "What if we stall, there's still seven guns to go!" And the White came to a dead stop . . . And Dad went rheumatic, he needed someone to warm his joints with a soldering iron, not only his knees, but his arms as well, he just gripped the steering-wheel and saw the lieutenant signalling at him from a distance to get the hell out of there, gesticulating: shoo, shoo! Like shooing chickens the lieutenant gesticulated to the White to get out of there, and Dad rallied himself, jumped out, lifted the bonnet, then returned to get his screwdriver and spanners, with quick motions he released the carburettor, and just as Dad unscrewed the float chamber and loosed the jet and blew into it, he saw the lieutenant listening to his radio, and then with a single dismissive flap of his hand he consigned Dad to perdition, he looked at his watch, raised his arm and glanced again at his wristwatch, and all the gunners were truly concentrating now, some of the soldiers clapped their hands to their ears . . . And then the lieutenant gave the command with a flap of his hand in the sunny morning air, and the first volley rang out, and with that first volley Dad saw how the side flaps were torn off the back of the White and all the fizzy drinks were swept away and a shower of glass like a snowstorm rose far into the landscape and glittered, and Dad felt a great buffet of air rip off the bonnet, and that was probably his saving grace, because away on that bonnet Dad flew as if carried on elephant's ears, over the ripening cornfield, hurtling through the air just like Mr Jirout once did at the fair, Jirout the maltster who in his younger days had himself shot out of a cannon at village carnivals, and when the force of air diminished, Dad landed with his bonnet on the ground, sailing across to the very edge of the ditch, still holding his carburettor, and then he was showered in a spray of glass and splinters ... The second volley spun the White right round and swept away any remaining cases with their already smashed fizzy drinks and the ripped-off side pieces flew over Dad's head ... Then came further blasts, Dad managed to pop up his head in time to see how the White was shifted a bit further each time and turned at another angle and with every blast there was a bit less of it, and Dad tried to peer through the dust to see what had happened to Uncle Pepin ... And after sliding into the ditch Dad saw that Uncle Pepin was there in the blackthorn and dog-rose bushes, still sitting on his lorry seat, which must have flown through the air likewise with him and landed him here on these springy bouncing bushes, and after each celebratory volley of artillery the bushes shook with the force of gusts of wind and Uncle rocked to and fro as if in an old wickerwork rocking pram. And then the solemn inauguration of the memorial to be unveiled in the town

square commenced with a speech broadcast and
amplified on loudspeakers which were distributed not
only on pillars by the verges of all the roads leading into
town, but also close by on a number of plum trees, and
the grand voice solemnly portrayed and narrated some
glorious episode in the general's life-story . . . And the
lieutenant came running over, and when he saw that
Dad only had a ripped coat and torn trousers, and
Uncle Pepin was still rocking away there on his seat in
the springy embrace of the bushes, he spread out his
hands, and Dad remarked that it was *force majeure*, it
was the first time in two years, the first time ever the
carburettor had played up, and that was a great
achievement, even if . . . Dad ran on pitifully, pointing
to the fragments and wreck of the lorry, which had been
carried off bodily by the force of the air current right
into the fields . . . And now two gunners, one on each
side, carted off Uncle Pepin enthroned on his lorry seat,
looking like a real monument to a Czech writer . . . And
they loaded Uncle on to a military vehicle. By the time
they reached the square a couple of minutes later the
monument was still to be unveiled, smartly dressed
soldiers and citizens had re-emerged from arcades and
houses, children in tunics and kerchiefs ran cautiously
out again, and the paving of the square all around the
statue glittered with shards and fragments and splinters
of glass from the bottles of refreshing lemonade and
other drinks, which the artillery fire had pounded and
shattered but the great gust of wind had carried even
this far, and one or two foreheads were peppered with
cuts, and nurses fixed sticking plasters and bound up
the scars . . . And so it happened that the music playing

was the national anthem, and the mayor pulled the rope, and as the sheet came floating down, the statue of the general rose, towering up, and the military saluted, and the soldiers put Uncle Pepin down, plonked him down on some boards on the trestles of a stall selling plaques and other mementos, so that they could salute the anthem too . . . But Uncle Pepin leaned over and fell together with the seat, the steel underframe of which made a terrible clang on the paving . . . But no one could do anything about it, because everybody has to stand to attention of course during the national anthem. And a military caterpillar tractor arrived on the square as well, pulling the shattered White lorry, which limped so badly on all its four wheels, that while the anthem was finishing, the caterpillar tractor stopped, and the soldiers saluted, but then with a great clashing of iron and steel on the paving of the square the whole White lorry caved in and collapsed like some antediluvian beast, wounded mastodon, or Loch Ness monster. And still the White's centre of gravity gave it no rest, a few more ounces of weight slumped it over to one side, enough to turn it on its back, showering out with a crash the last splinters and remains of bottles left stuck at the bottom and in the chassis and interstices of the engine. And the national anthem finished, and those already pockmarked by the glass couldn't help themselves, when they saw that second monument at the lower end of the square they fled into the side streets and passageways and arcades. Then the military towed Dad and the White lorry off home, not on its own axles, but on top of a trailer. And they hauled that battle-scarred lorry into the yard and put it right beside the Škoda,

they carried in Uncle Pepin, still sitting on his lorry
cabin seat, and because Dad's hip was a little out of
joint, they carried him across the yard on that bonnet on
which he had earlier sailed through the landscape, and
Dad was still holding his carburettor . . . And from then
on Dad never really got himself back to rights again,
because he could never get the White lorry back to
rights either, there Uncle Pepin would sit, while Dad
outlined joyful prospects for the future over the two
vehicle wrecks, just have to spend a couple of thousand
crowns on the bodywork, then the engines will roar into
action again, and the White model lorry will deliver its
vegetables again and off they'll go in the family Škoda
to visit their old home town . . . So then one day Dad
went over the level crossing to the cooper's to get some
oak beams, and there he stopped for a while to watch a
painter painting stripes on the level crossing poles, but
just as he started to paint, the poles went slowly up, to
the clear position. So the painter brought a step-ladder
and mounted it and carried on painting from the ladder,
but the paint on his brush ran out, so the painter got
down and took his tin and brought it up the ladder and
hung it on a hook, and just as he dipped his brush, he'd
scarcely begun, when the poles came slowly down
again . . . The painter looked round, but no one was
watching, only Dad gave a smile, and the painter came
quite calmly down the steps, removing the paint tin first
and dipping his brush in the paint. But scarcely had he
begun to paint the second black stripe when suddenly
the poles went up again, there the painter stood, with
the paint dripping off his brush, he waited, but it took
too long, so he climbed up the steps again, but the paint

had run out on his brush, so he came down, but by the time he'd taken his paint tin up and hung it on a hook, the poles came down again, and he hadn't managed a single stroke . . . Nobody noticed, only Dad, who had seen this conspiracy of fate against him, he gave a smile, but still didn't see what it meant for himself. And so, while Dad kept on watching from the cooper's shop over the level crossing, as the poles rose and fell, as a train passed, and locomotives and goods trains shunted, the master painter, instead of getting angry, got calmer and calmer, as he climbed the steps and the poles went down, every time he forgot his paint tin, but he returned patiently to fetch it, only to find the pole moving away from him again after a couple of strokes, and making him change his set-up . . . And Dad suddenly saw in this a symbol of himself, he identified himself with this painting of the poles, he saw in it the image of his own fate, he waited in anticipation, and sure enough, the master painter painted away and finished only a single black stroke. And Dad went on changing the beams and battens and boards, ignoring the fact that the White lorry had broken axles and a smashed-up engine, that every wheel had broken gears and brake drums, he concentrated on the details and refused to contemplate the fundamentals. About the same time the doctor advised that Uncle Pepin had to get some exercise, otherwise he'd stop being able to walk altogether, so every morning Dad set Uncle at the pump and asked him to pump a barrel of water, a two-hundred-litre barrel of water, Uncle pumped away, while Dad went on repairing his vehicles, from the yard you could hear the regular knocking of the arm on the cast-iron neck of the pump and the gurgle of fresh spring water, and Uncle Pepin constantly went over and reached into the barrel to see how the water was rising, and when he felt the level of the water he smiled and pumped on, the neighbours gathered just as before, they asked Uncle questions and Uncle waved his hand and stood there in the sunshine and pumped, made content by the fresh water gushing up from the bowels of the earth, and when he felt the water-level and the barrel was full, it would be afternoon by then, he shuffled his feet, shuffled over towards the yard as if his legs were tied together, felt for the wall, and when he found it, he followed it round till he reached the yard and reported that the barrel was now full. Then in the evening Dad poured the water out over the garden, and when it rained, he bored a hole in the barrel and let the water run out and then he bunged up the hole with a peg. And so the two brothers worked, pegging away, but the result of their work was the same as the contents of the barrel, it began not to have any sense, really just like all of that time, which had stood still, not only on that wonky clock on the church tower which had stopped and nobody came to mend it, but all around them that time was slowly standing still, in some places it had already stopped altogether, while another time, of different people, was out there full of its own *élan* and new energy and endeavour, but Uncle Pepin and Francin had stopped knowing about that, they no longer bothered about the fact that the time of the cattle markets had stood still, the time of the annual fairs and Advent markets had stood still, the time of the Sunday morning and daily evening promenades had passed away, political parties no longer laid on outings to the woods, joint outings where they had tombolas and jailhouses and shooting booths, gone were the fancy-dress balls and the festive balls and the village horse-rides, gone were the masquerades and the allegorical processions and the winter processions of Bacchus at Lent, the local amenity societies had ceased to vie amongst themselves for the finest windows in town, the five theatres were closed down and of the two cinemas only one was in operation. Gone too was the time of the Sokol athletic academies and the summer exercise grounds, where at four o'clock in the afternoon the boy and girl juniors filed up and then the novices, gone was the time of the early evening exercises for men and women, nobody in town organised a symphony orchestra any more or a choir, gone were the pensioners walking in procession through the municipal parks, the time of the evening strolls of lovers by the river or through the woods had vanished, the time of the wreaths given to school-leavers had stopped, nobody gambled with cards at the pub, there were none of the establishments with ladies' service any more, gone with those times were the famous local black puddings and famous sausages, which assistants brought over to the pubs at four in the afternoon and then the players of Mariage put away their cards and bought two sausages and a roll, gone was the time of the carpenters' and maltsters' songs to accompany their work, no musical boxes wafted music out through windows, everything linked with the old era had fallen anti-clockwise into a slumber, or as if a lump of food had stuck in its throat, it had choked on it and was slowly dying, the old time had stopped just like Sleeping Beauty eating a poisoned apple, and the Prince didn't come, couldn't even come, because the old society no longer had the required strength and courage, and so we had the era of great posters and great meetings, at which fists were shaken against everything that was old, and those who were living by the old time were at home, living quietly on memory . . . And Dad started getting annoyed by the noise of that pump, that constant tapping of the pump arm against the cast-iron neck, he began to be sorry for Uncle and sorry for himself, because Uncle's pumping up of two hundred litres of water, which Dad let out secretly again in the evening, began to glow in his mind's eye like a symbol of all that he was doing himself . . . And so, not as a plain substitute, but as a quieter means of keeping Uncle Pepin moving and thereby alive, Dad fetched two enormous inner tubes from the White's tyres, and every morning he screwed the pump into the valve and all morning Uncle pumped up the tube, with slow movements, it rose, it reared up like a jumping jack, that toy, that figure with strings that children pull, and the jumping jack lifts its legs and arms . . . And so, as Uncle Pepin's lungs and heart were fine, because he'd never been a smoker, he pumped away, felt the tyre, the inner tube, offered it to Francin to feel, but Francin tapped with a little hammer, praised his brother, and Uncle went pumping on, in the afternoon he pumped up the other tube . . . And at nightfall, when Uncle was sitting in the kitchen and eating his potatoes, Francin let both the tubes down, so that Uncle Pepin would have enough exercise to do again the following day. Whenever Dad heard the sound of the water flowing from the barrel, or heard that strong, but then weakening expiration of air from the inner tube, he couldn't help thinking that both his and his brother's, and indeed everyone's life was the same as what he was doing with the inner tube or the barrel, and later he would return quite pale, with a momentary ghastly pallor, into the kitchen, trembling all over, just like when he had to slaughter a cock, and he did, or slit a rabbit's throat, and he did, after first stunning it with his fist. Uncle Pepin sat there all evening motionless by the kitchen dresser, the old tomcat Celestine sat just behind, eaten away by time just like Uncle's face, a tomcat who, when young, slept only under roses and peonies, only he got round almost all the female cats in the district, only he failed to turn up at home for a fortnight, and when he did, he roared out the whole way, "Open up, I'm home! Give me the best you've got, quick!" . . . And he got it too, for a long time, just like Uncle Pepin, and he wouldn't be stroked either, and if you tried, Celestine attacked you straight away, and always he was victorious, like a soldier of the old Austria, he even jumped on Dad's back when he scolded him with a broom. And Celestine's face was scarred from brawls, just like Uncle Pepin's was scarred by wrinkles left from nights on the town and early morning rising, hard graft in the wash-house and boiler-room and ice chambers and sewers. Now they sat together, Uncle Pepin felt for the tomcat's head and said quietly, "Is that you there?" And the tomcat rumbled at Uncle and purred, there he sat, like an owl on a prophetess's shoulder, close behind Uncle, and the tomcat was snug and so was Uncle. Every evening they sat there, just the two of them, they talked together, just the two of them, they no longer had any communication with others. And then it happened, one day Uncle felt twice for Celestine's head, and twice there was no purred response back to the question "Are you there?" and Uncle Pepin gave up walking altogether, he never got out of his bed again, just as Celestine, the old tomcat, never came home, because that is not the place where tomcats die.

ELEVEN

The old people's home is in a lovely château. When you pass the little town where time stood still and go down the avenue of lime trees, the château still remains out of sight, you keep going up the hill, in the flat countryside even quite a little rise gives the impression of a hill down which you could sledge nicely in winter. Then there is a lodge by the road, hidden in the flowering tops of lime trees buzzing loud with bees, and suddenly from the gate you see the beige-walled monastery. A long time ago the Dominicans were here and their hobby and occupation here apart from scholarship was to cultivate a botanic garden. But when under Joseph II the days of the monastery were numbered, the Dominicans were disbanded and the monastery abandoned, the botanic garden went to seed. The first plants and flowers to perish were those unable to survive without human attention, only those flowers and bushes remained which managed to adapt. Only a small number of the original plants were left, and these not only maintained themselves in the abandoned garden, but as the wind blew, it carried their fruits and seeds over the boundary into the countryside around, so that now, two hundred years after the abandonment of that garden, there are still strange flowers and bushes growing in the area, the descendants of those plants whose seeds climbed over the fence and adapted themselves to the habitat. Altogether it was a kind of tradition in our area to adapt yourself and merge with new and different times. Under Maria Theresa the country round about was populated with German peasants, whole villages and farmsteads, but as time went by, not only did these Germans adapt, but finally they merged with the land and the language, just like those plants from the botanic garden, and so now there is not a trace of the original Germans in this area, only the German names, whose bearers speak and feel themselves to be Czech. Dad entered the courtyard and then the garden, down from the galleries of the former monastery and château there ran thick eiderdowns of red geraniums, like you can see on pictures of farmhouses and hotels in the Tyrol or Switzerland, and out there in the sunshine, on benches, old men and women were sitting, all looking sort of solemn and special, because it was visiting time and every old person here was under the illusion that his daughter or son might turn up, or at least some friend or other, maybe he hadn't come, maybe he never came, but always he might come, because every old person has at least some friends or relations. Dad stood and looked at these old people, comparing them with himself, and observing that they weren't much older than himself, some were even a bit younger, but Dad was a youngster to these people here, because he came from outside, and whoever is outside, is young, and can look after himself, and for these people, for whom time had stood still, to look after yourself and not to be a burden to others meant everything. Dad stood there holding a large bag inscribed with the name of the firm Alois Šisler, he listened to every sound, and because in the softest hints of sounds and notes and happenings he was accustomed to hear approaching disaster, as life had taught him to do, he noted distant music, wafting out not from a single centre but from several places at once. And so he looked round, wondering where it might come from, and saw open windows and blowing curtains, but that orchestra was playing gentle string music, which grew louder as he walked up to the main gate, and then Dad heard and saw how along all the galleries and corridors, even on the trees, like little feeding boxes for the birds, tiny little amplifiers were hung on cables, radio receivers protected from the rain by polythene sheets, so that the music would play all the time, even when rain was falling or snow, and all the time the music played "Harlequin's Millions", a sweet sentimental programmatic intermezzo, which enhanced the solemn chocolate-box mood of the expectant old-age pensioners, and they, leaning on their sticks or with arms folded in their laps or over their chests, their hats pressed down against the sunlight, gazed sharply at the main gate to see if anyone they might be expecting would arrive. Even if someone were to come, no great joy or excitement would be displayed, the main thing was that it was the time of waiting and expectation, and like that state of mind of children awaiting the bell to tell them that Jesus had come to the

Christmas tree, that state of nervous tension when children go to look on the window ledge to see if Santa Claus or St Barbara has put their presents on the plate or in their stocking, that expectant state of grace was enough to make pleasant this day on which visits were permitted. And a few of the inmates recognised Dad and got up, these were people who spent all Saturday and the following night and Sunday morning helping Dad to repair his Orion motorbike all those years ago, these were the people who never came to help again, who were terrified of meeting Dad, who fled from the threat of more repair work and hid themselves from Dad as he approached in cellars . . . Today these people got up and came to meet Dad, stretching out their hands, hoping and trusting that Dad would suggest they came and did some more of this maintenance work, anything at all, but Dad's hand gestured that the days of motor-car maintenance were over, finished, it was all over, finished . . . So Dad listened five times to the music of "Harlequin's Millions" and stepped into the cool air of the whitewashed Baroque passage, up the wide staircase he climbed as more "Harlequin's Millions" wafted down to meet him. On the first floor there was a corridor full of flowers, all the flower stands were overflowing with cascades of geraniums, petunias, and snapdragons and asparagus fern, just like the music from boxes on wall brackets floating down from the string orchestra, unfurling its strands and filaments and motley calligraphic initials billowing and swirling in the current of the musical threads. And Dad peeped through the half-open doors into the knights' hall, and again, there on every table in the common refectory a flowerpot shone bright or a vase with rearing stems of colourful blooms, and again, as knights jousted their way across the tapestry along the whole length of the wall, from the same little boxes the music poured out once more, inexhaustibly, amongst the poor pensioners, playing "Harlequin's Millions". And then he was touched by a woman's pink hand, and when Dad turned round, in front of him there stood a corpulent nun with a kindly face in spectacles, the spectacle rims were jammed down on to her nose and cheeks, just like the white starched collar which cut into the nun's fat pink neck and gave her a permanent ring mark like doves have. Dad said he was looking for his brother, Uncle Pepin. And the nun took Dad over to a window, to an alcove with such thick walls, that there was room for a small table and four chairs, and the nun looked out of the window and said to Dad with a joyful countenance that very soon Uncle Pepin would be passing on ahead of the rest, he wouldn't remain more than a fortnight on this earth, Uncle kept falling down, so she'd had them put Uncle Pepin in the ward for the immobile. And, she added, without dropping the joyful look in her eyes, did Uncle have any relatives, and if so, they should come to take their leave, in such imminent circumstances access and visits were permitted on any day and at any hour, for Uncle's time had come. And the sister spoke with such bliss and joy that Dad suddenly thought that if ever he was a burden to people, that he'd like to be with someone like this sister for his remaining days. And so Dad went in with his bag in his fingers, he was holding that bag rather like most visitors to the home used to hold the edge of their hats, feverishly, as if the hat brim were a lifebelt. In the ward for the immobile there was deep shade, outside the large windows the sun shone all the more brightly through the tall trees, as if the trees were illuminated from below by strong floodlights, so brightly were the windows packed with foliage, fluttering and issuing a steady rustling rushing noise that penetrated glass and walls, as if apart from the trees there had to be a waterfall or soaring fountain. When he got used to the half-gloom and dazzle of the windows, Dad saw that the sister was standing at the head of a bed. There lay a slight little man – so small, almost a child, his arms thrown back and bent behind his head, and he was staring fixedly at the ceiling, his eyes no longer expected anyone, looked forward to anything, they were eyes in which time had almost stopped. It was Uncle Pepin. The sister leant over, lifted Uncle like a child, with her arms round his back, so light he was, like a girl picking up her doll from a child's pram. "Look dear," said the sister, "look who's come to see you." Then she uncovered Uncle's legs, and his legs were white, as though they had been lying in lime water. Dad noticed, with a modicum of horror and disgust, like all healthy folk, that Uncle Pepin had nappies and pads under him like little children. And the sister unfastened those nappies and pads and said cheerfully, "Let's see if he's wet himself." Then she added, "Would you like to go on the gramophone, dear?" And Uncle Pepin said nothing, he went on staring at the ceiling and his eyes were blue like pallid blue lilacs, like a pair of frozen forget-me-nots. And the sister brought the gramophone over, a sort of stool it was, she took off the lid and sat

Uncle on this commode with a chamber pot underneath, and Uncle fell, keeled over like a statue, Dad supported his brother and looked at his legs, his blue, leached feet, Uncle was naked, with a towel thrown across his front, he sat like Christ crowned with thorns. And all of a sudden Dad groaned, uttered a long moan, releasing everything that had tightened his coat till the buttons practically snapped, and then he opened the bag and took out of it into the semi-darkness of the immobile ward a white sea-captain's cap, with an anchor and the inscription BREMEN-HAMBURG . . . And he put it in front of Uncle's eyes, but though Uncle looked at that cap, he looked right through it and elsewhere, that sailor's cap was transparent and Uncle gazed on into the very heart of time as it was stopping. "Old Šisler sewed it for you," Dad whispered and put it on Uncle's head, and he added, "He made it to measure . . ." But the cap fell right down over Uncle's ears, he'd got so terribly thin that even his head had shrunk several sizes. The sister said sorrowfully, "He doesn't eat his food." And she straightened Uncle's bed, and Dad looked round at the other beds in the room, they were all watching Dad as if he were the visit they would like to have themselves, which hadn't come or wouldn't come, or had already been and gone. An old man stood by the window piping away timorously: "Ah, the horror of it, I'm ninety-six years old and I can't die, ah, it's awful, it's a misfortune, I've a good heart and lungs, what a destiny, eh?" He nodded his head at Dad's watching eyes. And Dad understood that none of them knew anything about Uncle Pepin, nothing about the lovely ladies, about his dances and sprees, about how he entered the town in that cap like a sovereign ruler or king, how everywhere the windows opened for Uncle, while for him, for Dad, the windows closed and the gates were shut and people fled, because he stole their precious time, while Uncle Pepin filled and fulfilled it. And then Dad shivered, he was expecting that awful sound of diarrhoea, that noise that horrifies every living breathing person, which the sister would hear too, but the sister considered all this simply part of humanity, as a little childish trifle, for no diarrhoea could deprive her of that radiance provided by her faith, that for all of this, when her time came, she would look upon the very face of God, into the radiance in fact into which she looked even now, and she did not muffle this radiance in her eyes, but issued it forth to all people, Dad as well, so that they could savour the sparkling glow of God's grace in the eyes of a believer. And Dad looked round at the other beds again, a paralysed man was lying there beside Uncle, instead of hands he had stumps twisted in on himself, like knuckles on the stems of an old vine, that man must have been constantly hungry, on his bedside table he had pieces of bread and bowls of tea, like a paralysed lapdog he bent his head over and grasped a piece of bread with his lips or lapped the tea with his tongue, and beside the window, on a bed propped up with planks, probably so that the immobile person could see better into the garden, there sat a young man with spectacles and in his fingers needles swiftly clacked and as he gazed out he was crocheting a big curtain, already as long as a blanket and running down almost to the ground, and on that curtain there were little crocheted birds and sprigs and foliage, and the immobile person looked as if he were reading music and playing the zither, he looked for a moment out at the rustling, fluttering foliage and then he crocheted what he saw into his threads. "There we are," said the sister, taking Uncle Pepin and wiping him, Dad took the sailor's cap, which had fallen off, turned away and waited till he could tell by the sound of the paper that the cleansing was over, he couldn't get a hold on himself and watch, and now he realised what a benefit it was for an old person to be able to do things for himself, not to be dependent on people. Now Uncle Pepin was back lying on the bed and staring at the ceiling. Dad sat down on the edge of the bed, and the sister stood there silhouetted in the window and watched the young man crocheting his curtain. Then all at once Uncle Pepin felt for Dad's hand and stroked the back of it, feeling the hard patches, Dad's hands all mucked up by the repair tools and spanners, then he looked at Dad and Dad sobbed, almost choked to see that Uncle was looking back at him out of that time which had stood still, there out of an inhuman realm. And then Uncle lay down on his back, threw one arm behind his head and crooked the other over his brow, and again with unblinking eyes he stared into the cold space which was approaching closer towards him. "Jožka, what are you thinking about?" inquired Dad. The sister came over and listened, she watched Uncle Pepin's purple lips. "What's tae become o' the love?" whispered Uncle. "What's that?" inquired Dad putting his ear up close to him. "What's tae become o' the love?" repeated Uncle, and the sister touched Dad's sleeve and nodded sweetly and Dad understood and got up, took the cap, put it on, but the sister took it off him and put it in his hand, and softly went away, and Dad followed, before the tall doors of the mansion closed Dad saw that the young man was looking at him sharply through the lenses of his spectacles, and the spectacles glittered just like the three crochet needles. In the corridor the radio on the walls again poured out "Harlequin's Millions", through the open doors into the knights' hall gushed the smell of soup and gravy, and the pensioners hobbled or walked into the refectory, where so many years ago the time of the Dominican and the aristocratic order had stood still, to be succeeded by the time of the old people who lived out their lives there amongst the flowers and the distant music. When Dad left the park, not a single bench was occupied, nobody was sitting there in the sun any more, no more visitors would be coming, it was time for food and lunch again, then time for a nap. Dad put on the sailor's cap, adjusted it carefully once more, and when he looked at the world around him under the shadow of the black peak, he felt a beautiful feeling, he even pulled himself up straight, straightened his back to its full extent till he was walking stiff as a soldier, dignified, when he went through the gate, where a mentally handicapped old man was on duty, Dad gave him a salute, and the old man clicked his heels and opened the whole of the main gate and bowed to Dad, and Dad give him a five-crown piece. "Have yourself a beer," said Dad, and he went down the avenue, crossing the alternate patches of sunlight and lime trees' shade. When he was passing the old cemetery, he stopped. As he could see, people had even got going on this old cemetery with picks, and block and tackle, and levers and jacks, even here it wasn't enough for people that time had stood still. Nearly all the monuments had been torn out of the ground, nearly all the graves and tombs were open, memorials had been dragged on skids and boards with chains on to open drays like heavy barrels of beer, monuments with inscriptions which for more than two hundred years had given addresses, status and age and favourite verses, all this hewn and carved into stone had now been carried off to another town, where grinding wheels and chisels had blotted out the names of people from the old time. Along with these they ripped up the old cypresses too, the thujas and arbores vitae and black elder bushes, and uprooted too from the earth were the remains of coffins and bones. And Dad just looked and saw that this work of abolishing the cemetery was done, not by people of the new time, they maybe only gave the instructions, but by people he had known ever since he had first moved into this little town where time had stood still. And for a while longer Dad almost delighted at how the graves had resisted, how they had had to bring caterpillar tractors, how the chains had burst, but in the end they had succeeded, they had to succeed, in tearing those old times out of the ground, and so Dad walked on and looked at the gravestones and saw the inscriptions, he read them and learnt that his time had truly died too, not with Uncle Pepin, but with this cemetery, and he felt contentment at what he had seen. And so, torn out of the ground were the tombs and gravestones of František Hulík, the fisherman known as Old Hobbler, Červinka known as Wee Brolly, Červinka The Perch, Červinka The Limp, Červinka Drampa, curly-headed Červinka Woolly, Červinka Práda, Červinka Skinny Whippet, fancy Červinka Bankrupt, Červinka Ciggy, Červinka Mincemeat, Červinka Made-Him-Sweat, and on the dray was the gravestone of Dlabač The Ducats, Dlabač The Pigman, Dlabač The Louser, Dlabač The Toff, Dlabač Big-Arse, and on another cart there's Votava The Dummy, Votava The Musician, Votava Vanity, and next to him Vohánka Lederer and Vohánka Laudon. And in a lorry which had stopped at the cemetery gates and couldn't get out through the mud there lay the stones of Zedrich The Corner and Zedrich Bubikopf, Procházka Robinson, and next to it the gravestone of Miss Tubitz known as Pull-Me-Pigtail, and other gravestones of people in this little town where time had stood still who also possessed a familiar name, an added nickname. And a good thing too, said Dad to himself, everything returns to its origin, now I can see that time really has stood still and the new time has really begun, but I have only the key to the old times and the one for the new is denied me, and I cannot live in the new time anyway, because I belong to the old time, which is dead. And so meditating, Dad came on to the bridge, and when he saw the beige-walled brewery there at the end of the suburbs, he leant over above the river and looked at the water flowing by. And he took off the sailor's cap, the famous cap of Uncle Pepin, and it was as if that sailor's cap symbolised the golden olden days, not only those of Uncle Pepin, but of Dad as well. Dad held the cap up to the wind and then he threw it into the air, into the sun, and the cap glided and fell into the water and the current carried it away, right up to the very last moment

Dad watched the cap as it was carried away by the flow of the Elbe, and the sailor's cap floated and Dad felt, not that it would never sink, but it couldn't, and even if it did, then that cap would go on shining radiant in his mind like a bright memory. And when Dad got home, Mum said, "We've just been told that Uncle Pepin has died." And Dad laughed cheerfully and confirmed it to her: "Yes," he said, "I know."

AFTERWORD

I wrote this *Little Town* in the early spring of 1973, when illness was in the offing, and I fondly imagined that I alone held the key to these stories of two brothers, that only I could sketch out their narrative, and if I were to die, someone else could finish it off somehow. Also, a year before that illness, I had a photographer come to Prague's Letná cemetery, and there I had him take my portrait with the black tombstones in the background, and then I had him take another picture of me in the same place, but this time waist-deep in an open grave, and finally the black crosses on their own, as if I had sunk down into the ground. I had a feeling in the small of my back that soon I'd be confined to a white bed, and so it was to be, and while I lay there believing for a certain critical moment that I was going on somewhere else, again I remembered about *The Little Town Where Time Stood Still*, and I had it sent over and every morning I made cuts and then more cuts, fondly imagining that I alone held the key to this little town. So again this text, like *The King of England*, is written by the spontaneous method of peril in lingering, and again as in *The King* I made only deletions to the first draft. But I think (now that I have recovered and start looking round at the world as I convalesce) that in future it will no longer make any difference if I place my Kersko woodlands in the close vicinity of the town, it won't matter if I enable my characters to walk out to my beloved woodlands and the lovely forest clearing. Perhaps it won't any longer matter one bit if I haul the little town away on the trailer of the imagination about fifteen kilometres west, just to enable my heroes to reach the portals of the woods and let them enter as needed into any landscape or green abode. For, if Pieter Breughel could put the Alps down right next to the backyards of his Low Country landscapes and towns, why shouldn't I use the same scissors and cut out of my landscape and people whatever suits my text, and why can't I cut out of my head only that which I dream about most intensely and hence most happily? So now having got over this illness, once again I fondly imagine that only I hold the key to certain events, and hence it is up to me and me alone to try to write it down. And not only do I know what to write, and what about, but I start to sense that the most important thing will be, how I will write in the future. And because the illness came by aeroplane and is leaving on foot, being weak, I set up tough prospects for myself and start to know that *Falling In Love*, this first book of mine, will be borne along by a tenderly sensual dynamics in the manner of Matisse's picture *Luxe, Calme et Volupté*, and that this text will be permeated with glowing pigments of light and space. The second text will be called *Surprise in the Woods*, and it will be full of fear and stress and vain adaptation in the manner of Edvard Munch's lyrical expressionism. I shall try in this text to achieve something I have been contemplating for some years, something which deriving itself from realistic drawing gradually arrives at deformation and finally crosses over into that which is the essence of gestural painting, as practised by Jackson Pollock. I am putting the bar so high that it vanishes in the glittering azure, because for what I shall be attempting, to join consciousness and unconsciousness, vitality and existentiality, to abolish the object as the outer and inner model, for that a leap is required, and only my illness, that university of mine, which I lived through in the hospital on Charles Square, only that may perhaps be able to prepare for me a jumping-off point, from which I shall jump head first into the gravitational field of emotionality. Up then towards that which as yet is not.